THE
HONEY
MOON

ALSO BY SHALINI BOLAND

THE HONEY MOON

SHALINI BOLAND

THOMAS & MERCER

Text copyright © 2024 by Shalini Boland
All rights reserved.

No part of this book may be reproduced, or stored in a retrieval system, or transmitted in any form or by any means, electronic, mechanical, photocopying, recording, or otherwise, without express written permission of the publisher.

Published by Thomas and Mercer, Seattle

www.apub.com

Amazon, the Amazon logo, and Thomas and Mercer are trademarks of Amazon.com, Inc., or its affiliates.

ISBN-13: 9781662507113
eISBN: 9781662507120

Cover design by The Brewster Project
Cover image: ©Laura Ranftler / Arcangel; ©r.nagy / Shutterstock

Printed in the United States of America

Firestarter888

I think you could be the one.

Space Dancer Girl

I was thinking the same thing about you.

Prologue

You relive each second with every footstep that rings out across the smooth flagstones.

You're making too much noise. Panting, thudding, jumping at shadows.

Calm down. Breathe.

The clear fresh night smells of blood and rot. Of betrayal and darkness. Of death and sorrow. Regret.

You stop. Heave out a breath. Dry retch, before getting hold of yourself again, staring at a puddle of lamplight on the pavement. You gaze up at the black sky, at the fingernail of cold moon and the winking stars, before glancing wildly around the unfamiliar street and up at the blank windows. People are sleeping all around while you're in turmoil. While your heart judders and the sweat oozes from every pore.

It all seemed so reasonable. So logical. So deserved. But now that it's over, reality tears at you.

What have you done?

Chapter One

NOW

'Wow. Venice is beautiful.' Austin stands next to the open shutters of the Juliet balcony, staring out across the dark expanse of the Grand Canal, lights glittering on the opposite shore. The chill April wind ruffles his dark wavy hair as he turns back to face me, a smile dimpling his cheeks, his green eyes sparkling. 'Almost as beautiful as you. I can't believe what an incredible place this is.'

My heart clenches with a fierce, desperate love. 'I can't believe we're married!' I reply, putting my phone down on the coffee table and crossing the living area of our honeymoon suite to take both his hands in mine. To stretch up on my tiptoes to kiss him. *My husband*. Even saying the words in my head sounds crazy. I'm a married woman. 'Stella Lewis.' I say my new name aloud, still not used to the sound of it on my tongue.

'*Mrs* Stella Lewis,' Austin adds, pulling me in close and kissing me harder, making my body react in all kinds of ways.

Although I was happy to take Austin's surname, I'll miss being Stella Goldsmith. I liked my old name. Austin suggested we both take the name Goldsmith-Lewis, but I prefer the simplicity of a single surname. I'll get used to it. And even though I'm an only child – same as

Austin – my parents aren't precious about it. Whichever name I ended up with was the least of Dad's concerns.

We turn back to face the Grand Canal. I'm slightly breathless, my pulse thrumming, my face heated. The clink of glassware and cutlery filters up from the hotel terrace below, late-night laughter, faint music, the pop of a prosecco cork. It's so surreal to be here in Italy, just the two of us, after the crazy lead-up to the wedding where we've been surrounded by friends and family, the centre of a non-stop whirl of activity and attention. I'd been anticipating tonight for so long. And now it's finally here. It feels like a dream. The cool air makes me shiver where only moments ago I was flushed from our kisses.

'You're cold,' Austin says, closing the glass balcony doors.

'Need you to warm me up again,' I reply, my gaze catching on the black-and-gold gondolas swaying gently in their stations.

Austin steps closer, puts his arms around me and starts to unzip my dress. 'That water taxi here was some real James Bond shit,' he murmurs, a smile in his voice.

'I know,' I reply, turning to loosen his belt and unbutton his shirt. I think back to this morning's exhilarating speedboat trip from the airport to the hotel. It felt as though we were starring in a movie. 'I think I could get used to this lifestyle.'

'It's a good job my parents own a travel company then,' he replies. 'Plenty more trips like this to come.' The honeymoon was their wedding present to us. A five-star luxury trip to Venice, followed by a week's skiing in the Dolomites. I'm not an accomplished skier, but I managed to fit in a few lessons on the dry-ski slope back home. Austin assured me it's a lot easier on snow. Luckily, despite it being April, there's still a lot of snow around on the higher peaks, and the bonus is that the slopes will be empty at this time of year.

As our kisses grow more urgent, I take Austin's hand and tug him towards the bedroom. His mouth, still on mine, tastes of

4

limoncello. His hands beneath my dress are warm and insistent. My soul is full of thankfulness. Happiness. I relax into his arms as we sink on to the pristine king-size bed, our clothes a memory as they slide to the floor. Is it my imagination or is he being more tender than usual? More present. Dare I hope that our marriage will be everything I want it to be?

He moves a wisp of my auburn hair away from my face and stares down at me. 'I love you, Stella. So much. I hope you know that.'

'Love you too,' I whisper, my voice suddenly choked with emotion.

'Are you crying? Don't be sad.' He looks surprised and wipes a tear from beneath my eye.

'I'm not sad. Just emotional,' I reply with a sniff. 'And a little drunk.' I give him a crooked smile.

He kisses away my rogue tear and I push all thoughts and worries from my mind. This is our honeymoon. I'm here in this beautiful city with my handsome husband. Perhaps everything will be all right.

As our bodies rock together, I let myself go, and it's as perfect as it was back in those heady first days when all I wanted was this.

Afterwards, I curl into his side and he kisses the top of my head. 'Stella, that was . . .' He trails off.

'I know,' I reply, content.

I turn over and he curves his body into my back, strokes my arm with his thumb. I feel cosy and safe. Austin is always so much warmer than me. Heats me up on cold nights. I call him my hot-water bottle. His breathing slows and I turn over, watch his face go slack. His dark lashes brush his cheeks and his lips part slightly with every rise and fall of his chest. His skin is golden, his stubbled jaw strong and infinitely kissable. I watch him as though seeing him for

5

the first time. Or the last. And I finally let myself relax. Roll over again and let sleep take me.

What seems like only moments later, I awaken. My back is cold, and I turn to see his side of the bed lies empty.

'Austin?'

A dark figure appears in the doorway, making me gasp.

'Go back to sleep, Stella,' Austin says.

'Why are you up?' I blink and try to focus. 'Are you *dressed*? What's wrong?' I ask, my heart juddering. I sit up and fumble for the bedside light.

'The restaurant just called. I left my credit card there. I was going to leave you a note in case you woke up while I was gone.' He waves a pad and pen at me.

'Call them back,' I say groggily. 'I'm sure they'll keep hold of your card until tomorrow.'

'Better not,' he replies with a sigh. 'Don't worry. It won't take long. I need to get a phone charger anyway. My battery's almost dead and I forgot to pack mine. I wish you'd get an iPhone. Do you want anything from the supermarket?'

'I'll come with you . . .'

'You're half asleep.'

'I don't mind,' I reply, trying to shake the wooziness from my brain. I really don't want him to go. To leave our cocoon. To break the spell. 'Wait for me. I'll get dressed.'

'No. It's fine, Stella. Stay. You're tired.' He comes over and leans down to kiss me, his clean, warm scent of cologne making me want to pull him closer. 'I'll be back before you know it.' I watch him slip on his suit jacket and leave the room, the door closing with a definitive clunk.

My phone shows that it's only 11.15 p.m., but it feels much later. I was exhausted from the hecticness of the past few weeks and today's early start. We got up at four thirty to catch our seven-thirty

6

flight from Bournemouth Airport, and I only managed to grab about three hours' sleep before that. I've been running on adrenaline and coffee all day. Those two glasses of wine at dinner followed by the shot of limoncello just about finished me off. But now I'm suddenly wide awake again.

Tonight's meal was another thoughtful surprise from Austin – he'd booked a restaurant called La Terrazza di Stella. It wasn't a posh place, but a family-run restaurant in a quiet side street. The food, however, was spectacular, and the owners – Nino and Elena – were the loveliest couple. When Austin explained to them that he'd booked their restaurant because my name is Stella, they made an extra-special fuss – as I share the name with their ten-year-old daughter – showering us with attention and free drinks. The whole evening was as near to perfect as it could be.

I touch my lips, thinking back to Austin's kisses. To his body against mine. To the promise of our night together. To the thought of our lives together. We've been a couple for almost four years. When he proposed last May, I didn't imagine it was possible to be so happy. How did a regular dance instructor like me end up with a handsome, successful business owner like Austin Lewis? I sink back down against the pillow, my eyes wanting to close.

But then I blink and stretch out my arms. I can't fall back to sleep. Not yet.

Barefoot, I pace the deep-red patterned Indian carpet that runs the length of the suite's living room, walking from the door to the Juliet balcony and back again. Past the chaise and the glass coffee table with its fruit platter and unopened bottle of champagne. Past the two gold-velvet armchairs, the carved armoires and the landscape paintings of Venice's canals. My dark-grey heels lie on their side, my jacket slung over one of our carry-on cases.

It's 12.40 a.m. – over an hour since Austin left the hotel. The restaurant's only fifteen minutes' walk away. Austin said he was going to the supermarket afterwards. It's possible he intended to have a late drink with the restaurant owners, Elena and Nino. Austin's great with people; usually manages to charm the pants off them. It's mainly why he's so successful in business and in his relationships. That, and possibly the fact that he comes from a wealthy and supportive family who gave him a leg up.

I'm wide awake now, more alert with every second that ticks by. Attuned to the door. To my phone. I've messaged him twice, and have also left a message at the restaurant. Either they're too busy to pick up or, more likely, they're closed; it's well after midnight. I call his number for the third time, and it goes to voicemail:

'*Hey, Austin, everything okay? Where are you?*'

I'm still aiming for light and breezy, but my voice sounds strangled. I end the message and stare at my phone screen, wondering how much longer I should wait before doing something. Maybe I should go to the restaurant . . . or the supermarket . . . speak to someone downstairs on reception . . . call the *police*? My chest contracts at the thought. I shouldn't panic, but my brain is already going into overdrive at all the terrible possibilities.

Chapter Two

THEN

'Dad, Austin and I have been together for over three years.' I try to make my voice calm. To keep things light. The last thing I want is an argument, but I can hear the tension and defensiveness behind my words. I put my fork down, having lost my appetite.

'Doesn't matter how long you've been with him, Stella. You don't throw good years after bad.' Dad takes a swig of his water and leans back in his chair, running a hand over his short greying hair.

'Leave it, Phil.' Mum reaches over and puts a freckled hand on his arm, as though her touch will magically make everything all right.

But Dad's face is hard, his eyes narrowing like a cornered cat's. 'I won't leave it,' Dad snaps, his voice filling the small kitchen of our rented terraced house. 'I know you want us to be all nicey-nice, Lindsay, but this is our daughter's life we're talking about.'

'I'm well aware of that,' Mum replies. 'But having a barney won't help.' She sighs. 'Honestly, you're both as pig-headed as each other.'

'I am here, you know,' I reply quietly. I knew telling my parents about Austin's marriage proposal wouldn't be a walk in the park, but I hadn't thought Dad would kick off quite as badly. 'I hoped you might have congratulated me. *Us*,' I say, unable to keep the hurt out of my voice.

'Sorry, love. Your dad's just worried about you. We both are.' Mum's always been the peacekeeper. Dad and I are close. But when we clash, we clash. Mum's more easy-going. She's always been nice to Austin, in contrast with Dad's silent disapproval. You'd think he would have got over it by now, because everyone else likes my boyfriend. Or should I say, my fiancé. Just thinking the word makes me smile.

'Glad you think this is funny, Stella,' Dad says, giving me a stern stare.

'I'm just happy, that's all. I love Austin and this is . . . well, it's the next step, isn't it? Getting married.'

Dad and Austin's first meeting three years ago was unfortunate. Austin had come straight to our house from a works do where he'd had a bit too much to drink. Dad's not a killjoy, but Austin came across as a bit brash and over-familiar, which isn't usually like him. He told Dad that he was going to treat me like a princess and provide a better life for me. I'd winced when he said that last part, knowing Dad would take it as a slight. If Dad would only have taken the time to get to know Austin properly instead of making a snap judgement over one comment, he'd have realised that Austin had spoken without thinking. That he was simply a little drunk and a little nervous. That he's a good guy.

But it was too late; that first meeting set the tone for their relationship. Dad thinks Austin is entitled and arrogant, and nothing either of us has been able to say or do can convince him otherwise. The more Austin tries to be nice, the more my dad resists. Dad's never said anything bad to Austin, he just gives off a disapproving vibe. I guess it doesn't help that we tend to spend more time as a couple with Austin's family than mine. It's a catch-22 – if Dad was nicer to Austin, we'd spend more time with my parents.

Last year, Mum accidentally let slip to me that Austin reminds Dad of her previous boyfriend, a local casino owner, who liked to flash his cash. Mum said she broke it off with him to be with Dad, but there was some unpleasantness at the time.

I probably should have made more of an effort earlier to smooth things over between Dad and Austin, but I didn't want any more unpleasantness so I swept it under the carpet.

'Is anybody going to eat this meal I've just cooked from scratch?' Mum asks, eyeing our untouched plates on the kitchen table. 'I didn't spend hours shopping and cooking just to throw this lot in the bin.'

'Sorry, Mum, it's really good.' I put a forkful of Spanish omelette with caramelised onions in my mouth and start to chew.

Dad does the same. 'You've outdone yourself, Lins. It's delicious.'

Mum's always experimenting with recipes to try to save on the grocery bill – some of which work, and some of which absolutely do not. But Dad and I always rave about her dishes, no matter how they turn out – even the one where she used demerara sugar instead of couscous. Thankfully, this is one of her better offerings. She's mollified by our praise. Although Mum and I look very similar – she's a slightly shorter, curvier version of me, her hair more pale brown than auburn – we're nothing alike in personality. She's softer, warmer, sweeter. I'm more like my dad.

'When did he propose?' Mum asks.

'Last week,' I reply, feeling warm and tingly at the memory. 'We went out on his dad's boat and moored up as the sun was setting. Then he got down on one knee. It was so romantic.'

'That does sound lovely,' Mum replies. 'But why did you wait a whole week to say anything? Why are you only just telling us now?'

'I wanted to wait until we were all together, not rushing to and from work.'

Dad grumbles something incoherent.

I hold out my hand to show Mum the ring and her eyes widen. I couldn't believe it when Austin flipped open the box and showed me the emerald. The whole proposal was such a shock, I could barely take it all in. Over the past year or so, I'd thought about bringing up the question of marriage and children with him, but hadn't known how to broach the subject. I'm over the moon that it was on his mind too.

'So,' I begin hesitantly, looking at my parents, 'I know he's not your first choice for me, but will you at least congratulate us? It would mean the world to Austin. And to me.'

'It would have been nice if he had the decency to speak to me first,' Dad says, avoiding the question.

'He wanted to,' I lie – he absolutely did not. 'But I told him it would be better if I spoke to you alone. Because I worried you'd be like this.' I mutter the last part under my breath.

'The man's a smarmy prat,' Dad adds.

'Now you're just being mean,' I reply, frustrated. 'He can't help having a posh accent. This is my life, Dad. You're not the one getting married. It doesn't affect you.'

'Your happiness affects me.' Dad sets his fork back down on the table with a clatter.

Mum huffs.

'If that's true,' I reply, 'then you being happy for me will make me happy.'

'You may be happy now,' Dad says. 'But marriage is a long-term commitment. What happens after you have a family and you realise he's not the one for you?'

I grit my teeth. 'No one knows what the future holds and if that happens – which it won't – then I'll deal with it at the time.'

'You'll understand when you have kids of your own,' he says.

I sigh, exasperated.

Dad's expression darkens further. 'He already made you give up your dream of dancing professionally. What else will he make you give up?'

'We've been over this. It's ancient history, and it was my decision, not his. I wanted to stay here in Christchurch with my friends and family. London and the rest of it wasn't for me.'

In truth, being a professional dancer was all I'd wanted during my younger years. Dad always liked to tell people how I could dance before I could walk. My parents were proud of me. They spent a lot of time and money making sure I got to performances and auditions, had the right costumes, and got into one of the top performing arts courses in the country. Mum's a cleaner for an agency and Dad's a delivery driver. They're hard-working and have sacrificed a lot for me.

It's not that I don't appreciate it, but does that mean I have to live the life they want for me, rather than the life I want for myself? I can't blame them for being disappointed when I turned down my big break three years ago – the opportunity to tour as a dancer with a famous singer. Instead, I took a modestly paid job locally as a dance instructor. I can admit to myself that I did it because I couldn't bear to be apart from my then-new boyfriend, Austin. Of course, I denied that at the time. But it wasn't Austin's decision. It was mine, so it's unfair of Dad to blame him. Although, if I'm being honest, I guess it was obvious why I stayed.

After my performing arts degree ended and I accepted a job with Millie Sessions as an instructor at her dance studio, Dad barely spoke to me for a month, he was so disappointed in my decision. But, despite his disapproval, he and Mum let me move back home. My job isn't well paid enough for me to buy my own place so I'd planned to live at home and save for a deposit. But that hasn't worked out too well. My parents rent their house so I chip in for rent and bills. And Austin and his friends are all well off so I don't like to be a cheapskate when we're out. Consequently, I spend far more than I should each month, leaving – let's be real here – nothing to save towards a deposit.

If I thought about it too deeply, I'd probably admit that I made the wrong career decision. That I should have taken the exciting gig that would have opened doors for me. I optimistically assumed that further opportunities like that would come my way if I wanted them. Only they haven't. I realise now that those types of things are usually once-in-a-lifetime dream situations, and I turned mine down. Instead, I opted for the once-in-a-lifetime dream boyfriend.

He literally is the perfect boyfriend though – attentive, loving, fun, impulsive, always planning romantic surprises. I'm lucky, and I don't regret my decision to stay in Christchurch. There are far worse places to live than this pretty Dorset town. Even if my family does live in a not-so-pretty part of it.

'What about Jake?' Dad says, interrupting my thoughts.

'What about him?' I reply, knowing exactly where this conversation's going. Our neighbours, the Pirellis, have a son called Jake, who I went to school with. He's a good friend, the sweetest guy. Kind and down to earth, works locally as a mechanic. I'm sure my parents have had numerous conversations about the two of us getting together. But I've never thought of Jake in that way. He's more like a brother.

'The lad's still in love with you, you know,' Dad says, as if it's news to me. 'You should give him a chance.'

'Dad! I've just told you I'm marrying Austin. Why are you trying to set me up with someone else?'

'Lindsay,' Dad says, 'back me up here. Jake's perfect for Stella, isn't he?'

'He's a lovely boy,' Mum replies noncommittally.

'Exactly! He's the boy next door,' Dad says. 'You know exactly what you're getting with Jake – he's down to earth, hard-working, loyal. And he makes you laugh – that's important. Me and your mother, we have a laugh, it's part of the glue that keeps us together. Jake is . . . well, he's a good man. Not some random person you met on the internet.'

'Everyone meets online these days! And Austin is hardly random. We've been together three years. You've met his family.' I always knew Dad didn't love my boyfriend, but I hadn't realised the sheer depth of his dislike. I guess he'd been keeping all this inside, hoping we'd eventually break up. Now he knows that's not happening, he's letting rip with his true feelings. I love my dad, but this isn't fair. I don't want to choose between my father and my fiancé. 'Why can't you just accept him?' I cry, unable to keep a lid on my emotions any more.

'Because you're my daughter and I know what's right for you,' Dad replies gruffly.

'Fine. Well, I think it's best if I stay over at Austin's tonight,' I say, getting to my feet. 'Give you a chance to get used to the idea.'

'Hmph. There's no getting used to you making the biggest mistake of your life,' Dad mutters.

I bite my tongue and mouth an apology to Mum before leaving the kitchen and heading upstairs to grab a change of clothes to take to Austin's, tears stinging the back of my eyes.

Don't let him get to you, I tell myself, throwing open the door to my childhood bedroom and picking out a few things from my wardrobe. But I know my father too well. He's stubborn as hell. Like me. Winning him over is going to be an uphill battle.

Chapter Three

NOW

Pacing the hotel suite is doing no good. My mind is racing, my breathing irregular. I realise I need to go looking for my husband. It's 12.50 a.m. – over an hour and a half since Austin left our hotel room. I must have called his phone at least half a dozen times. With trembling fingers, I slip off my robe and pull on a pair of dark jeans, a cream jumper and tan boots. I'll go to the restaurant. See if he showed up there.

Google Maps is telling me it should only take thirteen minutes on foot so I head downstairs to the hotel lobby where I walk across the vast expanse of grey marble floor, nodding at the receptionist and concierge before leaving. I take a left out of the glass double doors and hurry along the narrow street, away from the Grand Canal and towards the interior of the city. I pass designer shops – closed and shuttered – bars, restaurants and a gelateria that's still open for business, but the streets are virtually empty at this late hour on a Sunday. The quietness of the city should make me wary, nervous – a female alone at night in a foreign place – but I'm too anxious to worry about my personal safety. Instead, I stride through the lanes, a woman on a mission.

I hurry up the steps of a small stone bridge. Beneath, the dark water of the canal laps against the mossy walls. A couple of boats knock against the wooden poles they're tied to, and a cold wind whispers along the canal, bringing with it the sulphury smell of drains and something rotting. My eyes water and I turn my face away from the boats, focusing on the way ahead and picking up my pace. I'm almost at the restaurant. I pause to check directions on my phone, and then turn right into the side street we visited earlier this evening.

There it is up ahead – La Terrazza di Stella. But it's nothing like it looked a few hours ago. Now it lies in darkness, aside from the haze of a streetlamp further down the lane. No lights twinkling from the canopies above the outdoor seating. No overhead heaters warming the customers. No bustling waiters, laughter, chatter or gentle music. Just the whistling breeze. I shiver and approach the building, unsure what to do.

The door to the restaurant is closed. I step on to the terrace and give it a push, just in case. But, of course, it doesn't budge. I pull on the handle. Locked. Pressing up close to the glass, I peer through a gap in the gauzy curtains, cupping my hands around my face to block out the faint glow of the streetlamp.

Inside, a single light has been left on behind the bar, illuminating the dark wood tables and the seating with its deep-red velvet upholstery. The tables are already set with plates, glasses and cutlery, a single red candle in the centre of each, ready for tomorrow's customers.

I take a breath and knock loudly on the glass door – three raps in succession. Maybe there's still a member of staff out the back, in the restaurant kitchen. I glance behind me, certain someone is going to start yelling at me for disturbing the peace. The buildings behind are a mix of restaurants, bars and shops. All closed, all in darkness. The windows above are similarly dark. I wonder if they're storerooms or flats up there.

I check my phone and see it's just after 1 a.m. I'm worried the owners will be at home, asleep. Do they live here, above the restaurant, or somewhere else? I desperately need to speak to them. To ask if they've seen my husband. I try calling Austin on my mobile again, but I just get put through to voicemail.

This time, I don't even try to sound calm. 'Austin, where are you? Are you back at the hotel? Please call me as soon as you get this message. I'm going out of my mind here.' A tear runs down my cheek and I wipe it away. I can't panic. I need to focus on what to do next.

I bang on the door once more, louder this time. If anyone's still in the restaurant, I need them to hear me. To take notice. '*Hello!*' I call through the letterbox. 'Hello! Is anybody there?'

There's a scraping noise above, and I take a few steps back from the terrace so that I'm on the street once again. I look up to see a green wooden shutter creaking open on the second floor. A dark-haired man in a white vest peers down at me, his face crumpled from sleep. He says something in Italian and I realise it's the restaurant owner, Nino, who Austin and I got on with so well earlier this evening.

'Sorry,' I call up.

'Stella?' He remembers me. That's good.

'Hi, Nino, I'm so sorry to disturb you, but—'

He puts a finger to his lips and gestures around to the other buildings before indicating that he's coming down.

I nod and wrap my arms around myself. My fingers and toes are numb with cold, or maybe with the shock of the situation. My lips are still throbbing from Austin's earlier kisses, my body still tingling from his touch. I try to stay calm, but I feel like I might lose control at any moment.

18

Seconds later, Nino emerges from a small door at the side of the restaurant, painted the same deep green as the shutters. He's wearing a smart blue robe with white piping and a pair of tan slippers. Behind him, down a steep flight of stairs, comes his wife, Elena, wearing navy silk pyjamas and a thick woollen cardigan. I feel bad for getting this hard-working couple out of bed, but I had no choice. I have to speak to them.

'Have you seen my husband this evening?' I ask without any preamble. 'Austin.'

'Austin? Your husband?' Nino replies. 'Yes. He came back this evening to collect his credit card. He left it on the table earlier. He's not back?'

I swallow down a burst of hysteria. 'No. He said he was coming here and then going to find a supermarket to get a phone charger. But that was almost two hours ago. He said he wouldn't be long.'

'Which supermarket?' Elena asks.

I shake my head. 'I don't know. Did he say anything to you about . . . anything?'

'No, no,' Nino replies with a frown. 'He was very quick. He came into the restaurant. We were closing down for the night, but I asked him if he wanted a drink. He said he had to get back to you. It's your honeymoon!'

'Okay,' I say, 'so how safe is it at night here? Do you think he could have been . . . attacked? Mugged?'

Nino shakes his head. 'It's a very safe city, aside from the pickpockets. You can easily walk around at night. Maybe he went for a drink somewhere? Or . . .' Nino turns to Elena and they converse in Italian for a moment, shrugging and frowning.

'You've called him?' Elena asks.

'Every ten minutes at least,' I reply. 'It just goes to voicemail.'

'Maybe he tripped and hurt himself?' Nino says, giving his wife another look. 'I think you must call the police. They will help you find him.'

'I can't believe this is happening,' I mutter, rubbing at my nose. 'He only came out to get his card back. He was supposed to be gone for half an hour or so at the most.'

'It will be fine,' Elena reassures. 'Try his phone again. Maybe he will answer now.'

I call him as Nino and Elena give me encouraging looks. But there's still no reply. I shake my head.

'Come inside,' Elena says. 'I'll make you a warm drink and we'll call the police together.'

'Are you sure?' I barely know this couple, but they're being so kind.

'It's fine. Come. We must be quiet. The children are sleeping.' She pauses. 'You said your husband was going to the supermarket after coming here.'

'Yes,' I confirm.

'The closest one is across the Ponte dei Dai,' Nino muses. 'You should go there next. Ask if they remember seeing him.'

'I'll go now. It's okay, I don't need a drink,' I reply, hesitating outside their front door. 'I'm so sorry to have brought this to you in the middle of the night. I'll go to the supermarket and then back to the hotel. They'll help me find Austin, or call the police. But thank you for your help and for being so kind.'

'It's no trouble,' Elena says, her dark eyes filled with compassion, pitying me for something that may or may not have happened.

'I'm just hoping he'll be back at the hotel already,' I say wistfully.

Nino gives me a nod. 'Yes, you should check back there too before you call the police. I'll walk with you to the late-night supermarket and then the hotel.'

I hold up my hands. 'No, you've already been really kind. Go back to bed, both of you.'

'He's going with you. No arguments,' Elena says.

'Let me just get changed.' He sprints up the stairs before I can dissuade him.

'It will be fine,' Elena says, taking my hand. 'Oh, you're cold.' She rubs my hands between hers. 'Your Austin will be waiting for you back at the hotel, and then you can shout at him for making you worry, okay?'

I nod, shivering, wanting so much to believe that it's true. That I'll get back to the room, and Austin will be sitting there and I'll tell him off for worrying me so much, and he'll apologise and tell me a tale about how he got caught up in some kind of drama and had to help someone, and how he lost his phone in the process. And everything will be fine and our honeymoon will get back on track. This will simply become an anecdote that we'll tell people when we get home. Something that we'll tell our grandchildren.

But after Nino kindly walks me to the supermarket – where no one remembers seeing him – and then back to the hotel, where I check our empty suite, it's clear that this is more serious than an amusing anecdote. This is something else. My husband is missing.

Chapter Four

THEN

I step off the bus and walk along the high street, beneath the glowing streetlamps, then past the priory towards Austin's riverside flat, where we'll live after we're married. I'd thought he might have asked me to move in sooner, but it feels better this way. More special, somehow. Like we'll be embarking on a fresh new chapter.

A cold wind blows across the empty graveyard, the May air damp with a lingering chill of winter, making me yearn for warm summer evenings and lazy days on the beach. I shiver, trying to shake off the nervousness I've recently developed about walking alone. It started a few months ago when I had the eerie feeling I was being followed. Nothing actually happened, just a vague sense of someone behind me – footsteps matching my own – and I've had a similar feeling several times since. I throw a glance over my shoulder and relax when I see an elderly couple come into view, walking their dog.

My thoughts return to home. The aftertaste of this evening's argument sits heavily on my chest. I'm not a confrontational person so the disagreement with Dad has left me anxious and out of sorts. What if he never comes around? What if he refuses to come to the wedding? I shouldn't let my worries take over but it's hard not to, especially when I know how stubborn Dad can be.

I reach the narrow path, overhung with branches, that leads through the car park and into the riverside development where Austin lives. Birds sing the last chorus of their evening song joined by the priory bells, which ring out across the graveyard, over the river and throughout the town. Sentimentally, I imagine that they're ringing to celebrate our engagement. I can hardly believe they'll soon be ringing to celebrate our marriage. We're thinking about setting a date for next spring. My belly fills with excited butterflies at the thought.

I want the traditional wedding with all the trimmings, Dad walking me down the aisle, proud of me, happy, and feeling warm towards Austin. I want to do the father-daughter dance. The speeches, all of it. The schmaltzier the better. Pretty sure I've overdosed on rom-coms, but that's the vision I have in my head. So if Dad doesn't give his blessing, what then?

My parents' reactions feel even worse because Austin's mum and dad were so over the moon when we told them the news, breaking out the champagne and calling up his grandparents. Talking about a get-together with both families. Goodness only knows how that's going to go.

As I cross the stone bridge that leads to Austin's road, I slow down a little. I'm not sure what I'm going to say to him when I get there. He knows what Dad's like, but I'm sure he was expecting a warmer response. I think he thought that after proposing, my dad would see how serious Austin is about me. How can I tell him that Dad doesn't approve? That he even suggested setting me up with our next-door neighbour? I can't. I'll have to lie and tell him I haven't told my parents yet. Either that or pretend it went well. Surely, with time, Dad will come around.

I could tone down his response and maybe say something along the lines of *Dad's getting used to the idea*. That's vague enough to sound plausible. But I know what Austin's like; he can read me like a book. He'll pick away at me until he gets the truth. I exhale and press the bell, waiting beneath the porch for him to buzz me in. He gave me a key last year, but I never like to use it unless he's expecting me. It will be strange to move in here. For it to be our place instead of his place.

I press the bell again. Still no reply. His electric Audi is charging on the driveway, so it seems like he's home. Maybe he's on the phone, or got his ear buds in. I call his mobile, but he doesn't pick up, which is odd, so I leave a message telling him I'm outside. Should I use the key? I dither for a moment and then send him a text telling him I'm going to let myself in and wait for him to come home, and then I do just that, opening the front door and walking up the three flights of stairs to his penthouse flat.

Austin has the whole top level to himself. His flat has two en-suite bedrooms – one of which he's turned into an office – and a large open-plan living-dining-kitchen area that leads on to a wide terrace overlooking the river. The bedroom also has a terrace, but without the river view. It's a beautiful home and I'm looking forward to living here, especially as it's walking distance to town and to Dance Sessions, the studio where I work. No more standing in the rain to wait for the bus.

I reach the small landing and am about to press the doorbell, just in case Austin's home, when I hear raised deep voices. I think they're coming from inside the flat. Sounds like he's having an argument with someone. A bad argument that's growing more heated by the second. Someone is really angry in there. I swallow and wonder what to do. Who could be shouting at Austin like that?

Maybe I should leave, but I don't want to go back home, not while Dad's in such a prickly mood. The shouting has now reached a crescendo. I feel as though I've escaped World War III only to crash headlong into World War IV. Should I stay or should I retreat? If Austin's in trouble, I want to help.

After I press the doorbell, the yelling stops for a moment. A low, angry conversation starts up instead. I ring the bell again and rap on the door. 'Austin, are you okay? It's Stella.'

Silence falls, followed by the sound of footsteps and the click of the door being opened. Austin's standing in the hallway, red-faced, wearing navy joggers and a white T-shirt, his arms still tanned from our week away in the Canaries. A man comes up behind him and I see that it's Bart Randall, Austin's business partner and friend from school. His face is stiff with anger and he's blinking furiously. 'This isn't over, Austin. I'm not fucking happy,' he retorts.

Austin shakes his head. 'You're not getting away with this, Bart.'

'Don't make me laugh,' Bart mutters.

I'm shocked to see both of them behaving this way towards one another. I've known Bart and his wife, Patsy, for years, and have never seen either one of them angry. Patsy isn't necessarily my type of person – she's a little superior for my taste – but Bart has never been anything but friendly.

There must be something in the air today. First my dad doesn't want me to marry Austin, and now his business partner is having a go.

'Stella.' Bart gives me a curt nod as he passes me.

I'm not sure how to reply, so I stay silent.

But then he stops and fixes me with a stare. 'Word of advice. Get as far away from that arsehole as you can.'

I screw up my face in confusion as Bart slams his way out through the landing door and thunders down the stairs.

I turn back to face Austin. 'What the hell was all that about?'

Austin sighs. 'You'd better come in.'

25

Chapter Five

NOW

'Missing?' Davide Rossi, the hotel's night manager, gives me a sceptical look. He's in his forties, dark-brown hair swept back off his face, and he seems irritated that I've taken his attention from his computer screen.

I often get this dismissive attitude from people in authority. I realise it's because I'm female and have a young-looking face. It usually irritates me, but right now it's bloody infuriating. I stop drumming my fingers on the dark marble reception desk and square my shoulders, staring the man in the eye and strengthening my voice. 'My name is Mrs Stella Lewis, and my husband and I are staying in the honeymoon suite in room 421. Like I said, my husband, Mr Austin Lewis, popped out at 11.15 to retrieve his credit card from La Terrazza di Stella, but he never returned.'

Davide raises an eyebrow. 'Perhaps he went to have a drink. You have called him?'

I restrain myself from rolling my eyes. 'Many times. And I went to the restaurant to look for him. The owners confirmed he was there. But he's still not back.'

'You said it's your honeymoon?'

'Yes, we arrived today. Well, I suppose it's yesterday now.'

'Okay, okay.' His face softens a little. 'You are worried because he is out late?'

I grit my teeth. 'I'm worried because he said he would be gone for half an hour, but it's been over two hours. It's one thirty a.m.'

'Don't worry. Maybe he got lost. He'll be back soon.' It's clear Davide thinks I'm overreacting.

'He had his phone – Google Maps – he wouldn't get lost.' But then I remember that his phone was running out of charge. I think back to how kind Nino and Elena were at the restaurant. How they offered to call the police for me. I wish I'd taken them up on their offer now. After walking me back, Nino even said he'd wait with me at the hotel, but I insisted he return home, not wanting to disturb his night further. They're such good people. I try to stay calm, but my brain is racing.

'Maybe his battery died,' Davide says. 'Do you have the app *Find My*? You can track the last place the phone was switched on with that.'

'No.'

'Ah, it's good. It allows you to see where the other person—'

'Would it help if I installed the app now?' I ask.

'No, sadly you must be connected already for it to work.'

'So that's no good then.'

Davide shrugs. 'You would like a drink while you wait for him to return? I can get you a coffee?'

'No thank you.'

'Some tea?'

I shake my head, thinking that a shot of something stronger to calm my nerves would be perfect. But I resist the temptation. I should stay as clear-headed as I can.

'Two hours is not too long. He will be back soon,' Davide says in a tone that suggests he's ending the conversation. His eyes stray back to his screen.

'It's been over two hours and it's the early hours of the morning,' I snap. I'm not normally so rude, but I can't think straight, I'm exhausted and I'm stressed, and I need this man's help, not his dismissal. I soften my tone. 'I think I need to call the police.'

Davide's dark eyes widen momentarily, but then he gives a short nod. 'I will call them for you.' He picks up the phone that sits behind the reception desk.

I let out a small sigh of relief. I was dreading ringing them myself, worrying about the language barrier. Worrying whether or not they would take me seriously. 'Thank you.'

He holds up a finger to stop me, and then begins talking in Italian to the person on the other end of the line.

I can't believe this is my honeymoon. That Austin isn't here with me. That I'm calling the Italian police! This feels like the start of a nightmare.

After a few minutes of conversation that I'm desperate to understand, Davide tells me the police are on their way here to take a statement.

'How long will they be?' I ask.

'Not long. The station is only five, ten minutes away.'

I nod and exhale. Hopefully, once I've told them, they can start the search, and then this whole nightmarish episode will be over.

'Why don't you sit and relax over there while you wait?' Davide offers, gesturing to a seating area at the far end of the lobby.

I'm not sure how he thinks I'm going to relax, but I do as he suggests and make my way over to a spacious open-plan lounge with smart bookshelves and dark-leaved potted plants. I spot a grey armchair that will give me a clear view of the entrance and reception area. As I cross the lobby in a daze, a smartly dressed young

American couple I recognise from earlier amble past and wish me a good night. I barely hear them, but manage to mutter something unintelligible in response, hoping they don't try to engage me in conversation. Thankfully, they head past reception towards the lifts.

I perch on the edge of the armchair and check my messages for the hundredth time, send Austin yet another text and leave another desperate voicemail. A slender blonde-haired receptionist has joined Davide and they start talking, heads bowed together. She glances over in my direction and I realise he must be filling her in on my husband's disappearance. I wonder if there are many situations where the hotel staff have to call the police for a resident. I guess there must be thefts, lost property, maybe even muggings. But do people ever go missing from this hotel? Or is this the first time?

Picking at the skin around my newly manicured French tips, my chest aches as I think back to when I last saw Austin here, his familiar frame filling the doorway, his kiss before he left. I feel my eyes prick with tears. I inhale and will myself to keep calm. If I start to cry now, I think I'll lose it completely. All the worst-case scenarios are flitting through my head in a carousel of horror. It's no good thinking this way. I have to be strong and positive.

Movement and voices at the reception desk have me jumping to my feet, holding my breath in anticipation, but it's just an older couple coming through the water doors at the Grand Canal entrance, having arrived by boat. A porter brings their luggage into the lobby while they start to check in with Davide. I think back to the previous morning, when Austin and I were doing exactly the same thing after arriving by water taxi. I can't believe that was less than twenty-four hours earlier. It seems like days ago. Like another lifetime.

Just as I'm about to sit back down, I hear the static and crackle of radios as two youngish police officers arrive through the side entrance. My heart is in my mouth and my legs feel almost too weak for me to stand. They look so official in their dark uniforms. Both are huge guys, tall and broad, intimidating; more like cartoon superheroes than real-life police.

I can't continue sitting here in a stupor. I need to get up and speak to them. I walk over, the low heels of my tan boots tapping across the marble floor. Davide is still busy with the new arrivals, but the receptionist – a tag on her lapel says her name is Sara Bruno – is chatting to the officers, laughing and twirling her long blonde ponytail between slim fingers. She stops laughing as I approach, but there's still an inappropriately flirty smile on her lips.

'Mrs Lewis,' she says. 'I am sorry to hear you can't locate your husband. I'm sure the police can help.'

I give her a nod of thanks and turn to both officers, one of whom is still gazing, rapt, at Sara. His slightly older colleague, who looks around my age, gives me a sympathetic nod. 'Mrs Lewis?'

'Yes.'

'I'm Officer Rocco Gallini and this is my colleague, Officer Diego Moro. Shall we sit?' he asks in almost flawless English, gesturing to the lounge area I've just come from. 'And you can tell me what's happened.'

Davide calls over to Sara and points towards the restaurant, which is now closed. Sara speaks to the officers in Italian and I feel like I'm invisible.

'What's going on?' I ask.

'If you'll follow me,' Sara says. She walks beside the younger officer, chattering away as though they're old friends, while Gallini and I follow in silence.

We pass through the archway that leads into the dimly lit dining area and Sara gestures to a table in the corner next to one of the breakfast-buffet tables laid out with empty baskets and small pots of jam. I realise that she's tucked us out of the way; Davide probably didn't want two hulking great police officers cluttering up his lobby and making people wonder what crime has been committed. I guess that wouldn't give quite the right ambience for a five-star hotel.

'Would you like a drink?' Sara asks, directing her question to Moro.

We all ask for a glass of water, which Sara pours from a cooler, and then she leaves us to it.

'Please, tell us what's happened,' the older officer says kindly.

I feel manic, stressed, like I'm not even here. What am I doing in this foreign country, talking to these police officers? I take a sip of water, try to focus, and then tell them about Austin leaving to retrieve his credit card from the restaurant. About how Elena and Nino spoke to my husband, but how the supermarket owner couldn't remember seeing him.

The officers are sympathetic, but they seem unworried, saying that the chances are he'll be back soon. I wonder how much of that they believe to be true, and how much is them trying to keep me calm.

'I can't help worrying that he might be out there hurt,' I say. 'What if he's been mugged, or he's fallen into one of the canals?' My voice cracks.

'We can check CCTV in the supermarket, and we can also check the city's security cameras,' Gallini adds. 'We'll start with the San Marco Quarter.'

'I read a news article about the new surveillance system in Venice that tracks phones,' I say. 'Are you able to track Austin's phone with it?'

'No.' Gallini shakes his head. 'The surveillance system is for flooding and for crowd control, to track how many tourists visit Venice at any one time, and where they're from. But there's no personal data recorded.'

'Oh,' I reply. 'But you do have some cameras you can check?'

'Yes.' He inclines his head. 'Did you call the hospitals at all? In case there's been an accident?'

'No. I should do that! I can't believe I didn't think of it.'

'We can check for you.'

I exhale. 'Okay. Thank you.'

'Do you have a photo of your husband?' Moro asks.

I show them one I took earlier on the water taxi, Austin's eyes shining with excitement as the speedboat bounced across the waves. Moro takes a copy of it on his phone and says they'll start searching the local area.

'Was this what he was wearing?' Moro asks, gesturing to the photo, where my husband is wearing his navy puffer jacket.

'No. He's wearing a dark-grey suit.'

I'd been convinced the police were going to tell me to wait twenty-four hours – that's what normally happens on TV shows – but it looks like they're going to take immediate action. That's something at least.

'Did you notice anything unusual in his behaviour recently?' Gallini asks. 'Anything out of the ordinary?'

'This whole trip is out of the ordinary,' I reply. 'We're on our honeymoon. It's a first for both of us. But we were happy, in love . . . I didn't notice anything wrong.'

'Is your husband on any medication?'

'Not that I know of. No.'

'Had he been drinking? Taking any drugs?'

'Just some wine with dinner, and a shot of limoncello. Nothing major. He wasn't drunk.'

'Okay, well, you'll tell us if you remember anything else?' Gallini asks, getting to his feet along with his colleague.

I nod, but my blood is pumping and sweat beads beneath my arms and slides between my breasts. What happens now? Do I just stay in the hotel by myself and wait for the police to get back to me?

Gallini must notice my panic because he stops and asks, 'Do you have any friends in Venice who can wait with you?'

I shake my head, not trusting myself to speak.

'Have you had any sleep?'

I shake my head. I did have an hour or so before Austin left, but that feels like it never happened.

'Okay, so I recommend you go to bed. Hopefully, when you wake up, your husband will be back and you can get on with enjoying your honeymoon.'

I nod, wanting to believe him. Wanting so much for him to be right. 'Thank you,' I manage to croak.

'You're welcome. Let's exchange numbers. Get some sleep and we'll be back in touch tomorrow. Sooner if we have any news.'

Once the officers have left, I stay seated at the table for a while longer, unable to move, unwilling to return to my empty honeymoon suite. My belly swirls with nausea, my throat fills with saliva. I am *not* about to throw up in the dining room. I grip the edge of the table and will myself to breathe calmly, to slow my spinning brain.

'Mrs Lewis?'

I look up to see Davide Rossi standing at the entrance to the dining room. 'You are all right? Can I get you anything?'

I shake my head and attempt to stand. 'I think I'm going to try to get some rest,' I say, not believing for a second that I'll be able to relax enough to fall asleep.

'This is a good idea. Maybe I can have room service send you up some herbal tea? It will help you sleep.'

'Thank you.'

'Okay. I will update my colleague when she comes on duty at eight. She will look after you until your husband returns.'

'You're very kind,' I say.

He gives me a gentle smile and leaves.

I somehow manage to get myself into the lift and back up to the hotel suite. The living room feels cold and strange, like it's haunted with the ghosts of yesterday. I stumble through to the bedroom and sit on the edge of the bed, numb. What will the police discover? What will they tell me tomorrow? Or, I guess, it will be later today.

After four years together, I don't know what to do without Austin at my side. He's the person I would normally seek help from. We've always been a team. Had each other's backs and been there through the tough times. I need him here to talk to about this. To worry with me. He's my rock. The thought of calling his parents with the news that he's missing makes me feel ill. And I don't want to stress my parents about this either. Not yet, anyway. I lay my head down and bring my knees up to my chest in the foetal position.

If only Austin hadn't left the hotel. If only he'd stayed asleep by my side.

I close my eyes and try to ignore the tears that slide out from beneath my lids.

Chapter Six

THEN

'What was that about?' I repeat, following Austin into the flat, still shell-shocked by Bart's outburst.

'So sorry you had to see that, Stella.' Austin massages the back of his neck and I tilt my face up to kiss him before kicking off my trainers and slipping off my coat, hanging it in the hall cupboard and retrieving my phone from the pocket.

Austin pulls me into a bear hug and I squeeze him back, feeling his speeding heartbeat against mine. 'Are you okay?' I ask.

'Not really.' He inhales and lets go of me, rubbing at his stubbled cheeks and letting out a frustrated growl.

All thoughts of my dad's negative reaction to my engagement news have fled as I wait for Austin to enlighten me on his altercation with Bart. He and Austin are joint directors in a security-gate company. They set it up after graduating from their respective universities, and it's been incredibly successful, starting out in our local area and gradually expanding nationwide.

'Do you want a drink?' Austin asks. 'I need a beer after that.'

I follow him into the living room, where he heads over to the kitchen area and yanks open the sleek black door to the integral fridge. He tears off a can of some fancy IPA from a four-pack, then reaches for two glasses from one of the walnut cabinets. He still hasn't explained what the argument with Bart was about, but he's so keyed up that I don't want to push him. I'll wait to let him explain in his own time.

Austin pours our drinks and passes me a glass as I sit on a stool at the long black-marble-topped island, tracing one of its cold, pale veins with my fingertip. He remains on the other side of the island, facing me, taking a long draught of his beer while I sip mine slowly, the bitter lemony taste fizzing on my tongue.

'I'm glad you showed up when you did, Stella,' he says eventually, exhaling slowly through his mouth. 'I think that could have turned really nasty.'

'*Could have?* Sounded like it was already there. Thought you and Bart were supposed to be lifelong friends.'

'We are! Or at least I thought we were.' Austin's expression darkens, his sea-green eyes clouding over. 'Anyway, how come you're here? Not that I'm not happy to see you, but I thought you were supposed to be talking to your parents tonight. Telling them about our engagement.'

'It didn't feel like quite the right time,' I reply, staring into my glass, not wanting to add Dad's doubts to Austin's already stressful evening.

'Oh.' Austin's shoulders droop. 'Because Mum's going on about arranging a date for us all to go out to dinner to celebrate.'

'Yeah, that's fine. I'll talk to my parents. Just . . . you know what they're like. Dad isn't a big fan of surprises.'

'He isn't a fan of me, you mean.' Austin gives me a sad smile.

'*What?* No. Course he is.' I start fiddling with my emerald engagement ring, twisting it round on my finger. It's the most perfect ring I could have imagined. Austin said he knew it was the one as soon as he saw it. 'Dad's just not an enthusiastic person. He's low key.'

'Hmm.' Austin isn't buying my explanation, and I don't really blame him.

'Anyway,' I say, rapidly changing the subject, 'do you think you'll be able to sort things out with Bart?'

'Unlikely.' Austin grimaces and sips his beer.

'Really? Is it that bad?'

'He's been taking money out of the company,' Austin says, rubbing his forehead wearily.

'What? Like *stealing*?'

Austin makes a back-and-forth motion with his hand. 'Kind of, but it's hard to prove. He's been fiddling expenses, buying personal stuff with company money.'

'Oh no. Austin, I'm so sorry.'

'Yeah, you and me both.' He drains his glass and turns back to the fridge to get another can.

'What are you going to do?'

He sighs. 'I honestly don't know what to do for the best. I thought he was my friend, but now I've confronted him, he's turning into a loose cannon, denying everything. I hope he doesn't trash the business. I've spent years building it up, creating our reputation.'

'Can I help at all?' I ask.

'I don't know.' The colour is draining from his face and he looks genuinely scared.

I hope I don't look as frightened as he does, because I want to be supportive.

'I'm really worried, Stella. I hope this doesn't put you off getting married.'

'Of course not!'

'It's just . . . I get the feeling that Bart's not going to stop at threats.'

'Hey, come here.' I slip off my stool and walk around the island, taking him by the hand and leading him across to the pale-grey sectional sofa. 'Nobody is going to trash your business, and nobody is breaking us up, okay?'

Austin sinks on to the sofa, crosses his arms and drops his head. 'You can't know that,' he replies.

'Bart can threaten and shout all he likes,' I say, with more certainty than I feel, 'but no one's going to believe his ranting. Not in a million years.'

'But what if they do?' he asks.

'They won't,' I reply confidently, sitting next to him.

'How do you know? What if he wrecks everything? You didn't hear him. He was so nasty, Stella.'

'Only because you caught him out. He's on the defensive. Was that the first time you've confronted him?'

Austin nods.

'Okay, so maybe once he's had time to think about it, he'll realise he's in the wrong and he'll have to apologise, sort things out.'

'I hope you're right.'

'Course I am. You've been friends since school. He's not going to throw that away. I'm sure you can fix it. Anyway, you have proof, right? So make a note of all the transactions and tell him that if he starts spreading lies you'll . . . I dunno, report him to whoever. The accounts people or tax people or fraud or whatever . . .'

Austin cracks a smile.

'What?'

'You're so cute when you're being protective.'

'That's me. The cute protector of boyfriends.'

'Um, I hope there's only the one. And it's fiancé, not boyfriend.'

'Oh, yeah, sorry.' I smile back at him, although he's gone serious again. 'It will all be okay, Austin.'

He takes a breath and seems a little calmer.

'Does Patsy know?' I wonder if Bart's wife, always so condescending, will stick by her husband or make him do the right thing.

'No idea,' Austin replies, a fresh expression of despair suddenly crossing his features.

'How much has he taken out of the business?' I ask.

Austin shakes his head. 'I don't know exactly, but it's thousands.'

'That's terrible.' I gaze at the sliding doors that lead out on to the dark terrace, our faint reflections looking sad, defeated. 'Can he pay it back? Will the business be okay?'

'I don't know if he'll pay it back, but I'm hoping the business will survive. We're booked up solid at the moment and cash flow's good.' Austin leans back and stares up at the ceiling. 'It's just our partnership that's a mess. How can I be in business with someone I don't trust?'

'We'll sort it out,' I say. 'Get him to pay back what he owes, split up the partnership if you need to. I'll help any way I can. I know I'm not experienced in business stuff, but I can do emotional support.' I snuggle into his side and take his hand, rubbing my thumb across his palm. 'I can listen, and tell you how amazing you are. And whatever accusations Bart throws out, I'll make sure no one believes them.'

'You're amazing, Stells. I don't know what I'd do without you.'

'Well, you don't have to worry about that, because you're stuck with me forever.'

'Promise?' he asks, tipping up my chin and looking into my eyes.

'Cross my heart.'

My phone starts buzzing on the kitchen island and I wonder if it might be Mum wanting me to come home and sort things out with Dad.

'Do you want to see who that is?' Austin tips his head in the direction of my phone.

'No, it's fine.'

'Honestly, take it. I'm going to jump in the shower, try to clear my head.' He kisses me and gets to his feet.

'Sure?'

'Yep.'

Austin leaves the room, but I don't answer my mobile straight-away. I'm still too shaken by the evening's events. First Dad, then Austin. I wonder if Austin will tell his parents what's happened. They have their own successful company so I'm sure they'd have some good, practical advice. Aside from that, Rob and Vicki would do anything for their son. They treat him like a prince. I'll suggest he speaks to them once he's out of the shower.

I get up off the sofa and walk back to the kitchen, where my phone screen shows a missed call from my best friend Claudia. We chat most evenings, but I don't have the emotional energy to talk to her right now. I'm still trying to process everything. And seeing Bart being so aggressive is giving me a bit of delayed shock.

I listen to Claudia's voicemail:

'Hey, Stella, call me back when you get this, but just in case you can't, check out Keri Wade's Insta. I'm sure it's nothing, but wanted you to know. Use my sign-in. Okay? Love you. Call me, call me, call me.'

Well, that doesn't sound ominous at all. I sit down heavily on one of the stools and open Instagram. Keri Wade is Austin's ex-girlfriend. They broke up just before he and I got together three years ago, but she's never got over him, and she absolutely hates my guts and isn't shy about showing it. Obviously I don't follow Keri on social media – she blocked me anyway – but Claudia and I share each other's sign-ins for situations just like this.

40

I open up my browser, sign in to my friend's account, and search for @keriwadeofficial

Keri's an influencer with over fifty thousand followers. Her pinned post is a selfie of her in a swanky bar that has a huge tree growing up through the centre of it. Dark-haired and blue-eyed, with too much lip filler, Keri's wearing a peach bodycon dress showing plenty of cleavage. Sitting by her side, staring up into her camera, is my fiancé, Austin. She's captioned it with: 'Keri and Austin sittin' in a tree . . .' And the date shows that it was posted yesterday.

What the hell?

Chapter Seven

NOW

After a surreal night where I only managed to snatch around two broken hours of sleep filled with nightmares, cold sweats and a racing brain, I hurry down the stairs, shunning the lift because I don't want to be in close proximity to anyone, forced to smile or make small talk. I head to breakfast feeling – and probably looking – like a zombie. But I don't care how I look. I only want this nightmare to be over. As I wait to be seated, I gaze around the busy dining room. It doesn't feel easy to be surrounded by all these contented people – loved-up couples, laughing friends, and happy families – when my world feels as if it's imploding.

Through the windows, beyond the terrace, the sun is so bright, the sky so blue, the Grand Canal so jewel-like. Everything is absolutely perfect here. But in my current state it feels as though I'm seeing everything from outside my body. As though I'm not even here. I probably should have ordered room service, but I had to get out of the suite. I was going crazy up there after my terrible night of missing Austin. Of calling and texting him repeatedly. Wondering if I should have been walking the streets instead of trying to sleep.

'Good morning,' one of the waiters says with a wide, practised smile. He's an older man, with movie-star good looks. 'Table for one, or . . .' He stares beyond me as though he's expecting to see someone else.

'Just one, please,' I reply brusquely, unable to summon a smile in return.

'Certainly. Your room number, please.'

'421.'

'Ah, the honeymoon suite. Your husband is not joining us this morning?'

I blink, determined not to cry. 'No.'

He nods, getting the message that all is not well. We pass by the table where I sat last night with the police officers. This morning, it's occupied by a family of five – a chic-looking couple in their thirties and their stunning doe-eyed kids with dark curls and full lips. The waiter leads me to a lovely table overlooking the canal.

'This is good?' he asks.

I nod. 'Thank you.' Although he could have sat me in a dark corner facing the wall and I wouldn't have cared.

I ask for a pot of coffee. My stomach is grinding with stress, but I know I need to eat something so I choose scrambled eggs on toast from the buffet. Back at the table, I force myself to chew and swallow, chew and swallow, the action of eating feeling alien to me, as if I've never done it before. It's strange how when one thing changes, *everything* changes. Like the universe has shifted position. Like I don't fit into it any more. Am I actually losing my mind here?

While I wait for my coffee, I check my phone messages and call Austin again. There's no news. No reply. My coffee arrives and I add two packets of sugar to my cup, even though I don't normally take any. After a couple of sips, I wince and close my eyes, forcing myself to think about what I need to do now. The police haven't called or left any messages, so I should call them. And then, if they

43

haven't found Austin, I'll have to go out looking myself. But where should I search? Everywhere. My hands begin to shake so I clench them into fists and push them against my thighs.

I'm wearing my new cream cargo pants, a sage-green cropped sweatshirt and my Nike trainers. I don't even remember getting dressed. I have a vague recollection of letting the shower pound my skin with cool water to wake me up, but that's about it.

I take a last sip of over-sweet coffee and get to my feet, avoiding eye contact with staff and residents. Should I call Austin's parents yet? No. First I'll check with reception. See if there's any news.

Walking over to the desk, I scan the staff on duty. No Davide. No Sara. I guess they worked the night shift. There's an older male concierge talking to a young woman, and an older woman on the main desk. As I draw closer, I see the name Paola Schiavone on her name badge. She's immaculately turned out, with wavy dark hair, red lips, and a suit with no creases in sight.

'Good morning.' She smiles with a question in her eyes.

'Morning,' I reply quietly. 'I'm Stella Lewis, room 421—'

'Ah, yes, Mrs Lewis. My colleague, Davide Rossi, he told me your husband did not return last night.' She looks beyond my shoulder as though he might materialise behind me. 'Still nothing?'

I swallow and shake my head. 'No.'

'I'm sorry. You spoke to the police, yes?'

'Yes, they said they'd call if they found him, but I haven't heard anything.'

'He will come back soon. Probably he had too much to drink. It's common when you go on holiday.'

'Not on your honeymoon, surely,' I reply, wondering in what universe it's common for your spouse to go missing on holiday.

'Maybe not,' Paola replies. 'But don't worry. The police will find him if not.'

'I'm going out to look for him,' I say, sounding more decisive than I feel. 'Will you call me if he comes back, or if you hear anything?'

'Of course, of course. We have your mobile number in our system?'

I scribble it on a pad and write my name next to it.

'Good luck,' she says, and I envy her light attitude. To her, this is just another ordinary day.

I sit in the lobby, in the same grey armchair I chose last night, and call the police station, asking to speak to Officer Gallini. But the man on the other end of the line tells me he's not on duty. I tell him who I am and explain my situation, but he already knows all about it, which is somewhat reassuring. However, he has no news for me. He tells me they're investigating and will call me with any new developments. I ask if they've contacted the local hospitals and he confirms that they have, but no one of Austin's name or description has been admitted. I thank him and end the call. I can feel the scrambled eggs and coffee lodged in my gullet. I swallow and take a few deep breaths, tell myself everything will be all right, and then get to my feet. Determined.

As I'm leaving the hotel, I hear a man's voice call out behind me. I turn to see the concierge, a crease of concern on his face.

'Your bag . . .' He points to my handbag. 'You must . . .' He mimes keeping it close to my body. 'They will take your wallet.'

'Oh. Thank you.' I rearrange it so the strap is across my body and the bag is at my front, rather than my side. The last thing I need is to have my belongings snatched.

Outside, the cool April air is bracing, the sun brighter than back home. Sharper. I root in my bag for my sunglasses, but I must have left them upstairs. I debate returning for them, but decide against it, unwilling to return to the suite that suddenly feels claustrophobic rather than sumptuous. I need to be out here, trawling the streets, searching. I'll start with the area around St Mark's Square, because that's the route Austin took last night. First, I'll check the square and the shops and cafés in the adjacent streets. And then I'll widen my search, moving outwards.

As I walk, I refuse to give in to the panic that's threatening to claw its way up through my chest. Again, I have the out-of-body feeling that everything around me is happening from a distance. The early-morning tourists, the shopkeepers, delivery guys, the wealthy shoppers with their designer dogs – all part of this floating city that's doing what it always does, while I stumble through the streets, removed from it all.

I go into each and every establishment, showing Austin's photo to the shopkeepers, waiters and bar staff. But every time I receive the same blank stare, followed by dismissal, or a glance of pity when I explain what's happened.

'You should come back this evening,' one young waitress suggests. 'Most people working this morning won't have been working late last night. You need to speak to the people who were working the late shifts.'

I realise she's right. But it can't hurt to keep showing Austin's photo. To keep asking. The more people I ask, the better.

After a couple of hours of trudging from place to place, I find myself outside La Terrazza di Stella. They're just opening up, and one of the waiters, Gilberto, recognises me from last night. 'Back so soon?' he asks. 'Table for one? Two?' He peers over my shoulder to see if Austin's with me, just like the waiter from breakfast.

Nino appears from inside the restaurant. 'Stella.' He leans in to kiss my cheeks. 'No news?'

I shake my head. 'I spoke to the police and they say they're looking. But something's definitely happened to him, because why else hasn't he come back?'

'Elena is out getting supplies, but come, sit on the terrace. I bring you coffee, on the house.' He fires off instructions to Gilberto, who nods and disappears inside. 'Don't worry,' Nino says, sitting opposite me. 'They will find him, and then you will both come back here for dinner and we will celebrate, after giving Austin hell for worrying his beautiful new bride.'

I let myself be buoyed by his words. Wishing with all my being that it could be true. Gilberto brings us both a coffee, a glass of water and a slice of cake encrusted with sugar. I don't feel at all hungry. Instead, I gulp down the glass of water.

'Eat,' Nino urges. 'You need energy.' He picks his cake up with his fingers and takes a large bite.

I take a smaller bite of mine. It melts in my mouth. 'Tastes like panettone.'

'It's called *fugassa*,' Nino says. 'Very special Venetian cake for Christmas and Easter. But also for couples in love who want to marry. So you must eat it to bring you luck that you will find your Austin today, okay?'

I nod, taking a sip of coffee to hide my distress at his talk of marriage. This was supposed to be our honeymoon. A time of love and newly wedded bliss, but instead . . .

'Now I must get back to work,' Nino says, polishing off his cake and standing again. 'But you stay as long as you like. And come back if there is anything Elena and I can do for you.'

'Thank you. I'll leave in a few minutes. Get back to finding Austin. Thanks again for the coffee and the support.'

'It's my pleasure.' He pauses. 'Maybe you should print some pictures of him, hand them out . . .'

'That's a great idea.'

'My friend Giulia owns a small printing company not far from here – Grafica Scarpa. She will do it for you.'

47

'Thank you. Can you put the address into Google Maps?' I ask, passing him my phone.

'Sure. It's only ten minutes' walk. I'll message her, let her know you're coming.' Nino enters the details and then heads back inside the restaurant to continue with his day.

The route pops up on my phone and I study it while I take a few bites of cake and drain my coffee, feeling a little more energised. I leave the terrace and head for the print company.

After a few wrong turns, I finally find the right street and head all the way to the end, where it opens out into a small deserted courtyard with terracotta walls and shuttered windows of varying shapes and sizes, an olive tree planted in a stone trough at its centre. I glance around, catching sight of a man in the alley I just left. We lock eyes for a brief moment before he turns and walks away. He's short, sandy-haired, maybe in his thirties, wearing jeans and a hoodie, black sunglasses pushed up on his head. That was weird – first he was headed my way, and now he's turned back. I guess he could have taken a wrong turn. Anyway, he's gone now.

I turn back to the courtyard, where I spy a little wooden door that has the signage 'Grafica Scarpa' on a square glass plaque, so I head over, press the buzzer and wait. In the distance, church bells ring, and there's a muted hum of crowd chatter somewhere nearby. In this sheltered space, the sun is warm on my back, the chill of the wind not so noticeable.

The door swings open and I'm greeted by a woman in her forties, dressed in a navy trouser suit, her hair tied back in a messy bun. 'Stella?' she asks.

'Yes. You must be Giulia.'

'Come in. Would you like a drink?'

'I'm fine, thanks. Just had a coffee with Nino.' I follow her into a hallway that leads to a characterful office space with three wooden

48

desks, but there are no other staff around. A tall barred window overlooks a narrow turquoise canal. It's peaceful in here, aside from the floorboards creaking beneath our feet.

Giulia half leans, half perches against one of the desks. 'Nino explained about your husband. That must be very worrying. Do you have a clear photograph we could use?'

I nod and retrieve my phone from my bag.

After half an hour of finding a good likeness of Austin, and selecting some text to add to the image, along with my mobile phone number, we finally have a decent template. Thankfully, Giulia doesn't pry into my situation, but simply gets on with the job in hand. She leaves the room and returns a short while later with a stack of flyers that announce Austin is missing. Seeing those words in bold across the top of the poster is like a weight on my chest. Giulia adds a box of drawing pins and three rolls of Sellotape to the bag of flyers. 'Come back if you need more,' she offers.

'I can't thank you enough,' I say. 'What do I owe you?'

'Nothing. I just hope you find your husband.' She touches my arm, and her kindness makes me blink back tears.

I'm overwhelmed by her generosity. This woman is a stranger to me and yet she's offered her time and expertise out of the goodness of her heart. 'No, I have to give you something. This is your business.' I take my wallet from my handbag.

Giulia stays my hand. 'When you find your husband, you can buy me a coffee,' she replies.

'Dinner,' I counter. 'We'll take you and Nino and Elena out to dinner.'

'Deal,' she says, her eyes crinkling at the edges.

Armed with my flyers, I leave the print shop to continue my search, but this time I ask each shop and café if they'll put up one of Giulia's flyers. Most of them agree. But nobody recognises my husband.

By 6 p.m., my throat is dry and my feet are killing me. I've called the police several times over the course of the day. I've called Austin and left numerous messages. In addition to the police, I've contacted the hospital myself. But not a single soul has seen or heard from my husband.

As the evening rolls on, I realise that it will soon be twenty-four hours since Austin went missing. How is it possible that I'm even in this situation? My nerves are taut, vibrating like plucked guitar strings. I'll have to call his parents to let them know. Vicki and Rob are lovely people who absolutely dote on their son. They'll be beside themselves with worry. How am I going to tell them that their only child is missing?

As I turn around to head back to the hotel, I'm filled with a growing sense of dread. I don't want to go back there. To that empty suite. To sit and do nothing. To try to rest. Even if I manage to grab some sleep, I know I'll be haunted by nightmares.

From the corner of my eye I see a man up ahead, walking purposefully like he has somewhere important to be. He's tall with brown wavy hair, and he's wearing a dark suit. I freeze. And then I start to run.

'Austin!' I cry. 'Austin, is that you?'

Chapter Eight

THEN

I can't stop staring at the image of Austin and Keri together. She posted it on Instagram yesterday, but when was it actually taken? I recognise the bar; it's in Penn Hill, only opened last November. Austin never mentioned running into her or having a drink together, so what does this mean? After he and I met for the first time, he reassured me that he had zero feelings for his ex, that she was too high maintenance and had made his life a misery when they were together, trying to control him, treating him like shit. So what the hell is he doing out drinking with her and taking loved-up-looking selfies?

I'm squeezing my phone so tightly that my fingers hurt. I grit my teeth and try not to jump to any conclusions, but it's not easy. I get up off the kitchen stool and step into the hall, hearing the faint hum of the power shower. Should I confront Austin with the image when he gets out? He's already in an edgy mood after his argument with Bart so now might not be the best time. But I can't just act as though nothing's the matter. I head back into the living room and over to the sliding terrace doors, unlock them and walk out on to the decking, the damp wood seeping through my socks.

As I breathe in the cool river air, my brain spins with all this evening's negativity. First Dad pouring cold water on the news of my engagement, then Bart's confrontation with Austin, and now this Instagram post of Austin and Keri. They say bad things come in threes. There had better not be anything else. I try to let my mind go blank. To calm my frazzled nerves, as I stare out across the dark river at the moored boats and the swishing trees, the laughter and clink of glasses coming from the sailing club further along the riverbank.

'What are you doing out here? It's freezing!'

I jump at the sound of Austin's voice, but I don't turn around.

'Are you coming back in?' he asks, completely unaware of the turmoil I'm experiencing.

I open my mouth to speak, and then close it again, the swirl of thoughts in my head too jumbled to form any kind of coherent sentence. Digging my nails into the palms of my hands, I imagine the little crescent indentations on my skin.

'Stella? What's up?' Austin asks, concern in his voice. 'Are you worrying about the Bart thing?'

'No,' I reply, taking a breath, trying not to lose my shit as the image of him and Keri burns itself into my brain again.

'You are, aren't you?'

'I'm not. It's not that at all.' Finally, I turn around and stare at Austin's puzzled expression. He's standing at the door, barefoot, in a fresh T-shirt and joggers, hair damp from his shower.

'Are you coming back in?' he asks again, staring down at my wet socks. 'Stella, you're freaking me out. Why are you looking at me like that? I really am sorry about what happened with Bart, but we'll—'

'It's nothing to do with Bart,' I snap.

He tightens his lips for a second, confused and a little shocked by my tone. We never normally have cross words. 'So . . . what's wrong?'

I hold up the Instagram image on my phone.

Austin's neck mottles with ugly crimson patches. 'Oh.'

'Yeah. *Oh*.'

'Shit, yeah, that's not what it . . . I bumped into Keri last week. I was out having a quick drink with Mike Bardsley – a client – in Penn Hill when she came over to us. She said she was upset after hearing about our engagement. It was awkward because I didn't want her to start any drama in front of Mike, who wants us to install gates on three of his new developments, which could lead to a lot more work down the line. Keri was a bit drunk and asked to take a selfie with us – which was a bit weird and uncomfortable – but Mike was into it, so I said okay. There were three of us in that photo, but she must have cropped Mike out. You can just about see his shoulder there, look . . .'

As he explains what happened, I feel my stress levels slowly subside. It's typical of Keri to manipulate the situation so it looks worse than it is. To try to drive a wedge between us, still, after all this time.

'Sorry if you got a shock seeing that. I wasn't sure whether to mention it or not.' He gives me a sheepish look that I ignore.

'Having a drink with your ex and taking a selfie with her would definitely come under the category of things to mention to your future wife,' I reply coldly. 'Just in case it comes up again, which I'd hope it wouldn't.'

'Of course. Of *course*, Stella. I am SO sorry. It was less than nothing. Like, an absolute non-event, and I'm furious with Keri for posting that up on social media. I suppose I should have known she'd want to stick it online, what with her being an influencer or whatever.'

I roll my eyes at that. Keri likes to call herself an influencer, but the only thing I've ever seen her try to influence is my relationship with Austin.

'I'll message her to take it down,' he continues. 'And I'll kill her if I ever see her again, which I won't. Well, not on purpose anyway. Will you come inside and talk to me?' He reaches out a hand, but I ignore it, stepping back into the living room alone, childishly enjoying the way Austin winces as my wet socks leave prints on his pale wool carpet.

'How does she even know we're engaged?' I ask. 'I thought we weren't going to tell anyone until after we'd let our families know? What if my parents heard about it from someone else?'

'I know, I know, I'm sorry.' Austin raises his hands and looks contrite. 'I only told Miles, but he must have let it slip to Liv. Even though I told him not to.'

'And Liv will have told the whole of Dorset by now,' I reply, plonking myself down on the sofa and peeling off my wet socks. Miles Grey and Austin have been good friends since their early twenties. Miles met Liv Middleton through work and they became a couple just after me and Austin, so we've been an inseparable foursome ever since. Miles is quiet and reserved and usually knows how to keep a secret, but Liv – although absolutely lovely – is one of the least discreet people I know. Thank goodness I told my parents tonight, even if I'm wishing I hadn't.

'So, are we good?' Austin asks, sitting next to me and tilting his head, trying to get me to look at him. 'Stella?'

I let my shoulders drop. 'I suppose so. But that was horrible – seeing that picture of you both, with that gross caption. What's her problem? Why does she still have such a thing for you? She was the one who wanted to end it, but she wants you back just so she can control you again. I wish she'd just move on already!'

'I know, I know. It's really annoying.'

'It's more than annoying. It's stalkerish. Can we not stealthily set her up with someone else so she'll leave us alone?'

'That's not a bad idea, actually.'

'Anyway, I don't want to talk about Keri-bloody-Wade any more. Let's change the subject.'

'Fine by me,' Austin replies. 'How about we ban all mention of Keri and Bart, and talk about our wedding instead?' He gives a lopsided smile, hopeful his suggestion will cheer me up.

But I shrug a reply. These aren't the circumstances in which I want to plan our wedding – with the ghosts of Austin's ex, my dad, and Austin's shifty business partner floating around us. I'd rather call it quits on today and start fresh tomorrow or the day after.

'Can we just watch a movie instead?' I ask, picking at my fingernails.

'Um, sure, if you want.' Austin frowns and reaches for the remote. 'Action? Comedy? You choose.'

'Whatever,' I reply, trying to patch up my frayed emotions, but there's a lump in my throat and my skin is still hot with the remnants of my anger and frustration. Today has been horrible. I really hope this is the end of all this crap. And not the beginning.

Chapter Nine

NOW

I hurry down the street, weaving between the dawdling tourists, calling for the tall, wavy-haired man to stop, but the crowd is so thick, so loud, that he can't hear me. My heart is hammering and I'm starting to sweat. 'Austin! Stop!' I cry again. Several people are pausing to stare, turning to see who I'm shouting at. I'm too agitated to worry about them. Instead, I continue edging through the press of bodies, certain it wasn't this busy a few moments ago.

I yell Austin's name once more and, through a gap in the crowds, I see him turn as though in slow motion. I stop, catching my breath, a wave of dizziness overtaking me. But as soon as he starts to turn, I can tell it's not Austin. It's nothing like him. The hair, the build, the suit. Of course it's not him! I'm so tired, I'm imagining things. The man raises an eyebrow at me and gives a leering smile that turns my stomach. I shake my head, cut eye contact and turn away. Walking fast in the opposite direction, losing him in the crowd. The disappointment is crushing.

As I continue to walk aimlessly, my thoughts spiral. What am I doing out here alone, chasing after strangers? This isn't rational. I need to get back to the hotel, get my head straight and work out what to do next. There must be some kind of procedure in place for this situation. I wonder if I should contact the British Embassy. Do they deal with missing people abroad? I'll go back to the room and google what to do. Order room service. I haven't eaten anything since that piece of cake at Nino's this morning. No wonder I'm light-headed and hallucinating.

I find myself at the foot of another of Venice's bridges. I don't even know what part of the city I'm in. I'll have to check the location on my phone. I sit on one of the stone steps for a moment, giving my aching feet a rest. A tour guide walks past and I hear snatches of her spiel: 'Venice has one hundred and fifty canals and no fewer than four hundred bridges . . . three thousand alleyways . . .' Her voice fades as she moves on quickly, followed by several eager tourists hanging on her every word, filming and photographing everything around them. That should have been me and Austin this afternoon. We'd booked on to a short tour to see the city and get our bearings. Well, I've certainly seen a lot of the city today, just not the parts I'd been expecting to see.

As I think about getting to my feet again, a man in shabby trousers and a tracksuit top approaches, carrying an armful of roses. Despite my refusing to look his way, he's still making a beeline for me. I stand up, dusting down the back of my cargos. Not sure which direction to head in, I hesitate an instant too long.

The flower seller pounces. 'Here, you take the rose. You take two. It's free, it's free for you. You are English, American?'

I take the proffered roses. Surely they can't be free. But I don't want them anyway. What am I going to do with two roses? Stick them behind my ears? Wave them around like Morrissey?

I shake my head and thrust the blooms back at him, but he smiles and holds his free hand up, refusing to take them. 'You have a boyfriend, yes? Or husband?' The man gestures to the crowds.

57

'Which one is your husband? He will buy you these flowers. He loves you, yes? You are beautiful. You deserve to have the flowers.'

I shake my head. 'No thank you. Please take them back.'

'You have flowers now. You must buy.'

I suddenly realise the scam. 'No, I don't want them.'

'Yes, you pay now.'

The man is too close, invading my personal space. I can see the stubble on his cheeks and the dirt beneath his fingernails. I get that he needs to earn a living, but I don't want the damn flowers.

'I have no cash,' I say, patting my pocket.

'Where is your boyfriend? He will buy.'

'No boyfriend,' I snap, trying to stuff the roses back with the others and stabbing my finger on a thorn in the process. One of the flowers falls to the ground, but I don't attempt to retrieve it. Instead, I take the opportunity to hurry away over the bridge, ignoring the man's agitated cries and sucking the puncture wound on the underside of my ring finger.

I'm close to tears, which is ridiculous. He was simply an over-enthusiastic flower seller, that's all. Nothing to get upset over.

As I walk along a narrow canal path, the setting sun glints on the water and casts an orange light across the buildings. It's breath-takingly beautiful, but I'm not in the right headspace to appreciate it right now. I turn down a deserted alley and head for a busier street up ahead, pulling my phone from my bag. Before I reach the end of the lane, I open up Maps and type in the hotel name, waiting for the route to pop up on my screen. But it suddenly goes blank. My heart plummets when I realise the battery's dead. *Great. What now?*

I'll have to ask someone for directions. I lick my lips and swallow, reaching into my bag for my water bottle, but it's almost empty. Draining the last few tepid drops, I leave the alley, glancing around for a café or convenience store among all the shops. I finally spot a crowded osteria and go inside, taking a seat at the bar.

'*Buona sera.*' The young woman behind the bar gives me a warm smile. She's pretty, with dark curls and a gold nose ring.

'*Buona sera,*' I reply. 'Is it possible to have a glass of water?'

'Of course. And maybe a little *aperitivo*? Some *cicchetti*?'

I give her what must be a blank stare because she laughs. 'A drink and some snacks,' she explains. 'Maybe a small glass of wine or an Aperol spritz?'

'That all sounds good.' I nod.

She pours me a glass of water, her bracelets jangling. 'Here . . .'

I take the water and down it in a few gulps.

She raises her eyebrows and pours me another. 'I'll order you a small plate, yes?'

'Yes, please. And an Aperol spritz. Do you have a bathroom?'

She points to a door at the back and I wind my way through the chattering crowd. It feels like a locals' bar rather than a tourist place. Austin would love it.

After using the loo and washing my hands, I stare into the gold-framed mirror above the sink. I barely recognise myself. Brown eyes smudged with exhaustion, tawny hair hanging in lank waves, sallow skin . . . but none of that matters. What matters is that I don't know the person staring out of those haunted eyes. Who is she? Who am I? Austin might be the one who's missing, but I'm the one who feels lost. Scared. He's been gone for almost a day and I've no idea what to do. My mind keeps lurching from one terrible thought to another, as though I'm riding a roller coaster with no end.

I pat my cheeks hard to try to bring myself back to some kind of reality. But, here in this medieval city, I feel as though I've stepped into a Gothic dream. A nightmare that's pulling and pushing me in all directions except for the place I need to go. I blink, willing myself to leave the bathroom. The door handle jerks up and down and a couple of people start talking outside. I've been in here long enough.

Back at the bar, the waitress presents me with a plate of delicious snacks and a drink that helps bring me back from the abyss, the alcohol rounding out the sharp edges in my brain. She also lets me charge my phone, lending me her cable, and tells me the quickest way to get back to my hotel, which is about half an hour's walk away. Everyone is so friendly here. Again, I can't help thinking that Austin would be in his element. I show her the poster and explain about my husband. She looks shocked, upset. Says that of course she'll pin it up for me, and make sure she asks around. She offers her sympathies. But she hasn't seen him.

Outside, dusk falls and streetlamps are popping on. Fortified with Aperol and *cicchetti*, I pay my bill, leave a good tip and thank the friendly waitress before heading out again, hopefully with enough charge on my phone to guide me back.

As I walk, the crowds thin out and the lanes grow quieter. Periodically, I cross a bridge, glancing down at the slivers of moonlight and lamplight rippling through the waters below. I try to stick to the main streets, but occasionally the route directs me down one of the high-sided alleyways that make me want to hold my breath until I reach the end.

I'm halfway along one such alley when a set of footsteps behind makes my skin tingle. There's someone back there at the entrance to the alleyway. I shouldn't let it worry me; there are plenty of people walking around the city. Doesn't mean they're up to anything bad. I remember having this same creeped-out feeling back home a few times when I thought someone was following me. I even considered the possibility that I might have a stalker. I was terrified then, and I'm starting to feel the same way now. Surely it can't be the same person. Not here in Italy.

I quicken my pace and come to the end of the alley, which brings me out alongside a dark canal. The path is narrow and the air is damp. The sound of a woman's laughter echoes out through one of the windows above. The thump of distant music is muted in the still air. I throw a brief look over my shoulder. There's no one there. So I stop and listen. My breathing is jagged. Water laps at the canal walls. And then the footsteps resume, growing louder.

I put a hand to my mouth and hurry along the canal path towards another looming bridge. My feet are raw with new blisters, but adrenaline keeps me moving, crossing the bridge as the footsteps follow, speeding up to match my pace. I daren't run, because if they run too then that will confirm it. And what if they're faster than me?

I glance back once more and gasp when I see the silhouette of a man, head bent, hands in his pockets, drawing closer. I think I recognise him. I can't be sure, but I think it's the same man I saw outside the print shop earlier. The one I locked eyes with.

Why is he following me?

Chapter Ten

THEN

I stand in front of Austin's mirror, putting soft waves into my hair with the curling tongs. Once I move in with him, I'd like to have some kind of dressing table where I can sit and do my make-up. Maybe beneath the side window where Austin currently keeps his weights. I guess we should talk about stuff like that. About what our day-to-day lives will look like once we're married.

It's been a couple of days since the evening from hell when Dad refused to give his blessing to me and Austin, followed by the whole Bart thing and then Keri's attempt to sabotage our relationship. Since then, I've been staying at Austin's place, which he's been totally cool with, even though I haven't told him about Dad's true feelings. I just made up some vague excuse about feeling stifled at home. Austin said he could relate, as he loves his parents but they can be a bit too doting.

I popped home to pick up some clothes while my parents were out because I'm too chicken to have another conversation just yet. Dad hasn't called, and Mum is cross with me for not trying harder with him. It's all a bit of a mess so, of course, I'm sticking my head in the sand and pretending nothing's wrong. For now, at least. I was hoping Dad would call and apologise, but realise I might be waiting a long time.

'What time are you going out?' Austin asks. He's lying on the bed, scrolling on his phone as I get ready to meet Claudia for drinks in Christchurch.

'I said I'd meet her in the Dog and Duck at seven thirty. It's supposed to be really lovely in there now it's had a makeover. It's opening night, so I'm guessing it's going to be busy.'

'Nice. We should go there for dinner sometime. Say hi from me.' He looks up from his screen.

'Of course.' I smile into the mirror at him.

'I like that top on you,' he says. 'I'm looking forward to taking it off later.'

My smile widens and I straighten out the top, which is one of my favourites – a bottle-green silk, off-the-shoulder blouse with cut-outs down the sleeves.

'It's been so good having you stay here,' Austin adds, setting down his phone and putting his hands behind his head. 'This is what it'll be like once we're married.'

'I know. It's weird.'

'Good weird, I hope?'

'Of course,' I reply. 'Weird is always good.'

Austin grins and my stomach flips. His smile always has the power to devastate me. I still can't believe we're getting married next year.

We've completely made up after Keri's attempt at sabotage. I'll be damned if I let Keri Wade be the reason that Austin and I get into a fight. That's just playing right into her hands. But despite getting over that obstacle, Austin has still been super-stressed over the past couple of days. This problem with Bart treating the company like his private piggy bank has really got Austin rattled. He thinks I don't notice the stress lines on his forehead, the tautness of his jaw and his tense shoulders. I wish there was something I could do to help fix it.

'Sure you're okay with me going out?' I ask. 'Claudia won't mind if I cancel.'

'What?' Austin frowns. 'Why would I mind?'

'I just mean, if you want to talk about stuff. You know, with Bart and the business.'

Austin takes a breath. 'I've decided I'm going to speak to a solicitor about it.'

I stop what I'm doing and turn to face him. 'You're going to sue him?'

He nods slowly. 'Yep. Possibly.'

'Isn't that . . . I mean, won't that be stressful? Is there no way to sort it out amicably?'

He barks out a bitter laugh. 'We're way past that. You saw him, Stella. Bart's gone completely on the defensive. He's now trying to blame *me*. But I figure if I sue him first, then it might make him think twice about trying to smear my name. All I want is to get it resolved quickly and quietly, but for some reason he wants a fight. So . . . I'm going to give him one.'

My heart drops, but I don't want Austin to see how much this is unsettling me. I need to be supportive. 'I'm sorry,' I say, coming over to the bed and sitting next to him. 'I suppose at least a solicitor will know how to do things the right way.'

'I hope so.'

'I'll definitely cancel Claudia.'

'No, no, you go out. I need to sort some admin stuff this evening anyway, so I won't be much company.'

'What do your mum and dad think about it?' I ask.

He screws up his face. 'I haven't told them yet.'

'Really? Don't you think you should? They might be able to help.'

'I don't want to burden them. I'm still hopeful I can get it all sorted without it becoming a big thing.'

I feel like it already is a big thing, but I don't voice that thought out loud.

'Don't worry about it,' Austin says, picking up his phone and getting off the bed. 'I'll leave you to get ready.'

'It's fine, I'll stay.'

'I'm going to make a start on that admin. Have a good evening.'

'You should come. Take your mind off things. Claudia won't mind. She always loves to see you.'

'No, you go. Have fun.' He comes around the bed and kisses me, his hands sliding beneath my top as he pulls me in closer. I'm breathless when he finally moves away. 'See you later,' he murmurs and leaves the room, eyes back on his phone.

Despite the hotness of my fiancé's kiss and the promise of a fun evening with my best friend, I still feel uneasy. Dealing with a court case in the run-up to our wedding is not going to be a walk in the park.

Chapter Eleven

NOW

Surely the man behind me isn't the same man I saw earlier. And if it is, then it must be a harmless coincidence. Either that or my exhaustion and stress has made me imagine the whole thing.

I keep moving through the Venice streets and alleyways at a steady pace. Up steps, over bridges and down again. The urge to speed up is so strong I feel sick, but I daren't run because if I do, I don't think I'll be able to stop. I'm on the precipice of losing it.

As I navigate my way back to the hotel, the only route open to me now is along another alleyway. Once I've made it through that, I'll almost be back at St Mark's Square, which is only ten minutes from the hotel. But the tapering, dark space ahead is the perfect place for someone to attack me, if that's what they want to do. So I give in to my fear and I run, lengthening my strides as I go. Eyes stinging, breath rasping, feet painfully striking the paving slabs. I can't tell if the man is still behind me and I daren't look to see.

Is he a random predator, or has he targeted me because he knows me? Is he Italian or has he followed me here from England?

I make it to the end of the alley, lungs burning, pulse racing. I'm physically fit, but terror has left me weak and winded.

I chance a look behind me and am horrified to see the silhouette of the man heading towards me. He's not running, but he's certainly walking with purpose. I'm not stopping to find out what he wants. At least I'm on one of the busier streets now, with people heading back from bars and restaurants, queuing for ice cream, and browsing the few tourist shops that are still open for business.

I realise that if he's still following me, I'll be leading him back to my hotel. But what other option do I have? Actually . . . I do have another option. As I walk, weaving between pedestrians and trying not to have a meltdown, I tap a new address into Google Maps.

Ten minutes later, hurrying past a Gothic church and turning a corner, I find myself outside a grand building with iron balconies and wooden shutters. The only hint at what lies beyond the doors are the metal grilles on the windows – those, and the plaque outside, indicating that I've reached my destination. I was expecting the police station to be a utilitarian building – ugly and functional. But I guess this is Venice, where everything is a work of art. I stare up at the stone-framed entrance, push at its carved wooden door, step inside, and open a further glass door in the lobby.

It's such a relief to be here. Safe. If that man really was up to no good, I'm banking on the fact that my coming to a police station will have deterred him from following me any further. I pause for a moment, panting, allowing my heart rate to slow and my thoughts to settle. Aside from being followed, I need to know if the police have made any progress, and what's going to happen next.

I'd been planning to ring Officer Gallini once I got back to the hotel, but coming here in person is a much better idea. Hopefully, once he sees how shaken and upset I am, he'll realise that this is serious, and not some trivial lovers' tiff. I also have to find out who's been following me.

I find myself standing in a reception area beneath an ornate lantern. Landscapes hang on the walls and to my left are a couple of freaky mannequins dressed in what look like military or police uniforms. I realise that a real uniformed police officer is talking to me from behind the reception desk.

'Can I help you, madam?' she asks.

I nod and approach the counter, relieved she speaks English. 'There was a man following me,' I say, still breathless.

'A man?'

I turn to look back over my shoulder. 'He's been following me for at least twenty minutes. I was too scared to go back to my hotel.'

'He's there now?' She comes out from behind the desk and walks towards the exit. 'Did you see his face?'

'Sort of. He's got short fair hair, he's maybe five foot seven, in his thirties, wearing jeans and a hoodie, black sunglasses pushed up on his head. I saw him earlier this morning, and then again this evening.' I don't add that I thought I was being followed back in the UK because I worry it might make the Italian police less inclined to help me.

'You stay there. I will look.' She exits the station, standing in the doorway and scanning the street. After a few moments, she returns. 'We can check the CCTV from the last minute or two. See if he shows up.' She pops back behind the counter and makes a call. Another officer comes out from a door behind the counter, and I see that it's Gallini from last night.

He stops when he sees me. 'Mrs Lewis, has your husband returned?'

I shake my head and bite my lip.

'I'm sorry to hear that. We have no news for you, I'm afraid.'

'Have you been looking?' I ask.

'Yes, yes, all our officers have been given his photo.'

'I put up posters today. But no one's seen him.'

'This lady says she was being followed by a man,' the female officer says to Gallini.

He replies in Italian and they have a short conversation – obviously about my situation. Gallini beckons me in closer and reaches up to turn a multi-split-screen monitor in my direction. He presses a few buttons beneath it and I watch the images rewind to just before I enter the station. We watch the footage several times, but there's no sign of the man.

'I guess he realised I was headed to the station,' I say.

'Do you think this man could be something to do with your husband's disappearance?' Gallini asks. 'Was Mr Lewis in any kind of trouble?'

'We don't know anyone in Italy, so I don't think so.'

'It seems a bit of a coincidence. Your husband goes missing, and now you are being followed.'

'Do you think I might be in danger?' I ask, unease creeping into my bones.

'How long was this man following you for?'

'Like I said to your colleague, I first noticed him this morning, but didn't think anything about it. Then, when it started to get dark, I saw him again. This time I realised he was definitely following me. Or, at least, he was walking behind me in the same direction for about twenty minutes to half an hour.' As I talk to the officer, I wonder if I might have been mistaken. Could the man simply have been walking the same route as me?

'Did he attempt to talk to you? Or harm you?' Gallini asks.

'No,' I reply.

'I wonder if he was tailing you for some reason . . .'

'Tailing me? Like a spy?' I ask.

'I'm just looking at possibilities,' Gallini replies.

'That doesn't seem very likely. I just assumed it was some creep.'

'It might be,' he says, frowning. 'What about at home? Did your husband owe money? Take drugs? Have any serious disagreements with anyone. That type of thing?'

My heart starts to pound. I should tell them about being followed back home. 'No drugs or owing money. The only thing I can think is that he does have a court case pending with his business partner. But that's all being handled by solicitors. There's nothing . . . shady, or anything like that. But . . .' I pause.

'Go on,' Gallini prompts.

'Well, there were a few times back in England where I thought I was being followed.'

'By this same man?'

'I don't know. I never got a look at him.'

'You reported it to the police at home?'

I shake my head and shrug. 'Nothing happened, so . . .'

Gallini looks thoughtful. 'This could all be related. Have you informed Austin's family and friends that he's missing?'

'Not yet. I didn't want to worry them. I thought he'd be back by now.' My voice has started to wobble.

Gallini comes out from behind the counter and gestures to a bench by the mannequins, where I sit gratefully. 'I think you need to call everyone you both know. One of them may have an idea of where your husband is. We're still keeping a lookout here, but there's a better chance that someone he knows can shed some light on where he's gone.'

I nod. 'You're right.'

'Do it as soon as possible,' he says. 'Once you've spoken to everyone, if there's still no answer, then you can file a report with your local police back home, and we'll liaise with them. We can look at things like phone records and bank withdrawals. Also, you should contact the British Consulate in Milan. They will support you with practicalities and assign a caseworker.'

Although Gallini is speaking perfect English, his words sound like a foreign language. I can't believe any of this is happening. I nod mutely.

'But hopefully it won't come to any of that,' he adds kindly. 'Would you like my colleague to walk you back to your hotel? It's very close.'

I'm about to refuse his offer, but the remnants of fear are still clinging to me. 'That would be really kind. Thank you.'

The female officer smiles and we leave the station together. As we walk, I notice that she's scanning the area. She tells me to do the same, in case I spot my stalker. But the route is quiet and dark, with only a few tourists strolling along the Grand Canal, and no strange men lurking in dark corners, not that either of us can see anyway.

Back at the hotel, I thank my temporary bodyguard and walk into the lobby alone, feeling dishevelled and half delirious with exhaustion. The thought of ringing everybody and telling them Austin has gone missing is terrifying. It will make it all so real.

Paola, the hotel manager, is on reception and my heart lurches as she beckons me over. Does she have some news?

'Mrs Lewis,' she says, 'we've been worrying about you today.'

'Is my husband back?' I ask.

'No. I wish it were so, but . . .' She shrugs, a mournful expression on her perfectly made-up face. 'We shall send some food to your room, yes?'

I shake my head, unable to think. My stomach is empty, but I'm not sure if I'll be able to swallow anything.

'I will get the kitchen to send up a simple plate of spaghetti and a glass of wine. Some water. You don't worry about it. It will arrive in ten, fifteen minutes.'

I nod, grateful, and drag myself over to the lifts. I don't think my legs will make it up four flights of stairs after all the walking and running I've done today. Thankfully, I'm the only person on the elevator ride.

Our suite is immaculate. Cleaned and tidied by invisible hands. I sink on to the chaise and plug my mobile into the charger, setting it down on the side table. I stare at its screen, the battery icon flashing. Gallini told me to call everyone who knows my husband and ask them if they know anything. But I can't think straight any more, let alone string a coherent sentence together. And besides, I can't speak to anyone else until I've made the phone call that's going to be the hardest of them all.

I'll give it another day. Do it in the morning when I'm fresh and can handle it better. After all, Rob and Vicki won't be able to get a flight over until tomorrow, so I may as well let them have a decent night's sleep. Because after I call them, they'll be joining me in my new nightmarish world. The one where their son is missing.

Chapter Twelve

THEN

I push open the door to the Dog and Duck, patting down my windswept hair and scanning the crowded bar for my friend while admiring the sleek new decor. Everyone in Christchurch seems to be here tonight. Claudia waves from a table in the corner and I walk over to give her a hug. She stands, tossing her dark locks back as she kisses my cheek. Even in her four-inch heels she's not as tall as me, and I'm only five foot five.

'Well done for getting a table.'

'It's my superpower. Love that top on you,' she says as I take off my coat.

'Thanks. Your dress is gorgeous. Is it new?'

'Borrowed it from Gina.'

'Does she know you borrowed it?' I ask, head cocked to the side.

'What do you think?'

I laugh. Claudia's older sister, Gina, is known for her fiery temper. They both still live at home and the shouting matches they've had over the years are a sight to behold. Claudia and I have known each other since we were four, having gone through school together.

But even now, at the age of twenty-eight, I'm still intimidated by her sister.

'Are you okay for a drink?' I ask, nodding at her half-full wine glass.

'Can you get me another glass of Sauvignon?'

After I return with our drinks, I sit opposite Claudia, still feeling uneasy about Austin's plan to sue Bart. I get that he has to do something about the guy, but he knows how stressful a court case could be, especially while we're trying to plan our wedding.

Thankfully, meeting up with Claudia is the perfect antidote to my worry. She's more like a sister than a friend. We always tell one another everything and have spent hours at each other's houses over the years. Her parents treat me like a daughter and vice versa.

'Cheers,' Claudia says, holding up her fresh glass, having already finished her first.

'Cheers,' I reply, and I take a long sip of the cold, crisp drink, relaxing into my seat.

Claudia already knows about my engagement as – after Austin confessed that he'd blabbed the news to Miles – I sent her a photo of my ring on WhatsApp. It felt a little awkward because she broke up with her long-term boyfriend a few months ago and has been a bit sad lately. But Claudia is genuinely pleased for us. She loves Austin, and has always said she thinks he's my soulmate.

'Let's see the ring in real life,' she asks, leaning forward to grab my hand. 'Ooh, it's beautiful, Stella. Your man has good taste.'

'I know.'

She frowns. 'Your nails could do with some love, though. Come into the salon this week and I'll sort you out – my treat.'

'Are you sure?' I can't usually afford to get my nails done professionally and I don't like to take advantage of Claudia being a beautician. She gets enough of that with her family always wanting freebies.

'Totally. It's not every day my best friend gets proposed to. Talking of which, how's life as an engaged woman?'

'Honestly . . . it's been a rough few days.'

'What's happened?' she asks. 'Is this about Keri bitchface posting up that photo on Instagram? I mean, who the hell does she think she is? The girl's deluded.'

'It's actually quite sad,' I reply.

'What does she hope to gain?' Claudia continues. 'Does she think she'll trick him into being her boyfriend again?'

'I've no idea. But when I first saw that post, I almost had a heart attack.'

'Yeah, sorry to have been the bearer of such horrid news.'

'It's fine. Austin was with a client at the time, and she barged her way into a photo. But Keri's not the problem.'

Claudia's dark eyes widen as I fill her in on Dad's reaction to my engagement.

'I can't believe your dad still isn't a fan of Austin,' Claudia says, commiserating.

'I know. It's rubbish. Why can't he be happy for me?'

'What are you going to do? Want me to have a word with him?'

'No, that's okay. I suppose I'll have to talk to him again. But it's such a pain. Especially as Austin really wants his approval. And his parents are fully on board.'

'Phil will come round. He's a big softie.'

'He's a softie with you,' I say. 'But not so much with my boyfriend.'

'Fiancé,' Claudia corrects.

'Oh yes, fiancé,' I reply in a posh accent, flashing my ring at her. 'I still can't get used to saying that.'

'So, have you started on the wedding plans yet?' Claudia asks.

'Not yet. We were supposed to get going this week, but things keep getting in the way.'

'Oh yeah?' She sips her wine. 'Like what?'

'Just everyday stuff, you know.' Even though Claudia and I usually tell each other everything, I don't want to talk about Austin's trouble with his business partner as I'm guessing it's not the kind of thing he'll want getting around.

'What about your honeymoon?' she asks, her eyes lighting up. 'You have to go to Italy. It's the most romantic place in the world.'

'Well, you have to say that, you're half Italian.'

'No, but seriously. You'll love it. Has Austin been?'

'I think he's been to one of the lakes, and he's also been skiing there.'

'Well, you should go to Tuscany, or the Amalfi Coast . . . no, you should go to Venice!' She gets a faraway dreamy look in her eyes.

'I'll talk to Austin about it. See what he thinks. I'm sure his parents will want to suggest somewhere, seeing as they own a travel company.'

'Oh, that's right. I bet they'll sort you out with something amazing.'

'That would be nice.' We sit in silence for a few moments, sipping our drinks and dreaming about faraway destinations, until Claudia mumbles something at me.

'What's the matter?' I ask.

'Bitchface alert,' Claudia hisses, her gaze drifting past my shoulder.

My heart drops when I realise she must be talking about Keri.

'Don't turn around,' Claudia whispers, just as I turn my head to see Keri and a couple of her friends walk over to the bar.

'Why is *she* here?' I ask. The last person I want to talk to this evening – or any other evening – is Keri Wade. Although I should have guessed she'd want to photograph herself at the new-look bar for her socials.

'Want me to go over and have a word?' Claudia starts to get to her feet.

'No, sit down. I don't want any fuss.'

Claudia tuts. 'She needs to know that what she did isn't cool, Stella. You might be too nice to call her out on it these days, but I'm not.'

'What do you mean, "these days"?' I ask.

'Well, you were more feisty back in the day.'

'I was not!'

'Uh, may I remind you about Samantha Dawkins and the Twix incident.'

'She stole my Twix and ate it!' I'd been looking forward to it all morning.

'Yeah, and then you got her suspended from school by pretending she'd stolen Mrs Cunningham's bracelet.'

'Oh. Yeah.' I pull a remorseful face. 'Well, we were kids back then, and I didn't know she'd get suspended. I thought she'd just get a detention.'

'Well, you've definitely mellowed in your old age. Keri's doing a lot worse than stealing a bar of chocolate. She's trying to wreck your relationship.'

'She can try.'

'Just let me have a quick word with her.' Claudia's eyes narrow. She's itching to give Keri a piece of her mind.

'Look, I honestly love that you're sticking up for me, Claud, but I just want a drama-free night with my best friend. I've been so looking forward to this evening. Once they've sat down, can we just discreetly leave and go somewhere else?'

'You can't let Keri dictate where you have a drink! We were here first, so—'

'*Please.*'

'Fine. But, seriously, the girl needs a good slap.'

77

I love Claudia's loyalty, but I just want to get out of here and go somewhere Keri-free. I guess this is the downside of living in a small town. There's no escape from your past. Or, more importantly, your fiancé's past.

And now it seems my hopes of making a sneaky exit aren't going to be possible either.

'Hello, Claudia. Stella.' Keri is hovering next to our table, glass of wine in hand, her friends standing awkwardly behind her. I don't recognise either of them, but they're dressed similarly to Keri in tight, bright clothes, with layers of fake tan, spidery eyelashes and precision make-up.

I look up and say a brief, unenthusiastic hello, hoping she'll move on and leave us alone. No such luck. Thankfully, Claudia doesn't respond, just takes a sip of her drink and scowls at Keri. I give my friend a warning glance, praying she's not going to start trouble. Keri used to be a regular at Claudia's salon until a couple of years ago, when Keri started visiting a swankier place over in Canford Cliffs. Claudia wouldn't have minded her defection as she was quite a demanding client – surprise, surprise – but a couple of her other customers mentioned that Keri had said some disparaging things about her work. Claudia had confronted Keri, but of course she denied it.

'It was so nice to catch up with Austin last week,' Keri says to me sweetly.

'Did he tell you he's getting married?' Claudia asks.

'Hm?' Keri feigns nonchalance, but I can see that she's pretending not to know. 'No. We were having too good a time to talk about anyone else.'

I bite my lip, refusing to be baited.

'Pathetic,' Claudia says, under her breath.

Keri turns back to me. 'I told him it's a shame the three of us can't all be friends like civilised people. I mean, I get that it might feel threatening to you, Stella, to have me such a big part of Austin's life. But you shouldn't dictate who he can and can't spend time with. Putting limits on our partners is the surest way to drive them into someone else's arms.'

Claudia gets to her feet and takes a step closer to Keri. 'I can see what you're up to, Keri, but it's not going to work. All it does is make you look desperate and pathetic.'

Keri gives Claudia a disdainful glare and turns back to me again. 'I'll always be a part of his life, Stella. So it's better to just get used to it. Accept it.'

My whole body is buzzing with outrage at her attitude, my skin hot and my mouth dry as I absorb her jibes. I'm starting to wonder if she knew I'd be here tonight. If she showed up specifically to taunt me. I look her in the eye. 'I'm sorry you still have a thing for my fiancé, Keri, but you should really try to accept that it's over. Get help if you need it. I know it's hard when someone doesn't feel the same way about you, but you can't force them to love you. Austin's moved on. You need to do the same.'

I don't know how I managed to keep my voice so calm. How I didn't tell her to piss off. How I'm stopping myself from slapping her face. But I can see from her reaction that my calmness is way more effective than my anger would have been.

Keri clenches her fists and her face flushes scarlet, her eyes pooling with tears of fury. 'You're such a smug bitch,' she hisses, 'but you're also wrong. You'll see.' She turns away and stalks off, her two friends giving each other a look before following.

My hands tremble and I take a slug of wine. Was that some kind of threat?

'That was awesome,' Claudia says, sitting back down, her eyes shining. 'I really wanted to punch her in the mouth, but your way was definitely better.'

'She's not going to let this go, is she?' I slump back in my seat. 'She's like a spoilt kid determined to get her favourite toy.'

'It'll be fine,' Claudia says. 'Now that you're engaged, she'll have to back off. That was just the final vicious bite of a dying creature, the last gasp of a loser.'

'Either that, or hearing about my engagement has triggered something, and made her think she needs to up her game to get him back.' I finish my wine, anxious to be anywhere else but here, in the same place as my fiancé's ex. I'm grateful for Claudia's confidence, but I'm not convinced that she's right. Because Keri's expression told me that this isn't over. Not by a long way.

Chapter Thirteen

NOW

After another hideously restless night where I didn't fall asleep until the birds started singing, I check my phone and send a hopeless text to Austin. I tear myself from my bed and stagger to the shower, letting the jets of water attempt to turn me into some semblance of a human. But what I'm really doing is delaying the inevitable. This is day two of Austin being missing. There's no putting it off any longer. I'm going to have to call his parents and everyone else he knows.

Reluctantly, I turn off the shower and step into the bathroom, trying to absorb my new reality. But over the past couple of days it's been hard to distinguish between my nightmares and my time awake, with every minute feeling more and more surreal. I'm newly married and my husband is missing.

After drying off and pulling on a pair of jeans and a sweatshirt, I shuffle into the living area and screw up my nose at last night's glass of wine and abandoned bowl of pasta, of which I managed three bites before throwing it all up down the toilet. Just looking at it makes me gag.

I hold my breath and place the tray outside my door, hoping some kindly maid will remove it for me, then I call room service to bring me up some coffee and dry toast. I promise myself that once I've had my breakfast, I will make the calls I need to make. Another half hour won't make a difference, and it's only 6 a.m. in England, so I doubt Rob or Vicki will be up yet.

Too soon, I've drunk my coffee and chewed on a piece of dry toast. I sit on the velvet club chair in the living room and steel myself to call Austin's parents. Through the balcony doors, I can see that it's another fresh, blue-sky day welcoming a vaporetto-load of tourists on to the dock at San Marco. I view it all as though it's happening in another dimension. Some place regular and normal, where people go on holiday and have a good time.

With ice-cold fingers, I bring up Austin's mum's contact details on WhatsApp, and press the call icon.

It's ringing.

Vicki answers. 'Stella! *Buongiorno!* How's Venice? I hope you're both having a wonderful time.' She pauses for a moment. 'Rob! It's Austin and Stella on the phone.'

My throat constricts. 'Hi, Vicki.'

'Stella, can we switch to video? I want to see your lovely faces.'

I don't reply straightaway, panicking at the thought of seeing them face to face with the news I have to deliver.

'Stella? You still there?'

'Um, yes.'

'Can you turn on your video?'

'Um, okay.' I press the video icon, feeling ill-prepared.

Austin's mum appears on the screen, standing in their contemporary pale-wood kitchen. She's wearing a pink satin dressing gown, her chestnut hair caught up in a messy bun. 'Stella! There you are!' Her face breaks into a wide smile. 'Gosh, you're up early. You look a bit pale, if you don't mind me saying. Is everything all right?'

Rob appears by her side in a grey striped T-shirt that could be a pyjama top. 'Morning, Stella. You two love birds having a good time? Didn't expect to hear from you on your honeymoon, but it's a nice surprise. Where's that husband of yours? I hope he's treating you like a princess.'

The smiles on both their faces are beginning to falter as I don't respond.

'Stella?' Vicki prompts. 'Everything is okay, right?'

'Something's happened . . .'

'Where's Austin?' Vicki asks, shooting an anxious glance at Rob and then back to me. 'Is he okay?'

'I don't know,' I reply. 'He's gone missing.'

Neither of them replies for a moment.

'Missing?' Rob asks. 'How do you mean?'

'I mean, on our first night here, he left his credit card at the restaurant, so he popped back to get it. But he never came back to the hotel.'

'What?' Rob frowns as he absorbs what I'm telling him.

Vicki's shaking her head, and I ache for them. For the shock they must be feeling. I'm still in shock too, but it's different. It's been settling and deepening over hours, whereas theirs is fresh and brutal.

'He's been missing for two nights?' Rob asks.

'Why didn't you call us straightaway?' Vicki cries.

'I'm sorry. I was sure he'd be back by now. I didn't want to worry you over nothing.'

'So he went back to the restaurant on his own?' Vicki asks. 'You didn't go with him?'

'We'd already gone to bed when he got the message. I woke up and told him to leave it until the morning. I did offer to go with him, but he told me not to worry, that he wouldn't be long.'

'Have you called the British Embassy?' Rob asks.

'Not yet,' I reply. 'The police said to speak to everyone we know. See if they might have a clue about where he went.'

'I can't believe this is happening!' Vicki cries, her tanned face taking on a greyish-green hue.

'Don't worry, Vicks, we'll find him,' Rob says gruffly.

'But where could he be?' she wails.

'Stella,' Rob says slowly, 'can you tell us again exactly what happened on the night he went missing?'

I repeat the events of the night we arrived. It feels horrible saying it all out loud again. I'm fighting down the hysteria in my body that's threatening to erupt any second.

'What about these restaurant owners?' Rob says. 'Could they have something to do with it? Seems they were the last people he saw before he disappeared.'

'Nino and Elena,' I say. 'They were nice. Really helpful. They put me in touch with their printer friend so I could get posters made. I've spent the past day trawling the city, putting them up and talking to shopkeepers and tourists, asking if anyone's seen him.'

'*Oh my God, oh my God, oh my God,*' Vicki moans, bringing her hands up to her cheeks. 'Our baby boy. Where can he be? Please God make him be safe. I couldn't even bear it if—'

'Of course he's safe!' Rob cuts her off. 'He's just got lost. Maybe he hurt himself and got disoriented. Got himself a concussion and had a bit of memory loss. That'll be what's happened.'

'What about the canals?' Vicki whispers. 'What if he fell in?'

'Right, Vicki,' Rob says, 'I need you to stop talking like that. No good thinking the worst. We'll fly over and meet you at the hotel later, Stella.'

'Yes,' Vicki replies, her face rigid, stunned. 'I'll get dressed, book tickets.' She disappears from the screen.

'How are you holding up, love?' Rob asks me.

I shake my head, unable to stammer out an answer.

'Don't you worry. We'll be there by this evening, and we'll get our boy back, all right? Meantime, I'll call the consulate in Milan, and the local police in Christchurch. Are you able to go out searching again today?'

'Yes,' I reply.'

'But you mustn't go into any rough areas on your own. Stick to the busy places.'

'I don't think he's going to be in the busy places, Rob.'

'No. Probably not. But you don't know that. He could be wandering around with memory loss. Have you tried homeless shelters or churches? Do they have a place for rough sleepers? But be careful. Stella, we need you to stay safe. What about the Venetian coppers? Are they doing much?'

'I'm in touch with one of them – Officer Rocco Gallini. He says they're looking. That they've circulated Austin's photo. But he thinks our best bet is to contact everyone Austin knows. Gallini said it's likely one of Austin's friends or colleagues might know where he is. If he's in some kind of trouble.'

'Trouble?' Rob looks sceptical.

'Like, personal or financial. I don't know. What about this thing with Bart Randall?'

'That waste of space?' Rob curls his face in disgust. 'He's put Austin through hell this past year.'

'I know. So do you think he's done something?'

'Like what?' Rob's face suddenly breaks up and goes pixelated.

'Rob? Rob, can you hear me?'

The screen cuts out and says it's reconnecting. I exhale. That was the hardest phone call I've ever had to make. Austin's mum is a wreck and I'm worried that she might think it's my fault for leaving her son to go back to the restaurant alone, and I'm not sure how long his dad will hold out before he breaks down too. At least he's being stoic for now. Goodness knows, one of us needs to be.

'Stella?' Rob's face reappears on the screen. 'Vicki needs my help. I'm going to end the call now, love. But we'll stay in touch, okay? Make sure you're safe.'

'Okay. Thanks, Rob.'

'And can you send me the contact details of that police officer.'

'Gallini.'

'Yeah.'

'Okay.'

'Thanks.' He pauses. 'We love you, Stells.'

'Love you too.'

'Have you told your parents?'

'No. I wanted to call you first. I don't think I'm going to let them know just yet. There's just too much to do here.'

'All right. I'll leave that up to you. Stay safe. And let us know the second you hear anything.'

'Of course, and you both have a safe flight.'

Rob ends the call and his face freezes on the screen, leaving me alone again.

I put down my phone and hug my knees to my chest, steeling myself for the day ahead. For another day of showing Austin's photograph to strangers and getting the same pitying looks. For another day of no answers. But this time, I'm going to have the added stress of Austin's parents arriving. I'd thought it might have been helpful to have them here with me for moral support, taking some of the strain. But seeing Austin's mum's face, witnessing her sheer panic and horror, I'm not sure how I'm going to stop myself from breaking down.

I can't face calling up all our friends individually, so instead I compose a message outlining what's happened and asking if anyone might know anything. I don't want to create a group chat because I can't bear the thought of everyone speculating and offering sympathy. Instead, I copy and paste the text into individual messages, leaving out my parents – because I can't cope with worrying about anyone else right now – and leaving out Bart for obvious reasons.

Less than a minute later, my phone starts vibrating with replies. I need to get out of this hotel suite, start tramping the streets again. I'll check the messages in a while.

After leaving the hotel, I head away from St Mark's Square, scanning the area as I go to check I'm not being followed. Strangely, I don't feel as nervous about that guy today. Maybe because I've got bigger things to worry about, but also because it's daylight. And things always seem less sinister in the light. I make a promise to myself that if I see him again, instead of running, I'm going to approach him and ask him what the hell he's up to. I'd also like to know if he's English or Italian. Chances are that if he's English, he could be my stalker from back home.

As I walk, I remember that Austin and I were supposed to go on a day trip to the islands of Murano and Burano today. We had such a great time planning our trips and walking tours. Instead, I'm trawling the streets, showing photos of my new husband to shopkeepers and bar staff.

Halfway through the morning, I stop at a café for a cold drink and a snack, and to message Austin's parents, who are already en route to London Heathrow. They found a flight that gets in at 16.50 this evening. Wearily, I call Austin's phone again and send him another text to which I receive no reply. Then I check my friends' messages. No one knows anything about what might have happened to my husband. The only people I haven't heard back from are Miles and Liv, who haven't read my message yet. But that's probably because they're busy at work. I also leave a message for Gallini to ask if there's any news at his end.

The hours blur into a sea of streets and faces, punctuated by text messages of shock and sympathy from friends. I reach a point where my blistered feet are throbbing and I can barely see straight.

My eyes are heavy, my brain sluggish. I need a nap, but how can I go to bed when Austin's missing? Maybe food will help.

Spying a kiosk, I order a warm Caprese sandwich and a bottle of water. There don't seem to be any benches in this city, so I sink on to the wide, low rim of a stone octagonal well, one of many that are dotted throughout Venice. The sandwich looks delicious, but I can barely taste it. Everything about my body is numb, including my taste buds.

The Lewises will be arriving in Venice soon. I should start making my way back to the hotel so I'm there when they arrive. I feel too exhausted to walk but there are no roads so it's not like I can grab a bus, a taxi or an Uber. Maybe I could try to get a water taxi – even if they are insanely expensive.

I heave myself up from my makeshift seat by the well and dust the crumbs from my sweatshirt and jeans before heading to one of the wider waterways. There, I spot a queue of people waiting by a pontoon. Of course! I can get a vaporetto, one of the city's water-buses. I spot a ticket machine, so I make my selection and slot in my credit card, going through the barrier and joining the queue.

The wait is only a few minutes and I find myself being funnelled on to the watercraft, along with commuters and tourists, where thankfully I manage to bag one of the green plastic seats.

Opposite me, an American mother is trying to stop her toddler son from falling asleep, telling him it's only a couple more stops. But his eyes are closing. I know how he feels.

The vaporetto windows are stained with dried splashes so I can barely see out, but I can make out the shapes of other watercraft passing by – water taxis, private boats, police craft, and a delivery boat piled way too high with parcels.

The water-bus stops at several stations, emptying out and filling up. The American mum scoops up her son, who couldn't stay awake, and leaves, replaced by a couple of young Italian girls, chattering and giggling.

Finally, I see my stop ahead, outside the hotel. I wish I'd thought to take a water-bus last night when I realised I was being followed. It would have saved me from scurrying through all those dark alleyways. The water-bus stops and I disembark with another crowd of people. I notice the rows of gondolas bobbing next to the pontoon, with queues of tourists waiting their turn to take an iconic ride. I'd pictured Austin and myself doing just that, leaning back against heart-shaped cushions while our gondolier serenaded us. I turn away from the sight and focus on making my way back to the hotel.

After the crush of the water-bus, it's a relief to be out in the open again. I take a few deep breaths and check the time. There's a message from Rob to say they've landed safely, and should be arriving at the hotel in around an hour. That will give me time for a short power nap.

As I turn into the street that leads to the hotel's side entrance, I stumble over something – a loose brick – stubbing my toe badly and almost sprawling face down across the pavement. A teenage boy takes my arm to steady me and asks if I'm okay. I nod, touched by his concern until I see him snag the eye of another boy in a designer-store doorway, and then it hits me that the brick, the concerned boy . . . it's all part of a scam.

I feel around for my handbag. The zip is open. I rummage inside and realise with a thud of panic and dismay that my wallet is missing.

'Hey!' I cry.

But the boy is already racing off down the street.

'Hey! He has my wallet!' I cry. 'That boy has my wallet!'

People stare in confusion, too late to make any attempt to stop him as he darts away into the crowd. His accomplice from the shop doorway is nowhere to be seen. I start to run down the street after the boy, fury and despair building up in my chest. My cash, credit card and driver's licence are all in my wallet. How could I have been so stupid? The concierge warned me to keep an eye on my bag. Why on earth didn't I pay more attention to him?

I stand in the street, dazed, gasping, my toe throbbing, my chest tight. My life feels as though it's spiralling out of control into something unrecognisable. It's not even about the theft of my wallet – it's just the shock of it, on top of everything else. And, to add to my exhaustion and misery, I'm about to face the anguish of Austin's parents. I blink back tears and order myself to keep it together. But that's not easy when all I want to do right now is sink down on to the pavement and weep.

Chapter Fourteen

THEN

'Well done! You were on fire today,' I call out to my ladies as they leave the studio, buzzing with adrenaline. It's my last class of the evening – street dance – and we've been practising the same tricky routine for a few weeks now. Everyone has been giving it one hundred and ten per cent, and tonight was the first time we were all in sync, all the way through. It was just the thing to take my mind off yesterday's unpleasant encounter with Keri.

'Hey, Jem,' I say to my colleague who's just sashayed into the studio, running a silver-ringed hand through her blonde pixie cut.

'Hey, Stella. I caught the end of your class through the window. It looked so good. Honestly, your talent's wasted here. Your choreography is on point.'

'Aw, thanks.'

'Was that another new routine?' she asks.

'Newish. We've been practising this one since Easter.'

'I just tweak mine a bit every year,' Jem says. 'Saves so much time and my classes still lap it up. It must take you hours. You care way too much, Stella. Your ladies wouldn't mind if you kept some of the same routines.'

'Maybe,' I reply. 'But I switch it up more for me than for them. I enjoy creating new stuff. I think I'd get bored otherwise.'

'Hm, yeah, I suppose.' Jem doesn't look convinced. I don't think she and the other instructors like the fact that my classes are always booked up, while theirs are half empty. For me, the more I put into it, the more job satisfaction I get out of it. I'd hate to treat it like a regular job, where I simply put in the hours for a pay cheque. The most enjoyable part of my job is seeing my classes' sheer pleasure when they get into the flow of a brand-new dance routine that pushes them out of their comfort zones. Same for the kids' classes. They love the challenge of mastering new steps, and I love the thrill of seeing it. And when it all comes together, like it did today, it's a natural high.

'Stella, darling . . .' My boss, Millie Sessions, pops her sleek blonde head around the door. 'Can you drop by my office when you're done?' Her plummy voice fills the large space.

'Hi, Millie. Yes, sure.'

'Great!' she replies and disappears down the corridor.

Jem gives me an *uh-oh* look, but I'm not worried. Millie needs me more than I need her. Jem heads out. 'Good luck with her ladyship. See you tomorrow.'

'Thanks. See you, Jem. Have a nice evening.'

'You too.' She leaves and I gather up my bits and pieces from the studio before heading down the hall to Millie's office, although it's more like a sumptuous lounge than a work room, with comfy chairs, rugs, artwork, and a selection of expensive dance-themed coffee-table books.

Millie's in her forties and owns Dance Sessions with her husband, Darrin, who also works in insurance. Darrin is as quiet and laid-back as Millie is flamboyant and enthusiastic. They have four beautiful children – two girls and two boys – and appear to be living the dream. Millie is a bit of a local celebrity as she was on *The X*

Factor a couple of times as a back-up dancer about fifteen years ago, a fact that features heavily on the Dance Sessions website.

I knock and enter. Millie waves me over to where she's sitting at her glass desk and I sit in one of the leopard-print velvet club chairs, placing my bag on my lap.

'I watched a bit of your latest class, Stella, and I have to say I'm impressed.'

'Thank you. It was fun.'

'We should video a clip for social media. We'll need to get permissions, but I'll get Darrin to sort that.'

'Sounds good,' I reply.

'Now, sweetie,' she says, leaning forward and giving me intense eye contact. 'There are a couple of other things I'd like to run by you.'

'Okay . . .' *Here we go.*

'What would you think about adding two more classes a week to your schedule?' She sits back in her chair, trying to come across like she's offering me an incredible opportunity, but this is a conversation we've had many times over the years. Millie is always asking if I'll increase my hours, but I'm happy with my work-life balance. Sure, I could use the extra money, but what's the point of working myself to death? I already work more hours than a regular job, especially when you factor in all the hours of preparation and choreography it takes to keep things fresh.

I open my mouth to reply, but she holds up her hand to stop me, sensing I'm about to turn her down. 'Don't answer right away. Go home and think about it. Really think about it. I value you, Stella, and I'd like you to take more of an active role in inspiring my other instructors. I see you as playing an integral part of Dance Sessions' long-term future. Honestly, if I had ten more like you, this place would be a force to be reckoned with.'

'That's very flattering, Millie, but—'

'Nuh, uh.' Her hand comes up again. 'I said think about it.'

I nod, but there's nothing for me to think about.

'Now, the other thing I wanted to talk to you about,' she continues, 'is the youth musical theatre showcase this year. Do you have any stand-out kids in mind for the lead roles? Because I was thinking Saskia would be perfect for the *Wicked* number, and possibly the *Annie* routine.'

Saskia is Millie's elder daughter and although she's good, there are other, stronger dancers I would want to recommend, including a couple who really have the X factor. But instead of being honest, I make a few positive noises about Saskia before promising to have a think about it and then finally making my escape.

The place is quiet now, all the studios empty. It used to be a match factory and the old brick building lay derelict for years until Millie and Darrin took it over and turned it into their dream business. The space is great when it's full of people, but it's as creepy as hell right now as I hurry along the corridor to the exit. I leave through the massive oak door, pulling it shut with a puff of relief.

Dusk is approaching, along with a light sprinkling of rain, but it's not quite dark enough for the streetlights to pop on. I was energised after my class, but that talk with Millie has brought me down. I don't want to have to disappoint my boss by rejecting her offer of taking on two more classes a week, or of recommending someone other than her daughter to take a lead in the showcase. The other kids and parents won't be happy if she gives both plum roles to her daughter. I shouldn't let it worry me. It's not my dance school. If Millie wants to do that, then that's her prerogative. Just please don't ask for my opinion if you don't want to hear the answer. I think she wants to shift the decision-making process on to me so that she doesn't get accused of nepotism.

I did wonder about trying to open my own studio, but seeing the hours that Millie works in her office, I'm not sure it's for me. I'd rather be doing the dancing than the organising. Plus, I don't have the funds for anything like that. Maybe it's something to think about for the future. A long-term goal.

The car park is silent as I wend my way across the damp concrete, around the puddled potholes, until I reach the road, taking the quiet back streets that lead to Austin's flat. Soft footsteps behind have me throwing a glance over my shoulder, but I don't see anyone. I lengthen my strides anyway, unsettled, dismayed to have this same feeling of being followed yet again. I'd since decided to blame my overactive imagination, but this is too similar to previous times. The last time I felt it was on my way home from a night out in Bournemouth – I'd had quite a bit to drink so my judgement was impaired. But this evening I'm stone cold sober, and I'm not imagining anything.

I feel a bit more reassured as a woman with a caramel cockapoo walks past on the opposite side of the road, knowing that the roads are quiet but not deserted, and I've walked this route many times before.

The footsteps are still there though, and I'm beginning to think I should have taken the main road, even though it's a longer journey. I cross to the opposite side of the street and my insides quiver as I hear the footsteps cross too. I'm less than fifteen minutes away from Austin's flat, but the rest of my route will take me down quieter paths; the ones that run alongside the ruined Norman House, and around the back of the priory. I don't want to turn down those deserted streets. Not if someone might be following me.

As I quicken my pace, I reach into my bag and take out my keys, threading them through my fingers like Wolverine's claws, certain I'd be too squeamish to use them as an actual weapon. But as I start to sweat, I realise I wouldn't have a choice. I would have to do it.

Am I overreacting? Perhaps. But I've always had a vivid imagination, my mind jumping forward to project worst-case scenarios.

My thoughts swing from convincing myself it's just a random, harmless person to worrying that I may have a stalker. But I absolutely cannot turn my head to look, because if it is someone with ill intent, then they'll know for sure that I'm aware of them. Although maybe I *should* turn around. Maybe I should stop and face whoever it is and tell them to back off. For a brief, wild moment, I consider doing just that. But just as I'm about to glance back, fear pulls at my belly and slides down my back. Stops me doing anything other than hurrying forward on soft legs.

Chapter Fifteen

NOW

My brief window of time to grab some rest before Austin's parents have been snatched away – literally, with the theft of my wallet. So, once again, I find myself at the police station, greeting the same female police officer who was on duty yesterday.

She gives me a smile of recognition. 'Hello, how can I help you?'

'My wallet,' I say. 'Two boys . . . there was a brick, I tripped and . . .' I don't seem to be able to string a sentence together. My throat is tight and my eyes are burning with unshed tears.

'Some boys stole your wallet?' she asks.

'Yes. I'm so stupid. I thought he was being helpful, but then . . .'

She sighs with irritation and for a moment I think she's annoyed with me for letting it happen, but then she says, 'This is the third time today. These kids are getting too cocky. I'm so sorry this happened. We'll try to catch them, but . . .' She throws up her hands. 'Usually they just take the cash and discard the wallet and the cards. We might find it. I'll take down the details and then we can look in the street where it happened. It's close by?'

I nod. 'Just outside the hotel. I was getting off the vaporetto when it happened.'

'Okay, yes, this seems to be a favourite spot for them at the moment. We have officers regularly checking the area, but these kids are like slippery fish. And they can sense when we're around.'

'At least I still have my phone. And my passport's in the hotel safe with some spare cash. But all my cards, my driving licence . . .' I shrug. 'I guess it's not that important. Not with everything else that's going on.'

She gives me a sympathetic look. 'Remember to cancel your cards.'

'I don't suppose there's any update on the search for my husband?'

'Sadly, no. My colleague, he spoke on the phone earlier to Mr Lewis's father. We are now liaising with your local police in the UK. They may also contact Interpol.'

My head suddenly swims, and I grip the edge of the reception desk to steady myself.

'You are okay?'

'Just a bit dizzy.'

'You need to sit down?'

'Maybe for a minute.' I reach for a half-empty bottle of water in my bag and take a few sips as I sink on to the bench. There's an elderly couple already seated there, and the woman pats my hand and says something in a German accent. I nod and smile, even though I didn't quite hear what she said.

Another uniformed police officer appears and ushers the couple through an arched doorway at the rear of the lobby.

My officer – whose name I still don't know – comes and sits next to me. After she takes down the details of how I lost my wallet, two police officers bustle into the station with a couple of young men, who don't look very happy. They're English and drunk, swearing at the officers, making me embarrassed to be British.

The policemen speak to my officer, who gives me a regretful look and says she won't be able to help me look for my wallet right now as she's needed here. But she assures me she'll come and take a look later. And adds that it can't hurt for me to scan the area now. 'Look inside doorways, and trash cans. You may see it sitting there. You're feeling any better?'

I nod and thank her, relieved to be leaving the station with all that commotion going on. My head is still swimming, but it's not far to the hotel and I'm hoping the fresh air will help.

My phone buzzes with a message from Rob. They're in a water taxi, about five minutes away from the hotel. I slip my phone into my bag and zip it closed, bringing it around to the front of my body – although it's a bit late to be taking security precautions now – and I make my way back to the hotel.

As soon as I walk into the hotel and turn into the lobby, I see Austin's parents checking in at reception. Normally, they're a glamorous, eye-catching couple who turn heads wherever they go. But this evening, they look muted. Almost drab. This shouldn't be surprising, given the trauma of the situation, but I can't help being shocked by it. Although I don't suppose my appearance is any better.

Vicki spots me first. 'Oh, Stella, darling.' She almost staggers towards me and clutches me tightly. Usually I'd be enveloped in clouds of Baccarat Rouge, but today all she smells of is deodorant, breath mints and fresh air.

Likewise, when Rob hugs me, there's no trace of his woody cologne, and his normally smooth face is scratchy with stubble.

They both look like shadows of their usual selves. And it scares me.

'Can you believe this?' she says.

I shake my head. 'It's terrible.'

'I feel so sick,' she whispers.

'Have you eaten anything?' I ask, feeling faint again.

'We couldn't face it,' Vicki replies. 'It all seems like a nightmare. Where is he, Stella? Where's our boy?'

'I wish I knew,' I reply. 'None of it makes sense.'

'Okay, well, now we're here, let's have something to eat,' Rob says. 'Build up our strength.'

'I can't eat,' Vicki says. 'How can I even think about doing anything remotely normal while Austin's missing, who knows where?'

Rob hugs her and then looks her in the eyes. 'One thing I know is that if we're going to find our boy, we'll need to eat properly, stay hydrated and get enough sleep. It won't do him any good if we're all too weak and exhausted to look for him.'

Vicki's whole body wilts. 'You're right. I know you are, but my body feels like it just wants to shut down.'

'I know how you feel,' I reply.

'Oh, you poor girl,' she says, turning to me. 'You've been coping with this all on your own. Where can he be?'

Rob tips the concierge, asks him to take their bags up to the room, and then ushers me and Vicki towards the restaurant, where we're early enough to get a table. The waiter seats us in the window, but none of us cares about the breathtaking view.

I think the waiter must have been briefed on our situation, because he's quiet and respectful, his eyes filled with concern. 'What would you like to drink?' he asks.

'A glass of white wine for me, please,' I say, feeling as if I could drink a whole bottle of the stuff right now and happily fall into oblivion.

'Are you sure we shouldn't keep a clear head?' Vicki asks.

'I've had a couple of rough days,' I reply. 'I'd really like a glass.'

'I'll join you,' Rob says, his talk of staying healthy and hydrated seemingly forgotten.

'May as well get a bottle then,' Vicki adds.

We order and the waiter pours our drinks. Rob and Vicki only have a small glass each, but I top mine up immediately. Now that Austin's parents are here, I feel as though everything has suddenly become really real.

The wine is crisp and clear and cold. It tastes of better, happier days and it blunts my senses. Everything blurs around the edges as I listen to Austin's parents worry and plan and quiz me over and over about everything that's happened so far. Somehow I manage to answer them coherently, but I feel as though I'm pretending to be normal, like I'm holding on to my sanity by torn fingernails.

The first bottle of wine is suddenly empty, so I order another. I catch the look that Rob and Vicki give one another but I can't find the words to explain that this isn't me. This isn't how I normally behave. It's just that now they're here, I can set aside the fear and tension for a couple of hours. I don't have to be the one in charge, sorting everything out. Because the grown-ups have finally arrived.

Food is set in front of us and I make a show of eating a couple of forkfuls of something that's hot and gooey, like rice pudding. I don't remember what I ordered and I'm sure it's probably delicious, but it's not something I want right now. I realise I'm shivering, my teeth clacking together like those wind-up fake dentures you get.

Vicki puts an arm around me and leads me out of the dining room. She takes me up to my suite, makes me sip some water, and somehow gets me changed and into bed. I manage to glean that she and Rob are staying in the room opposite. She tells me the number, but I've already forgotten it. I want to apologise, but I can't stop shivering.

'It's delayed shock, Stella,' she says. 'We shouldn't have let you drink so much. You should get some rest. I'll sit with you for a bit.'

I should let her go to be with her husband, to finish their meal, but before I can formulate the words, I'm asleep.

Chapter Sixteen

THEN

My back prickles with the knowledge that someone is there. The footsteps are still behind me, matching my pace.

Keeping the keys in my hand as a makeshift weapon, I manage to call Austin on my mobile.

'Hey, Stella, you almost home?' he asks.

Just the sound of his voice gives me courage. I speak quietly and hurriedly into the phone. 'Can you come and pick me up? I think someone's following me.'

'*What?* Where are you?'

I give him directions and he tells me to get away from the quiet back roads as fast as possible and walk towards the high street. Even though the shops are shut, there will be bars and restaurants open there, cars driving past. Difficult for anyone to accost me. I tell him I'm already heading that way.

A few minutes later, I almost cry with relief when Austin's grey Audi pulls up alongside me. I'm almost at the high street anyway, but it's so good to see him.

'Thank God you're here. That was quick.'

'Hey,' he says, concern in his eyes. He glances back along the road, and I do too, braver now that Austin's arrived. But I can't see anyone at all.

I get into the passenger seat, my heart still drumming. Not owning a car, I'm used to walking everywhere, often alone, but after yet another scary experience, I'm going to have to rethink my walking habits. This evening has really shaken me.

'I can't see anyone there now,' Austin says. 'Did you get a look at whoever it was?'

'No.'

'Shall we drive around, see if we can spot them?'

'Thanks, but there's no point. I don't even know what they look like. I should've turned around to get a look, but I was too chicken. The thing is . . .' I swallow. 'It's something that's happened before.'

'What do you mean?' Austin's expression darkens.

'Yeah, a couple of other times I've had the same feeling I was being followed. I could be wrong, but—'

'Jeez, Stella. Maybe we should call the police. If there's some kind of predator or stalker on the loose . . .'

I shake my head, worried about turning this into something bigger than it is. Now that I'm safe in the car with Austin, the last thing I want to do is talk about it with the police. I'm sure they'll think I'm being paranoid. 'No. It's fine. Nothing happened. It was probably just someone innocently walking behind me. Could've been harmless. Probably was.' But my expression isn't convincing him.

'Come here.' Austin unclicks his seat belt and leans across to give me a hug.

My breathing gradually slows as I try to relax. 'Can we just go home?' I ask.

'Yeah, course. Shall we skip dinner this evening?'

'Dinner?' I ask, before remembering we have plans with Miles and Liv tonight. 'No, let's go, I'll be fine and it'll be nice. Don't tell them about my freak-out though. I feel a bit silly now. Like I let my imagination get the better of me.'

Austin shakes his head and rubs my knee. 'It's not silly. It's horrible. And I won't tell them if you don't want, but they'll be just as worried as I was.'

Austin drives me home and it doesn't take us long to get ready. I throw on some fresh clothes in a daze, unable to shake the remnants of my fear, but I'm hoping that a fun evening out with friends will clear my head and get me back to my regular frame of mind. Although, recently, I've been finding it harder and harder to stay on an even keel. Things just seem off kilter lately. Mainly due to falling out with my dad. And I also need to put Keri's words out of my head. When I got home last night, I told Austin about our encounter at the pub. He was annoyed that she'd hassled me, but just told me to ignore her, said she thrives on the drama, that it gives her oxygen. He's right, of course. But it's easier said than done when she invades my space like that.

This should be the happiest time of my life. I'm with the man I love, looking forward to getting married, the two of us starting a life together. It's everybody else who seems to have a problem with it. Thankfully, tonight we'll be spending time with two of the loveliest people on the planet.

Suited and booted, Austin and I walk to the Lebanese restaurant where we're meeting our friends. That's the beauty of living so close to town, although it's started drizzling again and we're huddled beneath his big umbrella.

'Part of me really wants to jump in one of those puddles,' Austin says, with a dangerous gleam in his eye.

'Ha! I know what you mean,' I reply. 'I used to love doing that as a kid. I remember my parents kitting me out in wellies and waterproofs, letting me splash to my heart's content.'

'We should do it,' he replies.

I raise an eyebrow.

He takes my hand and points to a particularly wide puddle at the edge of the kerb.

'Are you crazy?' I laugh. 'This dress is dry-clean only, and I don't fancy sitting in a restaurant covered in muddy rainwater.'

'Ahh, I guess you're right,' Austin says, pulling me in close, giving my waist a squeeze. 'Would've been fun though.'

I stare up at him, not quite sure if he would have actually gone through with it. He's usually quite fastidious about his clothes, but he can also be impulsive when the mood takes him. 'What's got into you today?' I grin.

'Nothing, just wanted to cheer you up after what happened earlier. Thought splashing about in puddles might help take your mind off things.'

'Yeah, it definitely would have done that. But can we maybe do something that doesn't involve mud?'

He laughs. 'Whatever you want, Stells.'

I lean into him, grateful for having such a thoughtful fiancé. It's nice to walk in the rain, feeling his strong arm around my shoulders.

I hope I can put today's incident behind me, because I'd hate to start feeling too scared to walk alone. I make a mental note to look into self-defence classes, because I can't rely on Austin speeding to my rescue every time I have a panic attack. I think knowing how to defend myself will give me the confidence that I need.

'Hey, guys!' Liv gets to her feet and holds out her arms for a hug. 'Congratulations on the engagement! Let's see that ring, Stella. Oh my goodness, it's bee-oo-ti-ful.'

Miles stands and bends to kiss my cheek. 'Congrats, Stella,' he says, giving me a warm smile before hugging Austin. 'Congrats, man.'

'Don't pretend you haven't already congratulated him, Miles,' I say, giving him a mock glare. 'He wasn't supposed to tell anyone yet.'

Miles gives me a rueful grin, running a hand over his dark hair.

'Oh, stop it,' Liv says to me teasingly. 'You have to shout news like that from the rooftops, not keep it a secret.'

'Who would have guessed you were in PR?' I smile, and slide in next to her on the banquette.

She waggles her finger at me. 'Listen, Stella, there's enough crap in the world. So when something good happens, celebrate it for all you're worth. Grab that joy and milk it. Even if it feels too much, it's not.'

Now I remember why I love this girl. She always has the power and the words to make me feel good.

We try to socialise with Liv and Miles at least once a month. Unlike us, they don't seem interested in getting married – too caught up in their careers. They both work for a successful marketing firm in Bournemouth, which is where they met. Miles works in analytics and Liv now heads up their PR department.

Miles was a bit of a geek before meeting Liv, but her bubbly personality complements his quiet nature. Plus, he's very easy on the eye with his swimmer's physique. They both do triathlons for fun.

The four of us spend the evening eating mezze, drinking and laughing far too much, but I notice that after his playful antics on the walk over, Austin is quieter than usual, checking his phone a lot.

'Put it away, Austin,' Liv chides, nodding at his mobile.

'What? Oh, yeah, sorry, just work stuff.'

'You're not at work now,' she says. 'Look, I'm normally glued to my phone too, but you've got to take a break.'

I silently thank Liv for saying out loud what I've been saying in my head for the past couple of days.

'Okay, okay.' Austin raises his hands and puts his phone back down on the table.

'Turn it over,' Liv says. 'So you can't be distracted by the screen.'

'Who are you, my mum?' he says to her with an eye roll. But he does as she asks.

'No, your mum's way nicer than me,' Liv replies.

'That's true,' Austin says.

Liv flicks one of her chickpeas at him.

'Very mature.'

'I aim to please.'

'Yeah, well, next time can you aim a bit better.' Austin picks at his shirt where the chickpea has left a small mark.

'Oops, sorry.'

But Austin's attention is elsewhere. 'Uh oh,' he says, catching my eye and shaking his head.

'What?' I mouth.

'Bart and Patsy just walked past. I think he saw me.'

'It'll be fine,' I say. 'He won't come in. Probably just on his way out.' They live in a flat around the corner from the restaurant, but it's bad luck they saw us. We shouldn't have sat in the window.

'What's going on?' Liv asks.

The door to the restaurant flies open and Bart strides in, followed by his wife.

'What the hell is this?' Bart waves a letter in front of Austin's face.

'Hey, Bart, chill,' Miles says.

'This is nothing to do with you, Miles,' Bart snaps.

For once, Liv stays silent.

'Did you know about this?' Patsy says to me. 'Was this your idea?'

'This is nothing to do with Stella,' Austin says. 'And this isn't the time or place for this conversation.'

'We were on our way round to see you,' Bart replies. 'You can't get away with—'

'Is everything all right, Bart?' One of the waiters has come over to see what the fuss is about and is obviously a friend of Bart's.

'No, it's not,' Bart retorts. 'Sorry to barge in, but this man is . . .'

'He's a crook,' Patsy cries.

'I don't know what he's told you, Patsy,' Austin starts, 'but—'

'Oh, save it, Austin.' Patsy waves a manicured hand at him. 'We're not interested in your lies.'

Austin looks at me in despair and my heart goes out to him. He turns back to Bart. 'Look, mate, you can see I'm—'

'I'm not your mate. I thought I was, but you obviously threw our friendship out of the window when you got some slimy solicitor to write *this*!' Bart crumples up the letter and throws it into the remnants of Austin's dinner. Splashes of garlicky, tomatoey sauce and hummus flick up on to Austin's shirt and face. But before any of us can respond further, Bart and Patsy stalk out.

Chapter Seventeen

NOW

I wake with a dry mouth and a fuzzy, sour tongue, remembering with shame how drunk I got last night in front of Rob and Vicki. What a shambles I was. I'm sure the last thing they needed was to have their missing son's wife get completely wasted.

I have a vague recollection of Vicki bringing me up to the suite and helping me into bed. I groan, my head throbbing. I'm pretty sure I polished off almost two bottles of wine on my own on a virtually empty stomach. I remember Rob trying to get me to eat something, and pushing a glass of water towards me. Every time he did that, I kept telling him that it was okay because I still had a bottle of water in my bag. Jesus, they must hate me right now.

'Of course we don't hate you,' Vicki replies half an hour later as we wait for the lift to take us down to breakfast. 'You've been under an enormous amount of stress. I'm sure there are a couple of bottles of vino with my name on them, just waiting for me to have my turn.'

'Even so,' I reply, 'I want you to know how sorry I am. This is traumatic enough without me adding to your stress.'

'Don't give it another thought,' Rob says. 'Let's be positive. We're going to make sure we find him. Preferably today. Then we can all go home together and celebrate. How does that sound?'

'Like a dream.' Vicki pats her husband's arm.

'How's your room?' I ask.

'Small, but absolutely fine. We were lucky to get anything at such short notice.'

'Take the suite,' I offer.

'Don't be daft,' Vicki says. 'We're fine where we are.'

'No, honestly, take it. There's two of you and one of me.' We all pause at the horrible significance of that sentence, but I plough on. 'I'd rather swap. That room reminds me of . . . I really don't like being in there.'

'Of course we'll swap,' Rob says. 'If that's what you want.'

'We'll do it later,' Vicki adds.

Downstairs in the lobby, Rob asks Paola, the hotel manager, if we can look at footage from their CCTV cameras the night Austin went missing. I mention that there's not much point, as we already know Austin made it back to the restaurant that night. But I guess it makes sense to cover all angles. As he talks to her, I glance around the lobby at the guests heading into the restaurant for breakfast, or leaving the hotel to start their day, oblivious to the nightmare I've found myself in.

Paola says to come back after we've had our breakfast, and she'll run through the footage with us.

At breakfast, Rob is in planning mode, running through what he thinks we should all be doing today. I nod along, but I keep zoning out. Vicki still looks shell-shocked, biting her lower lip and nibbling on the corner of a croissant, checking her phone obsessively.

I'm actually starving this morning, finding that food is taking the edge off my hangover. I've already polished off a plate of scrambled eggs on toast. And a couple of the little custard-filled doughnuts. Messages keep pinging on my phone, mainly from friends asking how I am and if there's been any news yet. Miles and Liv finally replied with texts, but they each gave quite a muted response, which has surprised and disappointed me. Maybe they don't understand the seriousness of what's happened.

'So, we're agreed?' Rob says. I realise I haven't been listening and he must have noticed my inattentiveness because he recaps for me. 'We'll take a water-bus to the train station at Ferrovia, and we'll work our way backwards to the hotel. I want to see if it's possible to check the cameras at the station, and speak to staff. It's also a good place to put posters up as they'll get a lot of foot traffic through there. Stella, do you have any posters left?'

I nod. 'Quite a few, but we can always get more copies.'

'Vicki, you made a start on the Facebook page last night, didn't you?'

She nods. 'I invited everyone I know to join the page and spread the word. Stella, can you do the same?'

'Yes,' I reply. 'But for today I think it makes more sense if we split up. We can cover more ground that way.'

Vicki blanches, but then she nods quickly. 'You're right.'

'Good idea,' Rob says, taking a gulp of coffee. 'Vicki, why don't you get off at the Piazzale Roma? That's where all the buses from the mainland stop. And, Stella, could you get off at the Rialto Bridge? That's another busy area with lots of people passing through. I think our aim should be to get as many posters up as possible, and to speak to as many shopkeepers and restaurant staff as we can. All it takes is for one person to have recognised Austin and give us a lead. I just wish there were more of us. We need an army of volunteers to search the city.'

'What about the restaurant?' Vicki asks, pushing her plate away. 'I'd really like to talk to the owners, and shouldn't we be searching around that area?'

'I searched all around that area on day one, but it can't hurt to search again.'

'Okay,' Rob says, pulling at his greying hair. 'How about Vicki and I go to the restaurant first? I'd like to speak to the owners too. Stella, what did you say their names were?'

'Nino and Elena Vianello. The restaurant's called La Terrazza di Stella.' I sit back in my chair. 'Austin booked it specially, because of the name . . .'

At this, Vicki chokes out a sob and takes my hand, squeezing it tightly. 'We'll get him back, Stella, don't you worry.'

After breakfast, I give the Lewises a stack of flyers and leave them to go through the hotel footage with Paola, while I catch the vaporetto to the Rialto Bridge. It's strange how quickly I've become used to having Austin's parents with me; it feels disconcerting to be on my own again. Like I'm not supposed to be here. I'm not a tourist, or a native, I'm not a worker. I'm nobody, nothing.

I show Austin's poster to everyone in the queue, and they throw me pitying glances, shaking their heads and wishing me success, then turning away, back to their lives. My sadness and desperation is a buzzkill and a downer for everyone I talk to. Who wants to be reminded of the fragility of everything? Of the way our lives can be upended without warning?

In the Rialto district, my morning takes on a rhythm as I get used to the strange activity of searching and asking, becoming accustomed to the same reaction over and over again. I find myself at the edge of a sad-looking market with hardly any customers selling fish, fruit, vegetables and dried pasta, among other things. I try to talk to a couple of the stallholders but they don't seem too friendly until I purchase a packet of spices from an older gentleman. I show him Austin's photo and he shakes his head. But then he passes the flyer to his neighbouring stallholder, who then passes it to another. The spice seller asks me for a few of the leaflets, and I gratefully hand him a thin stack.

The time passes quickly as the hours are eaten up. I keep trying Austin's mobile, but it consistently goes to voicemail. I know there's no point leaving yet more messages, but I do it anyway. Both Rob and Vicki are good at staying in touch, and I get texts every hour or so that I reply to straightaway with updates of my own.

I'd never realised what a massive task it is to try to locate a missing person. It's almost impossible. In a city of thousands, how do you find one? No wonder the police can do so little. They must know what a Herculean undertaking it is.

By one o'clock, I'm hungry again. Luckily, even in my hungover state, I remembered to take some euros from the safe this morning. I cancelled my cards too and it doesn't look like there's been any suspicious activity on my account. Hopefully, the officer was right when she said those boys just wanted the cash. I buy a cheese and spinach panini and a Coke and sit at the edge of the water to eat.

The white stone Rialto Bridge curves gracefully across the slimmest point of the Grand Canal, its central portico like a gateway to another time. Its walkways are heaving with people, mainly tourists in bright clothing taking photos and videos from every angle, something Austin and I would have been doing, but the sights hold no appeal for me now.

I've just taken my first bite of panini when my mobile starts ringing from my bag. I fumble for it, dropping my lunch into the canal when I see who's calling, my heart missing a beat.

It's Bart Randall.

My immediate thought is to ignore it. But if I do that, I'll only spend the afternoon wondering what he wants. Before I can change my mind, I reply, watching my panini sink beneath the surface of the water.

'Hello,' I say tersely.

'Stella, is that you?'

'Yes.'

'I heard Austin's gone missing.'

I don't reply.

'Stella?'

'What?'

'I said, I heard Austin's missing. I hope he hasn't done a runner.'

'Why the hell would he do a runner, Bart? He's not the one who's done anything wrong!'

'You have no idea, do you?' he sneers.

'I can't believe you're harassing me on my honeymoon while my husband's disappeared. Have you no shame? Or are you deflecting because this is something to do with you?'

'With me? Don't be ridiculous.'

'Well,' I continue. 'You're the only person with a grudge against my husband, so I think you'd be the main suspect if anything's happened to him.'

'The last thing I want is for Austin to go missing and make things even more complicated. I've no idea where he is and I'm not happy about any of it. The man has made my life a living hell this past year, with this court case of his.'

'You shouldn't have stolen from him then, should you?'

'I haven't stolen anything!'

'You would say that.'

'I haven't been able to sleep, Patsy's been having panic attacks—'

'If you've called me up to tell me what a hard time you're having, then I'm hanging up. In case you've forgotten, my husband's gone missing in a foreign country, so forgive me if I'm not sympathetic.'

'Where is he, Stella? What are you two plotting?'

'You sound deluded, Bart.'

'I won't let you do this to me. I'm going to counter-sue.'

'My husband is missing!' I cry, drawing stares from a nearby group of tourists. I give them a dirty look and turn away, lowering my voice. 'Just leave me alone, Bart.' He starts to say something but I end the call, cutting him off. My hands are shaking and I feel perilously close to tears again. What was all that about? Why is he calling me up?

That earlier bite of panini has lodged in my gullet. I take a swig of water, but it has no effect. My lunch is ruined, my morning has been a waste of time, so I stuff my phone into my bag and start to head back towards the hotel. All these hours of searching are starting to feel surreal, as though I'm trying to complete a quest in a video game that's impossible to finish.

I find myself walking against the flow of the crowd. It's become even more busy since I got here, with everyone homing in on the Rialto Bridge, taking photos, desperate to climb its steps and walk across. To tick that iconic sight off their bucket list.

A tall man with short dark hair, in a black-and-white baseball cap and wraparound sunglasses, overtakes me from behind and I clutch my handbag, nervous about being targeted again. I need to get away from these crowds, from the noise and heat; I'm starting to feel really claustrophobic. There's no space anywhere in my immediate vicinity. I consider getting a vaporetto, but the queue is horrendous. I don't think I could face standing in that crush.

As I weave through the crowds, I try to keep calm, try to remember to breathe, and then, miracle of miracles, I spot a quiet alley. Even though it's dark and narrow, I duck into it, walking until I'm almost halfway along before I lean with my back against the crumbling brick wall, breathing in and out slowly, my hands still cradling my bag.

A silhouette fills the entrance where I turned into the alley. The space isn't wide enough for more than one person abreast, so I have no choice but to start walking again. But there's something familiar about the figure – I think it might be the man who passed me earlier. The one in the baseball cap and sunglasses. Or am I imagining things, projecting a scary situation because I'm so stressed? Surely there can't be multiple people following me!

I'm not hanging around to find out. I stride down the alley, wishing it were shorter, or lighter or wider or busier, trying to ignore the feeling of the walls closing in. My head is pounding and I can't even feel my feet as I hasten to the end.

I glance back to see he's still coming. His head is down and it's dark in the alley so I still can't see his face, but I can tell by his clothes it's the same guy. Turning into a busier street, I reach into my bag, pull out my phone and call Vicki, almost sobbing with relief as she answers.

'Get yourself into a busy café,' she says after I tell her through panicked gasps that I'm being followed. 'I'll stay on the line. You tell me where you are and I'll come and find you.'

I turn to look behind me, but the street is crowded and I can't see the man anywhere. Was he even there in the first place, or am I so stressed that I'm losing my mind?

Chapter Eighteen

THEN

I step off the bus and walk past the short row of shops on the main road before turning into the side street where I live with my parents. I'm not sure if I'll be staying here tonight. That all depends on how things go with my family, and on how Austin's feeling after Bart and Patsy gatecrashed our dinner last night. Austin managed to laugh it off in front of Liv and Miles, but I could tell he was really shaken. He didn't want to talk about it after we got back to the flat, and he left early this morning to meet a client. I'll call him in a while to see how he's doing.

Mum rang earlier today to say that Dad's been miserable ever since our falling-out on Sunday, and that he wants to talk to me. It's only been four days, but it feels like longer. I'm a little annoyed Dad didn't call me himself, but it's a step in the right direction. At least the weather's warmed up today. I tilt my face up to the sky; everything looks and feels a little better in the sunshine.

Our house is the second in a row of four in the end-terrace block – lounge at the front, kitchen-diner at the rear, two bedrooms and a shower room upstairs, and a small garden out the back. I'm almost there when a figure on a bicycle speeds past. It's our neighbour, Jake Pirelli, who lives in the first house on the row, so they have a side alley that leads around to their garden. Like me, he still lives at home, with his mum, Antonia. We went to school together, and he's like this sweet but annoying brother.

As I walk up to my front door, Jake is taking off his cycle helmet.

'Hey, Stella.'

'Hey, how you doing?' I ask, rummaging in my bag for the front-door key.

'Just finished work so I'm doing great, thanks.'

'It's funny that you're a mechanic, but you cycle everywhere,' I tease.

'Haven't heard that one before,' he replies with a grin, attempting to smooth his dark-brown curls. 'Have I got helmet hair?'

I snort. 'It's fine.'

'Anyway,' he adds, 'I didn't tell you, but I work two jobs now. I'm branching out into security.'

'Oh, cool,' I reply, noticing that Jake's shoulders are a lot wider than they used to be. He must have been working out. 'How are you finding it?'

'Yeah, it's different – mostly quite boring, waiting around, that kind of thing, but it can get hectic quickly. And the money's not too bad.'

'Nice.'

'Heard you're getting married. You didn't tell me.' A hurt expression crosses his face. He pauses. 'Congratulations.'

'Sorry, yeah, thanks,' I reply, twirling my ring. 'We didn't tell anyone for a while because I was waiting for the right time to tell Mum and Dad. Dad's not exactly over the moon though.'

'He'll come around. You're his daughter. He's just being protective.'

'Hmm.'

Jake laughs at my expression.

'How are things with you, anyway?' I ask. 'You might live next door, but I hardly ever see you these days.'

'Yeah, same old. Eat, sleep, work, repeat. Thinking about jacking it all in and travelling round the world. Hence the second job. I'm trying to save up.'

'Sounds amazing.'

'You're welcome to tag along,' he jokes.

'Thanks, but I don't think Austin would be too thrilled with that idea.'

'Yeah, maybe not.' At his side, Jake swings his cycle helmet back and forth by its strap. He notices me looking and stops.

'Must be hard, working two jobs,' I say. 'Although I know what you mean about trying to save. I never have any spare cash.'

'It's not too bad,' he replies. 'As long as you don't mind not having much sleep, or a social life. Or any sort of life, come to that.' He laughs.

'Anyway,' we both say at once.

'Nice to see you,' I add, wondering why our conversation feels so stilted. Normally, we can't stop talking.

'Yeah, you too. Take care, Stella.' He gives me a half-smile that I can't quite decipher.

'Say hi to your mum from me,' I add, feeling a bit daft because I only saw her a few days ago.

He opens his mouth as though he's about to say something further, and then snaps it shut again.

'You okay?' I ask.

He nods and waves goodbye, wheeling his bike around the side of his house while I watch him go, wondering if I should double-check. But then I tell myself not to be so daft. I turn and slot my key into the front door.

'You're home!' Mum calls from the kitchen.

'Hi, Mum.' I slip off my shoes and hang my jacket on the peg.

'Is that Stella?' I hear Dad ask. I can glimpse him through the open kitchen door, sitting at the kitchen table with a cup of tea, watching Mum assemble one of her concoctions.

'Yes,' she answers. And then, more quietly, 'Be nice.'

'I'm always nice,' Dad replies, with no attempt to keep his voice low.

Mum flicks a tea towel in his direction.

'Mind my tea, woman,' he teases.

'I wasn't aiming for your tea,' she replies.

'Nice to hear nothing's changed round here,' I say, walking into the kitchen, determined to be calm. To be forgiving and conciliatory and all those sensible things.

'Hi, Stella, love,' Dad says, as I kiss Mum's cheek.

'Hi, Dad.' I sit next to him and he taps his cheek for a kiss too.

'How was work?' he asks.

'Yeah, it was fine. Millie asked me to up my hours again.'

'You should ask her for a pay rise,' Dad grumbles. 'I've seen the woman driving round town in her new Mercedes. If she wants more out of you, then she should pay a decent hourly wage.'

'It's fine, Dad.'

'Let's not go over all that,' Mum says, turning down the hob and coming to sit at the table with us. 'Your dad and I have something we'd like to talk to you about.'

I wince in anticipation. I hope Mum hasn't got me here on false pretences so they can have another attempt at talking me out of marrying Austin.

'Haven't we, Phil?' Mum gives him a pointed stare.

'What? Oh. Yes.' He clears his throat. 'We'd just like to say that, well, if Austin is the man you'd like to marry, then me and your mother are very happy for you. Congratulations.'

121

I stare at him for a moment, waiting for some kind of catch.

'Well?' he says.

'You mean it?' I feel as though a weight has fallen from my shoulders.

'Of course,' Mum says. 'We just want you to be happy, love.'

Dad nods. 'You already know that Austin wouldn't be my choice for you – I won't pretend he is – but if you really love him, then we'll support you.' His expression isn't exactly joyful, but his words mean everything.

'You don't know how happy this has made me.' My voice cracks and I'm suddenly wiping tears from my eyes. I hadn't realised how miserable I'd been about our falling-out. I feel lighter already.

'Oh, love.' Mum gives me a warm hug, and Dad sniffs with what I think is emotion, but I can't be sure.

'We'd also like to pay for the wedding,' he says.

'What?' I reply, stunned by their offer. 'Oh, no, that's okay, we'll pay for all that.'

'We want to,' Mum replies.

I think about the type of wedding Austin and I are envisaging and know for a fact that my parents would never be able to afford even a fraction of it. They barely have enough to make rent and bills each month. And it's not like they aren't the hardest-working people I know. They earn a decent wage, but it's just not enough for any extras. There's no way I'm going to let them fork out for what is, in effect, a massive party.

'I know what you're thinking,' Mum says. 'You're worried we can't afford it. But we've—'

'We've been saving since you were a baby,' Dad says. 'And now we have a nice lump sum for you to spend on the wedding of your dreams.'

'Are you joking?' I ask, overwhelmed. 'You've been saving for my wedding?'

Mum nods, and Dad pulls me in for a hug. 'We love you more than life itself, Stellabella. And we want you to have the best day. We don't want you thinking we can't provide for you.'

'I've never thought that. I don't even know what to say.' I realise I'm still crying. So is Mum. 'Are you absolutely sure?' I ask. 'Because, honestly, Austin's parents have also offered to pay for it. Maybe you could use the money for a holiday for the two of you. Or . . . a deposit on a flat. Or—'

'Stella,' Dad says. 'We're doing this, okay?'

I nod, feeling emotional, but also slightly panicky. Dad's proud and won't want Austin's parents thinking they can't afford to pay. My mind spools forward. We'll do a low-key wedding instead, which is absolutely fine by me. I'd originally envisioned something fancier, but I realise I'm not that bothered about it after all. I'm going to have to scale back Austin's family's expectations though. Which might be tricky.

I also realise that, despite their generous offer, Dad's still not exactly thrilled about the marriage. Mum has probably spent the past few days talking him round. Things might all seem like sunshine and roses between us right now, but I just hope it's not too good to be true.

Chapter Nineteen

NOW

'Okay, just breathe, nice and slowly,' Vicki says, putting her arm around my shoulders as she slides on to the bench next to me after taking a water taxi from the train station to come to my aid. 'I'm here now, and it's all going to be okay. Breathe in . . . and out . . . That's it, in, two three, four, and out, two, three, four, five, six . . .'

I want to apologise. To tell her that I'm not normally like this. That I really have been keeping it together and searching hard for Austin. That I've been nothing like the gibbering mess she's looking at this minute, and the drunken mess I was last night. But right now I can barely breathe, let alone talk. I need to pull myself together. Be a rock for them, instead of relying on their support. They're here for their son, not for me. That thought clears my head like a cold tidal wave, and I take a last long exhale, before sitting up.

'Feeling better now?' she asks, as the waitress brings over our drinks.

'I think so.'

'Good.'

'I'm sorry I freaked out,' I say.

'There's nothing to apologise for,' she replies, taking a sip of her orange juice. 'So the man didn't follow you into the café?'

'I don't think so. I saw him once walking past me, but then I think I saw him again at the end of the alley, which would have meant he doubled back to follow me. But . . . well, I'm not exactly clear-headed today, especially as I'd just had this weird call from Bart.'

'Bart Randall?' Vicki's face pales.

'Yes. He was really aggressive and horrible.'

'Well, if he calls again, ignore it. In fact, let it go to voicemail. Austin might be able to use Bart's threats as evidence in the court case. Does he know about Austin . . . going missing?'

'Yes. That's the reason he called. He had the nerve to suggest that Austin planned his disappearance on purpose. Which makes absolutely no sense.'

Vicki shakes her head, her pale-pink lips pressed into a thin line. 'I can't believe Bart Randall called you to have a go when he knows how upset you must be that Austin's missing. What kind of a person does something like that? I feel like calling him back myself and using some not very polite language.'

'I wouldn't recommend it,' I say. 'He sounded unhinged.'

'You don't think he might have had something to do with this, do you?' Vicki asks. 'Maybe we should tell the police.'

'I was thinking the same thing.'

Vicki puts her hands to her temples and starts rubbing them. 'Nothing about any of this makes sense. The only thing I'm sure of is that Austin would never disappear like this on purpose. He would never want to put us through this kind of stress.'

'I agree,' I reply. 'And I'm sorry for giving you extra stress this morning and last night. I'm here for you and Rob. I promise I won't be so useless from now on.'

'It's a miracle any of us are functioning right now,' she replies, her voice starting to waver. 'I don't blame you one bit for having a panic attack. I feel like I'm constantly on the edge of one. But we need to be strong for Austin. So we can find him. Yes?'

I nod. 'Definitely.'

'Good,' she replies, taking my hand and pulling me to my feet. 'Shall we go back to the hotel for a break and something to eat? I think we need an hour or so to regroup. And to fill Rob in on this call from Bart.'

We take a water taxi back to the hotel to see that my father-in-law is already waiting for us on the dock by the terrace, where guests are enjoying lunch in the sunshine. He waves and holds out his hand, helping us both off the boat and paying the driver.

'I've got us a table outside,' he says.

I feel grubby and tired from my long morning, but I follow Rob and Vicki past the diners to a table already laid with bread, olives and a carafe of water. No wine, I see. Probably just as well.

As we sit, the waiter comes to take our orders. I think longingly of my cheese and spinach panini which is probably at the bottom of the Grand Canal by now, along with my Coke. I order another Coke, and decide on a margherita pizza. Hopefully, I'll get to eat it without being interrupted this time. Still light-headed, I reach for some bread and tear off a warm crust, popping it into my mouth and chewing slowly.

Rob starts to update us on his fruitless search at the train station, but Vicki interrupts to tell him about Bart's phone call.

'That little weasel,' Rob growls. 'Austin should never have gone into business with him. Even when they were at the grammar school together, Bart was a right cocky little know-it-all. I always thought there was something devious about him, but I don't like to interfere in Austin's life. Are you all right, Stella? Want me to call him, have a sharp word?'

'I don't think you'll need to call him,' Vicki says, nodding at the hotel dock.

Rob and I look where she's indicating. I see a smartly dressed man wearing beige chinos, a white shirt with the cuffs rolled back and aviator sunglasses. He's stepping off a water taxi carrying a navy cabin bag, and with a sinking heart I realise it's Bart Randall.

'What the hell is he doing here?' Rob gets to his feet, his face darkening with anger.

'Sit down, Rob,' Vicki urges. 'Let's hear what he has to say. Maybe he knows something about where Austin went.'

Rob hesitates, but then does as she says. 'Fine.'

Bart darts a glance up at the hotel before casting his gaze across the terrace. He stops and removes his sunglasses and then heads our way, a scowl across his handsome features as he wheels his bag noisily across the flagstones.

'Where is he?' Bart asks as he reaches our table.

'Sit down,' Vicki says sternly. 'You're making a scene.'

Bart doesn't move from where he's standing, casting a shadow over us all.

'Bart, what are you doing here?' I ask, shocked to see him in the flesh. 'Why didn't you mention you were in Italy when you called earlier? You're not staying at this hotel, are you?'

'No, I'm not. I've only just arrived. I came straight here to see you.'

'Have you got something to do with Austin's disappearance?' Rob asks, wiping his mouth with his napkin and getting to his feet again, squaring up to him.

'Will both of you please sit down?' Vicki begs, staring at me in despair.

'Me?' Bart sneers at Rob. 'Of course I'm nothing to do with it. I came here to check he hasn't done a runner.'

'This was supposed to be our honeymoon!' I cry. 'Why would he want to disappear? It was our first night here. We were having an amazing time.'

Vicki gives up on trying to turn this into a civilised conversation. Instead, she stands up too and steps closer to Bart, clutching at his arm. 'If you know something about Austin, Bart, please just tell us. I promise we won't be angry, or go to the police.' She throws a look at her husband. 'Will we, Rob? We just want our son back safe and sound. We'll get him to drop the court case, if that's why you're here.'

Bart shakes her hand off his arm and stares at her as though she's mad. 'You really think I had something to do with Austin going missing?'

'How did you find out?' I ask.

'It's all over the local news back home. They've interviewed his ex, Keri, on *South Today*. Apparently, she's just got back from a photoshoot in Tuscany. I wouldn't recommend watching the interview, Stella – she doesn't paint you in a particularly good light.'

'*Keri?*' I go to say something scathing about her, but then I stop – I can't let myself worry about Austin's ex right now.

'It's all a bit convenient, isn't it?' Bart says. 'Austin disappearing right before the court case.'

'You're the one being sued, Bart,' Rob says. 'Austin's got nothing to hide. Why should he "disappear", as you put it?'

'He's stolen thousands from the business,' Bart spits. 'And you're all too blind to see it, because you think he's this perfect son and husband.'

'That's enough now, Bart,' Rob says, his voice loaded with warning. 'We know what you've done, and blaming Austin for your crimes isn't going to help anyone. Victim blaming, they call it, don't they? Like my wife says, if you've done something stupid, you need to come clean instead of blaming everyone else.'

'Is everything all right here?' We all turn to see that the maître d' has come over, his expression hovering between concerned and annoyed.

I also notice that most of the other diners are throwing curious or worried glances our way.

'Would you like me to lay an extra place for the gentleman?' the maître d' asks carefully.

'No!' we all reply.

'Don't worry, I'm leaving,' Bart replies.

'Very well.' The maître d' turns away to check on another table while keeping one eye still on us.

'You need to tell us why you're here,' Rob hisses.

'I'm here because I'm worried about what your son is up to.' Bart turns to me. 'And I don't trust you either, Stella. You and Austin seem to be as bad as each other.'

His words shock me. I knew Bart had been fiddling the business expenses, but he'd always been quite civil towards me. To see him full mask off like this is horrible.

'Don't you dare talk to our daughter-in-law that way,' Vicki cries. 'And you will *not* make slanderous accusations about our son.' Vicki isn't even attempting to keep her voice down now.

The maître d' returns and tells us to stay calm or he regrets that we'll all have to leave as we're disturbing the other guests.

'That's fine,' Vicki replies. 'I've totally lost my appetite now.' She scrapes her chair back and jabs a finger in Bart's direction. 'I look forward to hearing a guilty verdict.' And then she winds her way between the tables towards the hotel entrance. Rob shakes his head at Bart before following his wife. Bart gives me a final, poisonous sneer before taking the street exit from the terrace, leaving me alone at the table to be stared at by the waiters and other diners, my face hot and my heart thundering.

Chapter Twenty

THEN

Although I've enjoyed the past few days staying at Austin's place, it's also been a bit stressful, what with him worrying about Bart and the business. He says it's been good having me there to support him, but I get the feeling he needs a bit of space. It'll be different when I've moved in properly after the wedding, but right now there's not enough room for my clothes in the wardrobe, and I feel like my stuff is cluttering up his immaculate pad. Although he's far too nice to tell me any of that.

So I've decided to move back in with my parents. Firstly, Austin hasn't explicitly asked me to move in yet, and secondly, I didn't want my mum and dad thinking I still held a grudge after their initial reaction to my news. I need to get back to our easy relationship because I couldn't bear for things to be permanently awkward between us. They're my parents, and despite any disagreements we might have, I love them to pieces.

Today, Mum and Dad are at work. It's my day off, and instead of working on my choreography, I'm sitting in the lounge, nursing a coffee, scrolling through wedding sites and saving stuff to my Pinterest boards. It's relaxing and nerve-racking at the same time.

My main worry is about keeping costs down. Mum hasn't told me how much is in their nest egg for me, and I don't like to ask, so I'm still not sure how much to budget for.

I've seen a couple of cute dresses on Etsy that could be perfect, and they're a fraction of the cost of the ones Claudia keeps sending me links to on WhatsApp. Mum keeps reassuring me not to scrimp. To have the wedding of my dreams. But I'm not sure what their version of scrimping is. My pared-back wedding could be their idea of a huge blowout. Honestly, I think I was less stressed when my dad was against the wedding. Austin's lucky his parents are supportive. Then again, he can never do any wrong in their eyes.

I click off Pinterest and get to my feet, doing some light stretches to work out the kinks in my neck. I need to focus on something other than the wedding for a while. Maybe I'll go for a walk, although I don't like the look of those black clouds out there.

A face at the window makes me squeal, my hand flying to my chest. I exhale when I realise it's only Jake. He grins and then knocks on the front door.

'You almost gave me a heart attack!' I cry, yanking the door open. 'What are you doing looking through the window?'

'Sorry.' He gives an embarrassed smile. 'I wasn't, though. I mean, I was, but not on purpose. I was just walking to the front door and happened to look in at the same time you looked out.'

'Hmm,' I reply.

'Can I come in?' he asks, scratching the side of his head and staring down at his trainers.

'Um, yeah, sure. You not working today?' I stand aside and follow him into the kitchen, where he sits at the table and I lean against the kitchen counter.

'No. I called in sick,' he replies.

'Jake Pirelli!'

He grins. 'I know. It's not like me, is it?'

131

'Not at all. You're the goodiest two shoes on the block.'

'No I'm not.' He screws up his nose.

'Yes you are.' Jake was always the sweetest, most timid child I knew. Despite that, he would always follow along on my hare-brained adventures. 'I remember when I dared you to steal a packet of Chewits from the Spar and you ended up crying and confessing to the woman on the counter.'

'I was seven!'

'You were nine, and I can't believe she felt so sorry for you, she let you have them anyway.'

'That was my strategy,' Jake replies. 'Tug on her heartstrings so she wouldn't send me to jail.'

I smile, thinking back to when Jake and I used to hang out all the time, before we grew up and grew apart. We're still good friends and pop in and out of each other's houses, but it's not the same as before I met Austin. 'I was so mean making you do that.' I remember how his face had paled before he went into the shop. Terrified but determined.

'I was a willing servant,' Jake replies. 'Still am.'

'Well, don't worry, I'm not going to make you steal anything else. Unless you're up for a wedding-dress heist?'

'Pass,' he replies.

'Anyway, I thought you said you were working two jobs to save up to go travelling. Chucking sickies isn't going to get you any nearer to that beach in Bali.'

'I had a good reason,' he says cryptically.

'Intriguing,' I say. 'Do you want a cuppa?'

'I'll make it,' he offers. 'Coffee?'

'You know me. Although I've literally just finished one, so make it a decaf or I'll get the shakes.' We switch places and I watch him move around our kitchen as though it's his own. 'How come you're not coupled up yet?' I ask. 'You're not bad looking.' He's actually very good looking, but I'm not about to flatter his ego. 'You've got a decent job – sorry, *two* decent jobs – passable sense of humour . . .'

He shakes his head and smiles.

'Seriously though,' I push.

The kettle boils and he busies himself making the coffee, ignoring my question.

'Biscuits are in the tin.' I point to a scratched Highland Shortbread tin that we've used since I was a kid.

Jake plonks the tin in the centre of the table and brings over our coffees. 'There you go, your highness.'

'Thanks.' I prise open the tin and take out a pink wafer before offering one to Jake, but he declines. 'So is this just a social call, or is there a reason you popped round while you're supposed to be at work?'

'Does there have to be a reason?' he asks.

'No, not at all. I was just wondering. Because you look like you've got something on your mind.'

'You know me too well,' he says, scratching his cheek.

'Well, we've lived next door our whole lives, so it's not surprising.'

Jake doesn't reply. Just blows on his coffee and takes a small sip.

'Jake?'

'Um . . .'

'What's up?' He's acting strangely and it's a little unsettling.

'Thing is, Stella . . .' He puts his mug back down on the table and blows out a long breath. 'Thing is, I've always had a bit of a thing for you. And I've never mentioned it because you're way out of my league. But now you're engaged and I've left it too late. And if I don't say anything, I'll regret it. So this is me saying something.' His face is bright red and he's staring at me so earnestly I think he's going to cry.

Shit. This was the last thing I expected. I know my parents always wished we'd get together, but I didn't think Jake was the type to air out his feelings. I'd hoped he would have found someone else by now. How do I let him down gently?

'What I mean to say,' he continues, 'is that I love you, Stella. Always have. And I'm an idiot for not telling you sooner.'

'Oh God, Jake. That's . . . that's so nice. That's so lovely. I . . .'

'It's fine.' He cuts off my stammering reply. 'I'm sorry. Of course you don't feel the same way. I just . . . if there was a millionth of a percentage chance, then I just had to find out.'

'Maybe if things had gone differently,' I say, scraping around for a decent reply and figuring honesty is probably best. 'But I'm in love with Austin, and we're getting married next year.'

'Yep. Totally understand. I will leave you to your coffee and biscuits.' He stands, banging his knee on the underside of the table with a painful-sounding thunk.

'Are you okay?'

'No, but I will be,' he replies. 'I'm really sorry for laying that on you.'

'No, I'm sorry,' I reply, and we exchange weak smiles. 'You don't have to go. At least finish your coffee.'

'I didn't come here for coffee,' he replies. 'See you, Stella.'

'Bye, Jake.'

I leave him to let himself out. The last thing he'd want is for me to watch his hasty, embarrassed retreat. I hope this hasn't ruined things. I'd really miss our light-hearted banter and comfortable friendship. Jake is such a good person. So easy to talk to. I don't want to lose him from my life. He's like family.

After he leaves, I pour our drinks down the sink and mop up the spillage on the table, glancing at my lonely, uneaten pink wafer biscuit. I'm not in love with Jake, but turning him down still felt unutterably sad.

Chapter Twenty-One

NOW

After Bart's appearance on the hotel terrace and the Lewises' angry exit I feel horribly uncomfortable staying at the table on my own, so I tip the maître d' twenty euros and ask for our food to be brought up to the suite. I realise I should probably go easy on the spending because, without my bank cards, my funds are dwindling fast.

Leaving the restaurant, I message my in-laws and ask them to meet me in my room. They're already waiting outside the door when I arrive.

'So sorry to have left you like that, Stella,' Vicki says, her eyes filled with remorse. 'I just couldn't bear to hear all those awful things that man was saying about Austin. I worried I was going to do something I might regret, like shoving him over the wall into the canal.'

'You and me both,' I reply. 'It's what he deserves.'

I slot in the key card and we go into the suite, dejected and still a little shaken from the encounter.

'He's ruined our lunch as well,' Rob says.

'Don't worry,' I reply. 'I've asked them to bring it up to the suite.'

'Well done,' Rob replies, patting my shoulder.

They sit on the chaise side by side, looking small and a little lost, while I take a seat on one of the armchairs. The waiter arrives, placing our lunch on the sideboard, and we dig in, balancing the plates on our laps. I think we're all too drained to talk much, concentrating on our food for now, trying to build up our physical and emotional energy supplies.

'What now?' Vicki asks, clearing the plates once we've eaten our fill. 'Austin's out there somewhere needing our help, and here we are stuffing our faces in a five-star hotel suite.'

'We can't feel guilty for eating, Vicks,' Rob says.

'I know, but—'

My phone starts to ring and Rob and Vicki look at me with hopeful eyes as I retrieve it from my bag. It's an unknown number. I answer it with trepidation.

'Hello?'

'Stella Lewis?' It's a man's voice, with a trace of an Italian accent.

'Yes, speaking.'

Vicki's eyes are wide with hope.

'This is Officer Rocco Gallini.'

'Hello.'

I mouth to my in-laws that it's the police.

Rob takes Vicki's hand. 'Can you put it on speaker?' he asks me.

I do as he says. 'I'm with Austin's parents now,' I tell Gallini. 'Have you got any news?'

'I'm afraid we still don't know where your husband is,' he says.

The Lewises slump at Gallini's words.

'But we have discovered that your husband withdrew two hundred euros on the night he went missing. He used an ATM that was

136

about fifteen minutes' walk from La Terrazza di Stella, and he used the same bank card that he paid for the meal with.'

'That means he withdrew the cash after he retrieved the card from the restaurant?' I confirm.

'Correct.'

'So he was on his way back to the hotel when he went missing?' Rob asks. 'Or on his way to the supermarket to get a phone charger. Maybe he was mugged for the cash.'

Gallini is silent.

'Hello?' I prompt.

'Sorry, yes, I'm still here. No. The machine he used is situated in a different direction to the hotel and to the supermarket.'

'So he was going somewhere else?' I ask. 'I'm sorry, I don't understand.'

'We need to determine if it was your husband who withdrew the cash, or if it was someone else,' Gallini says.

'Sounds like it was someone else, if the cash machine was in a different direction,' Vicki says. 'Are there cameras you can check?'

'Yes. We'll check the security footage today.'

'We need to tell him about Bart,' Rob says to me and Vicki.

'Who?' Gallini asks.

'Bart Randall,' I say. 'Austin's business partner.'

'He showed up in Venice today, and was very aggressive,' Vicki explains.

There's a short pause on the line. 'Okay,' Gallini says. 'Can you come into the station?'

Rob and Vicki nod vigorously.

'Um, yes, no problem,' I reply. 'Shall we come now?'

'If that's okay.'

'We'll be there in about twenty minutes.'

We end the call and spend five minutes freshening up in our rooms before meeting in the lobby.

'Do you think they'll want to interview Bart?' I ask, as we leave the hotel.

'They'd better,' Rob mutters.

'Keep hold of your bag, Vicki,' I say, remembering what happened just around the corner from here. 'Rob, make sure your wallet and phone are safe.'

'It's okay, we travel a lot,' Vicki says, adjusting her bag anyway.

'I know, but I had my wallet stolen yesterday. I forgot to tell you.'

'Oh, Stella,' Vicki says, moving in front of me as we have to walk in single file to squeeze across a crowded bridge. 'That's awful.'

'It's okay,' I reply, 'I've cancelled my cards, and I've still got a little cash left in the safe.'

'What about your passport?' Rob asks. We're finally able to walk side by side again, making our way past the Giardini Ex Reali, the former royal palace gardens that run alongside the Grand Canal.

'Luckily, I left my passport in the safe,' I reply.

'Well, that's something at least,' Vicki says. 'Because there's not much else that's lucky in that scenario.'

'Do you need us to give you some cash?' Rob asks.

'Thanks. I'm okay for now, but I'll let you know if I need to borrow some.'

We weave our way through the throngs of tourists hovering around the souvenir kiosks and queuing at the vaporetto stop. We stride along the wide promenade of the Riva degli Schiavoni, past ornate buildings with wide colonnades and over the Ponte della Paglia, where people are clustering to take photographs. I glance along the narrow canal to see the Bridge of Sighs, that famous arched walkway named for the sighs of the convicted who used to cross it en route from the Palazzo Ducale to the prison, and I can't help feeling a little of the same despair as those prisoners.

Finally, we leave the bustle of the Grand Canal and make our way along the street that leads towards the police station.

'Is this it?' Vicki asks, looking up at the ornate stone building. 'This is the police station? It's a bit different to the one back home.'

We enter the building to find the lobby crowded with stressed-looking tourists while a couple of officers deal with the queue. I'm just wondering how long we'll have to wait when I spy Gallini through an arched door at the back of the reception, beckoning us over.

'Come on,' I say to my in-laws, who seem less confident in here.

Once we're through the door, we find ourselves in a huge courtyard. It's strangely quiet out here. I make the introductions and Gallini leads us beneath the arch of a cloister and into a warm, nondescript office with three scuffed wooden desks and a few plastic chairs.

'Please, take a seat,' he says, sitting behind one of the desks and gesturing to the chairs. 'I must get back to help my colleagues in a few minutes, but let's take a statement about this person . . . ?'

'Bart Randall.' Rob supplies the name. 'With two Ls.'

'Okay, Bart Randall,' Gallini confirms.

Vicki and I stay mainly quiet while Rob tells Gallini about our lunchtime encounter with Bart, and how Austin is suing him.

'You say Mr Randall arrived in Venice today,' Gallini says. 'How certain are you of this?'

'He told us he'd just arrived, and he had his suitcase with him . . .' I reply, realising that that doesn't necessarily mean anything.

'We can check his passport,' Gallini says. 'Do you have an address for Mr Randall while he's here?'

'We should have asked where he's staying,' Vicki says, shielding her eyes from a shaft of sunlight beaming through the office window.

'Probably wouldn't have told us anyway,' Rob replies.

I give Gallini Bart's phone number and he assures us he'll bring him in for questioning.

Vicki looks sideways at me. 'You should tell him about that man who was following you this morning.'

I shake my head. 'It was probably nothing.'

'A man?' Gallini asks. 'The same man as before?'

'No. This man was taller, broader. He was wearing a baseball cap and sunglasses.' As I say the words, I realise how delusional they sound. *As if I'd have two separate stalkers!* 'I thought he was following me, but I could have been mistaken.'

'Hm, okay.' Gallini places his palms on the desk and pushes himself up. 'We'll let you know when we have more news.'

'And you're still looking for our son?' Rob asks.

'Of course.' He makes a circular motion with his hands. 'This is all related to our investigation, okay?'

'Please find him,' Vicki begs as we all stand.

'I will do my very best,' Gallini replies.

Austin's parents and I leave the station and head slowly back to the hotel, none of us saying much. While there are things to do, tasks to perform, interviews, conversations etcetera, we can kid ourselves that we're making progress. That what we're doing is actually going to lead to a positive outcome. But in these quiet pauses between activity, that's when doubt and despair creep in, nibbling away at hope and splintering positivity.

It's late afternoon, and the sun is sinking lower in the pale-blue sky, but the crowds by the canal are still as thick as ever. I pass them as though in a bubble. Separated from the rest of humanity by this hellish limbo. What will my life back home look like now? I can't even think about it.

Soon enough we're back at the hotel, and just as Rob is pulling open one of the etched-glass doors, my breath catches as I see someone with a familiar face walking down the street towards us.

Chapter Twenty-Two

THEN

'Hi, love, it's only me!' My mum comes straight through to the kitchen and I hand her a cup of tea.

'Hey, Mum.'

'Oh, you're an angel. This is just what I need.' She sits at the table and closes her eyes. 'Some of my clients live like pigs. Honestly.'

'What's happened?' I ask, sitting opposite her and letting her vent. Mum always has a tale to tell after work, and I think it relaxes her to let it all out as soon as she gets home.

'Well,' Mum says. 'You know the Coopers who I clean for down on River Way?'

I nod. I feel like I know each of Mum's clients intimately because she's told me all about them in detail.

'Well,' she continues, 'I haven't been able to get to them for a few weeks because of illness and bank holidays, and they literally don't do a thing in between cleans. It's bad enough week to week, but this time the kitchen was piled high with dirty plates and crusted pans. The toilet was disgusting. And the floors were muddy.

I mean properly muddy. And the dog! You don't even want to know what I had to clean up.'

'Oh, Mum! Can you ask to change clients?'

'I already did, but Mandy said no. Apparently, they only want me.'

'That's because you're too good,' I reply. 'You should slack off and then they'll soon ask Mandy for a replacement.'

'You know me,' Mum says with a sigh, 'I can't do a half-arsed job.'

Mandy and Clyde are the couple who own the cleaning agency. I've told Mum she should set up on her own, but she's too nervous about being self-employed. The thing is, the agency take half Mum's earnings, so she's working for near enough minimum wage. But I know that the thought of going self-employed is nerve-racking. I've had the same thoughts myself.

'I'm going up for a quick shower,' Mum says, standing up and swigging the rest of her tea. 'I feel so grotty.'

'No probs. Before you go, you'll never guess what happened this afternoon.'

'What?'

'Jake from next door . . . he only went and declared his love for me.'

Mum sits back down. 'Did he now? And what did you say? He's such a nice lad.'

'You don't seem surprised, Mum.' I'm watching her expression and she seems shifty somehow – her face is flushed and she's not looking directly at me, which isn't like Mum at all.

'Well, he's always liked you, hasn't he? So, what did you say?'

'What do you think I said? I told him that he's a great guy, but I'm in love with Austin, and we're getting married next year. It was so awkward.'

'Oh. Well. That's . . . I'm sure he'll be fine.' She gets to her feet. 'Okay, I'm going up to have that shower.'

143

'Mum!'

'Yes, love?'

'Is that all you've got to say? I'd have thought you'd want to talk about it.'

'What's there to say?' she replies snippily, walking towards the door.

'Why are you acting funny?' I ask.

'I'm not.'

'Did you . . . did you have something to do with this?' I stand and turn.

She tuts and walks off down the hall, but I follow her.

'Was this Dad's doing?'

'What are you talking about?' She shakes her head as she starts up the stairs. 'Honestly, Stella, you do talk nonsense sometimes.'

'It was, wasn't it! He's been filling Jake's head with ideas. Giving him false hope. Do you know how excruciatingly embarrassing this afternoon was? For both of us. Poor Jake.'

Mum stops halfway up the stairs and sighs. She turns around to look at me. 'That boy has had a crush on you since he was a teenager. I'm glad he finally plucked up the courage to say something. Even if it was only to give him some closure. He deserves to be in a nice relationship, but he can't do that while he's mooning about after you.'

'So you did this for Jake's benefit?' I ask sceptically.

'I didn't do anything!'

'No, but Dad did. *What*, did he take Jake out for a drink and have a chat man to man about how the boy next door should declare his love for me? Save me from the dreaded Austin?'

Mum purses her lips.

'I'm right, aren't I? I thought you guys had got over all that? I thought Austin and I had your blessing and you wanted to pay for the wedding. Or was that all just hot air to keep me sweet while you were concocting your plan?'

'Don't be so dramatic, Stella. I didn't just finish the shift from hell so I could get a load of earache off you.'

'Sorry, Mum, but can't you see how hurtful this was? Not just for me, but for Jake too. Not to mention poor Austin, who hasn't even done anything wrong.'

The front door opens behind me and we both turn to see Dad coming in from work.

'What?' he says at our expressions.

'You can fill him in,' I say disgustedly, slipping past Mum on the stairs and heading into my room. I try not to slam the door like a sulky teenager, but it's loud enough to let them know I'm not happy.

'What's up with Stella?' I hear him ask.

The stairs creak and the front door shuts. I hear them go into the kitchen and close the door, their muffled voices filtering up through the floorboards, Mum's high and anxious, Dad's low and rumbling.

Sitting heavily on my single bed, I try not to let my emotions take over, but it's such a blow to know that they went behind my back like this. On what planet did they think their scheme would work? As if I'd magically fall for Jake and ditch my boyfriend of three years. I sit brooding for a while, not sure what to do with myself. I can't run back to Austin's. Not while this is still unresolved. Not while there's this hard knot in the pit of my stomach.

I jump at the sound of a soft knock on my bedroom door.

'Stella, love. It's your dad. Can I come in?'

The childish part of me wants to say no. 'Fine,' I call out, my voice quivering.

He pushes open the door, walks in and stands before me. 'I've made a right pig's ear of this, haven't I?'

145

I don't reply.

Dad sighs. 'Yes, I spoke to Jake. But it wasn't a premeditated thing. I saw him out the front and he looked a bit dejected, so I asked what was up. He told me he was gutted about your engagement and that he wished he'd had the courage to tell you how he felt years ago. I stupidly commented that "it's never too late". But I shouldn't have said it. And I'm sorry.'

I let his explanation sink in. It's not as bad as I'd imagined it to be, but it's still annoying. Although I realise now that I probably overreacted. I just want them to like my fiancé. Is that too much to ask?

'Can you forgive me?' he asks, twisting his fingers in front of him. Dad isn't usually the apologetic type; he's gruff and no-nonsense. But I can see that he's genuinely upset.

I'd be quite within my rights to give him a hard time. But I don't want to. I just want to put this whole episode behind us. My parents and I don't normally fight. We don't normally have a cross word to say to one another. So all these tensions and disagreements over my engagement have been horrible.

'Of course I forgive you,' I say, rolling my eyes.

He nods and his shoulders drop. 'Good. I'll make an effort to get to know Austin better.'

'You mean it?'

'I said so, didn't I?' He goes to the window and peers down at the garden. 'Can't believe that grass needs cutting again. I only did it at the weekend.'

'Because his parents want us all to have dinner together,' I continue. 'To start planning things.'

Dad takes a deep breath. 'Sure, that's fine.'

'So, can we get a date in the diary?'

'Sort out dates with your mother. You know she likes to organise those things.'

'Thanks, Dad.' I get up from the bed and join him at the window.

He puts an arm around my shoulders. 'Love you, Stellabella.'

'Love you too, Dad.'

I'm hopeful that things really are sorted between us now. As long as we can get through the dinner with Austin's family then I think we'll be okay. But I'm not looking forward to it at all. Rob and Vicki Lewis are super-sociable. They're what Dad would call schmoozers. Whereas Mum can be shy in social situations, Dad always calls a spade a spade; he's not one for niceties and flattery. I really want it to be a warm, happy occasion where everyone gets on. Or, at the very least, I just need for it not to be excruciatingly awkward.

Chapter Twenty-Three

NOW

'Not again,' I say, stopping in my tracks.

Rob and Vicki turn to see what I'm talking about, and the three of us stand outside the hotel doors watching Bart Randall walk down the street towards us. This time he's more hesitant, holding up his hands in a gesture of appeasement.

'What's he doing back here?' my father-in-law says through gritted teeth.

'Don't do anything stupid, Rob,' Vicki warns, even though she was the one who wanted to push Bart into the canal earlier.

'I don't suppose you know anything about the man following Stella?' Rob asks as Bart draws closer.

Bart looks bemused. 'What man?'

'Someone's been following Stella,' Rob replies.

Bart shifts his gaze over to me. 'Maybe you imagined it. With the stress of everything.'

'Oh, so now I'm "stressed",' I say. 'Earlier, you were accusing me of planning all this.'

'Stella, can we talk?' Bart gives me an earnest look.

'We are talking,' I reply.

'I mean, just the two of us.'

I give Bart a sharp glare, trying to find any hint in his expression of what he may want to tell me without Austin's parents present. But his face is now blank. My skin prickles a warning.

'Stella?' Bart pushes.

My heart is pounding, but I guess if he's got something to say about Austin, then I need to hear it.

'We're not going to let you whisk Stella off on her own!' Vicki says, pushing her sunglasses up on to her head and scowling at him.

I touch Vicki's arm. 'It's okay. I'll hear him out.'

'I'm not sure this is a good idea,' Rob says to me.

'I'm not going to do anything!' Bart retorts. 'I just want ten, fifteen minutes of your time, Stella. We can go to that bar.' He points down the street. 'It's a public place.'

'I'll be fine,' I say to the Lewises, unsure if that's true or not. 'Don't worry, I won't be long.'

'Fine,' Vicki says, turning to Bart. 'But I'm holding you responsible if anything happens to Stella.'

'Sure, whatever,' Bart replies, with barely concealed disdain.

'I think we should wait outside the bar,' Rob says.

'I'll be fine, honestly.' I rummage in my bag, looking for my hotel key card. 'Why don't you move into the suite while I'm with Bart? Most of our stuff is still in our cases, so it shouldn't take long.'

'I'm not sure we should leave you with him,' Rob says.

'I'm not going to do anything!' Bart snaps again. 'I just need to talk to her.'

'If she's not back in twenty minutes, we're coming to find you,' Rob says, glaring at Bart.

I hand Vicki the key card.

'Thanks, Stella.' She squeezes my hand as she takes it.

I walk with my husband's business partner to the bar, feeling my in-laws' stares boring into our backs. As we reach the entrance,

I glance back down the street to see the couple still huddled in the hotel doorway. I give them a short wave and follow Bart into the lively bar.

He orders an Aperol spritz and I join him, despite having told myself I wasn't going to touch a drop of alcohol today. There are no spare seats, so we stand at the bar.

'If you know what's happened to Austin, will you please just tell me, Bart? Like his parents said, we're not worried about who's to blame, we just want him back in one piece.'

'Contrary to what you think, Stella, Austin going missing is nothing to do with me.' Bart picks up a cocktail stick and skewers an olive, putting it into his mouth and chewing, using the empty stick to stab at the surface of the metal bar.

'I still don't understand what you're even doing here, Bart. You're the only person with a grudge against Austin, so you can see why you being here looks so questionable. Your story about why you came to Italy makes no sense.'

Bart discards the cocktail stick and turns to look at me. 'It makes no sense if you think I'm a fraudster and a liar, if you think I'm a bad person. But say, for one minute, that you accept I'm telling the truth about everything. That Austin is the one who's been defrauding the company and when I discovered the truth and confronted him, he denied it and accused me of doing the same thing, tying me up with this ridiculous court case and smearing my name with all our clients.' He rubs his chin, his anger suddenly evaporating to be replaced by a weary expression. 'Say you believe that, then you can see how it makes perfect sense why I'm here – to find out where Austin is, and to discover what he's done with all the money he's taken out of our business.'

I really don't like how sincere Bart sounds. How plausible. Either he's a bloody good liar or . . .

'He's made my life a living hell this past year,' Bart continues. 'Patsy and I have been beyond stressed.'

'And you think we haven't?' I reply. 'Try planning a wedding while there's a court case pending. It's not fun, I can assure you.'

'That was Austin's doing. I was fully prepared to sort it out without lawyers getting involved.'

'That's not what Austin said.'

The barman puts our drinks in front of us, and I take a long sip through the paper straw while Bart does the same.

'Austin's the one with the connected family,' Bart continues. 'He's the one who's known most of our clients since he was a kid because of who his parents are, with their successful business. Who do you think our clients believe? Him or me? I'm just a nobody to them. He's the face of our company. People think I'm just a lackey riding Austin's coat-tails.

'But what they don't know is that I'm a hard worker. I'm trust-worthy, the person who gets the job done. That's why Austin went into partnership with me in the first place. We're a good team – or at least I thought we were. He's connected and charming but, let's face it, he's lazy. I'm the grafter, the one with the smart brain who keeps the business going.'

'Says you,' I mutter.

'You know, I could just about accept that our partnership was unequal because, without him, it would have been hard for me to take our business to the next level. I could never have hoped to get those CEOs and other wealthy clients to take a chance on me – a nobody. But what I couldn't accept was Austin using our business as his own personal piggy bank. Leaving me with a pittance in dividends every year.'

'But that's what Austin said *you*'ve been doing,' I reply. 'Why would I believe you, over my husband?'

'Because you know in your gut it's true.' Bart glowers at me.

'I certainly don't!'

'You can tell yourself that, Stella, but you're not stupid. Or maybe you are.'

I'm annoyed with myself for letting Bart get under my skin. For making me feel even worse than I already do. I take another sip of my drink, feeling the bitter orange fizz of alcohol heighten my emotions. I suddenly want to lash out at this man. To yell at him. To throw the rest of my drink in his face.

'Look, Stella, there is one thing that I can tell you . . .'

I snap my head around to glare at him.

'It's something I feel bad about, but I had to do it.'

'What?' I steel myself in anticipation of more upsetting news.

'You haven't been imagining things,' he says. 'I did hire a private investigator.'

'*What?*'

'First to investigate Austin, to see if I could get any clear evidence against him. But then to follow *you*.'

'So I'm *not* going crazy!' I cry. 'I can't believe you did that!' I shake my head in disbelief, thinking back to earlier today when Rob asked Bart if he knew anything about my stalker and Bart denied it so convincingly. He's obviously an accomplished liar.

'Sorry about that,' Bart replies, looking a little sheepish. 'But now will you believe me when I say I don't trust Austin? Why would I put a tail on you otherwise? I wanted to see if you'd lead me to him. But it's clear you have no idea of his location.'

'That's what I've been telling you! I'm glad you finally realise. What made you change your mind?'

'I just had a report from my PI. He says you've been putting up posters and searching non-stop to find him.'

'Of course I have. Because he really is missing. There is no elaborate ruse, Austin isn't trying to hide from you, because he hasn't done anything wrong. Please tell me you've told your man to stop tailing me now.'

'I haven't, but I will.'

'Straightaway, this evening.'

'Sure. I'll do it in a minute.'

I let my shoulders relax a little, grateful that at least one awful thing has been resolved. 'How long has it been going on? Him tailing me, I mean. Did it start back in the UK?'

Bart shakes his head. 'No. Just here. Like I said, I instructed him to start tailing you after Austin went missing.'

'Are you sure?' I ask, thinking back to those times at home when I was sure someone was following me.

'Yes.'

I give him a sceptical look.

'I swear.'

I stir the ice in my drink, my mind trying to process this new information. Unsure if I still need to be worried about Bart. But at least he's been somewhat upfront with me this evening. 'Oh . . .'

'What?'

'I should probably let you know – we gave your name to the local police earlier.'

'You did *what?*' Bart tenses up and gives me a disbelieving glare. 'Why would you do that?'

'Because Austin's missing and you've just happened to show up in Italy at the same time.'

'Um, I arrived after he went missing. I only came here *because* he went missing.'

'Fine. Well, you can tell that to the police then,' I snap.

'You're just as bad as Austin,' Bart says, shaking his head. 'A few moments ago, I thought I might have been getting through to you, but either you don't want to believe what he's like, or you know

153

what he's done and you're defending him. Blaming me instead of him. Going to the police, for Christ's sake!'

I shake my head with a weary sense of déjà vu. 'We're going round in circles,' I reply.

'You're right,' he says dismissively, throwing some folded euros on to the bar. 'This was a waste of time.'

'This private investigator,' I say, as he starts to leave. 'Small guy, fair hair, right?'

Bart frowns. 'Yes, actually.'

'Because he hasn't done a very good job of being stealthy. I thought he was some weird stalker trying to kill me.'

'Oh.' Bart swallows. 'Well, sorry about that. It wasn't my intention to scare you.'

'No. Just to have me followed. Oh well, that's all right then.' I shake my head in disgust before adding, 'Was it just one PI you used, or were there two of them?'

'Just one,' he replies with a scowl, irritated that I'm delaying his departure.

My skin prickles with apprehension. 'Are you sure? Maybe your guy works with a colleague – tall, dark hair.' An image crawls into my head of the man in the baseball cap I saw at the Rialto Bridge.

'No. I think I know how many people I've hired. Anyway, I'm sure my investigator works alone.'

I discard my straw and gulp down the rest of my Aperol, trying not to panic. Because if my other stalker isn't Bart's guy, then who the hell is he, and why has he been following me?

Chapter Twenty-Four

THEN

'Come in, come in!' Rob says, a wide smile on his face. He's dressed in belted chino shorts, a white short-sleeved shirt and brown leather deck shoes, a chunky gold watch on his wrist. 'We're so excited to have you guys over at last.'

My parents and I step through the cedarwood double doors into the Lewises' spacious hallway, dominated by a grand wood-and-glass staircase where Rob and Austin now stand side by side, peas in a pod. Dad holds out his hand and Rob takes it in both of his, pumping it up and down like a jackhammer. In the end, we decided to have a Sunday lunch get-together with the parents instead of an evening meal, as it somehow feels less formal.

'It's very good of you to have us over, Robert,' Dad says, handing over a bottle of red.

'Rob, please. My dad's Robert, so I've always been a Rob.' He looks at the wine label. 'Oh, lovely! Lyme Bay Pinot Noir. I've been meaning to try this for a while. It's from Devon, isn't it?'

Dad nods, having done a bit of wine research after I told him Austin's dad's a bit of a connoisseur. 'I don't know much about wine, but Lindsay and I always like to support local where we can. Not that Devon's that local, but this one's had good reviews.'

'Well, it's much appreciated,' Rob replies. 'Hello, Lindsay, so great to see you again. Are these roses for us? They're beautiful. Thank you. You shouldn't have. Stella, come here, you gorgeous girl.' He pulls me in for a hug, his cologne sharp and spicy, while Dad shakes Austin's hand.

'Vicki will be down in a minute.' Rob glances at his watch and then up at the staircase just as Austin's mum appears, looking elegant in a white fitted dress, a gold pendant and tan heels, her shiny chestnut hair held back with a large gold butterfly clip. 'Here she is, now.'

I told Mum and Dad we were far too early, but Dad always has to be on time or early to everything.

'Look at those roses,' Vicki says, walking down the stairs. 'They're gorgeous! So lovely to have you here. Can you believe our kids are getting married next year?'

Austin and I grin at one another. I'm so happy, I can barely see straight. I've been nervous about this meeting for days, but it seems to be going really well, so hopefully I can start to relax. I just need Dad not to say anything blunt or inappropriate and Mum not to get overwhelmed and flustered.

Our parents have met briefly before. Once at Christchurch Regatta, when Austin and I were with his family cheering on some friends who were competing that day. Dad's a bit of a boat enthusiast and had come along to gawk. And another time when I was out having lunch with my parents for Dad's birthday and Austin's mum and dad happened to be in the same pub. Awkward hellos were exchanged on both occasions, and that was about it. But today is a whole other kettle of fish. This is the 'parents getting to know each other' before our official engagement party next month.

'You have such a beautiful home,' Mum says to Vicki.

'Thank you, Lindsay. We do love it here.' Austin's parents live in a large modern chalet bungalow in west Christchurch. The plots here are bigger, the roads wider, and yet it's still only ten minutes' drive to the town centre.

'And it's absolutely immaculate,' Mum adds, glancing around at the polished stone floors and the gleaming woodwork.

'I can't take credit for that – we have a wonderful cleaner who comes in twice a . . . um, twice a week.' Vicki flushes, obviously remembering that Mum cleans for a living.

But Mum puts her at ease. 'Oh, yes, it would be too much for you to keep all this clean and run your company at the same time. Most of the families I clean for have demanding jobs. You run a travel business, don't you?'

'Yes, that's right.' Vicki and Mum start chattering away like old friends, and I sigh with relief.

Meanwhile, Dad's quizzing Rob about his boat.

'I didn't know you were into boating?' Rob says. 'Austin, you never told me Phil liked boats.'

Austin smiles and shrugs.

'It's a hobby of mine,' Dad replies. 'Not that we have a boat; I just enjoy the idea of them. The craftsmanship, the freedom of setting sail or motoring around the bay.'

'I know what you mean.' Rob claps Dad on the shoulder. 'Well, we'll go out one day this month. Tell me when you're next free and the six of us can have an afternoon on Poole Harbour, weather permitting. Or just the two of us. Right, come through to the kitchen, we've got some champagne in the cooler.'

We all troop through to the open-plan kitchen-diner, where Rob heads for the wine fridge and pulls out a bottle of Krug.

The circular glass dining table has been set in a white-and-gold theme, helium 'Congratulations' balloons floating from its centre with gold streamers and a scattering of metallic confetti. I realise that Rob and Vicki match the table decor and I wonder if they did that on purpose.

Austin and his mum hand round the champagne glasses while Rob opens the bottle with a practised subtle pop of the cork. He fills our glasses and raises his.

'To a beautiful couple,' he says. 'Here's wishing you a long and happy life together. Congratulations, you two.'

'Congratulations!' our parents cry as Austin and I kiss, gazing into each other's eyes with joy and hope, like we can't believe this is actually happening.

Lunch is delicious and the atmosphere is relaxed and fun. I feel as though today could not be going any better. Dad's even making a real effort with Austin, asking him about his security-gate business and how it started.

'Vicki, this food is sensational,' Mum says. 'I love how you've done the parsnips.'

'Thanks,' Vicki replies, 'but I have to admit it was mostly Rob.'

'I do a great roast,' he says. 'Even if I do say so myself.'

'Yes, but it's the only meal you do,' Vicki says with an indulgent smile.

'True!' Rob laughs and sips his wine. 'Vicki's a wonderful cook, but I do like to show off with a roast dinner.'

'Mum's a great cook too,' I say.

Mum blushes and looks down at her plate.

'She's always creating new dishes,' I continue.

'I'd love to be able to do that,' Vicki says, 'but I'm more of a recipe book cook. I need to follow instructions or I wouldn't have a clue.'

'I don't have the patience for recipe books,' Mum replies. 'I just put in a bit of this and a bit of that, and hope for the best!'

'Story of my life,' Rob says, and we all laugh. 'Now, Phil,' he continues, after the laughter dies down, 'I know you and Lindsay said you wanted to pay for the wedding, but it's going to be quite a shindig, so we'd like to chip in too. Go halves with you and Lindsay.'

I hold my breath, willing my dad to accept their offer.

Dad doesn't blink. 'Nice of you to offer, Rob, but—'

'Now, now,' Rob says in a patronising tone that's bound to get Dad's back up. 'We're going to be family, and Austin's our only child, so we'd really like to give these kids a good send-off.'

I really wish Rob hadn't said that last part, because it implies that my parents won't be able to give us a great wedding without the Lewises' help. I can see that Dad has already taken offence, his body tensing and his expression hardening.

'It's tradition for the bride's parents to pay, so we'd like to foot the bill,' Dad says gruffly. 'Maybe you can help with the honeymoon, seeing as how you've got a travel firm.'

Rob opens his mouth to protest, but Vicki places a hand on his forearm. 'That's very generous of you, Phil,' she says. 'We're grateful and so are the kids.'

Rob grunts, put out by Dad's rebuttal, and Dad still isn't appeased by Vicki's attempt to smooth things over. Austin and Vicki start talking about honeymoon locations, attempting to move past the awkwardness, but I feel sick. I wish Dad had accepted their offer of going halves because, savings or no savings, weddings are expensive and I don't want my parents to be stressed about money. I know I originally wanted a traditional ceremony with all the extravagant trimmings, but all that has changed. Right now, I'd be happy with a simple wedding in a pub with dancing afterwards, but the Lewises will never go for that. Not in a million years.

Lunch continues without any further mention of who's paying for what, but the atmosphere has dulled from everyone's initial warmth and joy, the strain making me lose my appetite. The Lewises don't seem to notice anything wrong. But Dad's face is tight, and Mum has lost her confidence, so it's mainly me, Austin and his parents who are carrying the conversation now. Austin can tell I'm ill at ease and he keeps squeezing my hand reassuringly under the table.

We don't linger after dessert – a strawberry pavlova with mountains of cream and gold-leaf shavings. Everyone is saying all the right things, talking about how exciting it is, and how lovely it's been to meet up properly, but there's no real feeling behind it. I think I'm going to have to accept that, just because our families are merging, our parents aren't necessarily going to be friends. Civility and the pretence of friendliness is probably the best I can hope for. I doubt chummy trips out on Rob's boat are going to happen either.

Back home, after a couple of hours watching TV, my parents go to bed earlier than usual, tired from socialising. They don't often go out and when they do, it's usually just the two of them, or with me. I go into the kitchen and make myself a camomile tea, mulling over the day, wishing it had gone a little differently, but also thankful it hadn't been any worse.

Dad's old Nokia buzzes on the counter. Neither of my parents like to take their phone up to the bedroom, claiming it disturbs their sleep. I glance across at the screen and see a message pop up on his phone from Burton Best Loans. Which is weird, because my parents are completely against going into debt. It must be spam.

I pick up my mobile and google the name. It comes up as a company based locally in Christchurch. There's not much information other than they offer payday loans and loans to people with bad credit. A sense of dread slides over me while at the same time I try to dismiss it. Dad wouldn't have taken a loan to pay for my wedding, would he? Especially not one from a company as dubious-looking as this one.

Before I can lecture myself on the ethics of snooping, I snatch up Dad's phone and click on the message. Frustratingly, it's asking

160

for a pin number. I don't want to guess in case he knows that I tried to get into his phone. *What am I doing?*

I set his phone back on the counter, anxiety scrambling my brain. Should I confront my parents about it, or leave well alone? If it is a loan, then they obviously don't want me to know about it. But I can't let them go into debt for me. How can I bring up the subject tactfully? I know how proud my dad is; today highlighted that in screaming fluorescent pink. I'll have to think about what to do for the best because, right now, I have absolutely no idea.

Chapter Twenty-Five

NOW

I walk back to the hotel, casting glances over my shoulder every twenty seconds, terrified I'm about to lock eyes with my stalker. Hopefully, I won't ever have to see Bart's investigator again, now that he's called him off. But that still leaves the dark-haired man I saw near the Rialto Bridge.

I hurry into the hotel lobby, trying to shake off my paranoia. Aside from my fears about being followed, my chat with Bart has thrown up more questions than answers. One minute I felt sorry for him, the next I was convinced he was lying. Maybe I'll have to hire an investigator of my own to find out the truth about that man.

Up on the fourth floor, I see that Rob and Vicki have almost finished switching our rooms around.

'Oh, Stella, thank goodness you're back,' Vicki cries, throwing her arms around me. 'Rob had to stop me from storming into the bar and checking on you about twenty times.'

'What did that slimy git have to say?' Rob asks.

We sit in the living room of the suite and I fill them in on how Bart tried to make me believe he was innocent.

'So he's basically sticking to his story that Austin's the one in the wrong?' Vicki asks.

'Well, it's obvious he's going to say that,' Rob snaps.

'Nothing about where Austin could be?' Vicki's hazel eyes are wide, hopeful.

I shake my head. 'No, that was what I was hoping for. He did, however, tell me he'd hired an investigator to spy on Austin and to follow me.'

'He did *what*?' Rob thunders.

'You're joking!' Vicki gets to her feet.

'Is that legal?' Rob asks. 'Surely it's a violation of your privacy.'

'So if he was having you both followed,' Vicki says, 'then surely he'd know what happened to Austin?'

'No. He said he hired the PI to investigate Austin's business. But then, after he went missing, that's when Bart asked him to follow me. To see if Austin really had disappeared, or if I might know where he was. But, obviously, all the PI would have seen was me searching for my husband.'

'This is hopeless!' Vicki cries, covering her face with her hands.

Rob gently pulls her back on to the chaise to comfort her as she sobs into his shoulder. I feel as though I'm intruding, and wonder whether to leave them to their grief, but Rob turns to me. 'What else did he say?'

'It turns out Bart's PI is the fair-haired man I first saw at the print shop. But the dark-haired man at Rialto isn't anything to do with Bart.' I give an internal shiver at the thought.

'So he says,' Rob snaps. 'Bart could be lying. Having two different people following you makes no sense.'

'None of it makes any sense.' Vicki pulls a tissue from her pocket, dabbing her eyes and blowing her nose.

I get the feeling the Lewises think I've imagined the second guy, due to the stress or whatever. That really he was just some random person who happened to be walking in the same direction as me. Maybe they're right, but I can't shake the feeling that there's more to it.

Vicki sniffs. 'I'm sorry for getting so upset, Stella. I just want us to find Austin. I don't care about the whys and hows and whos. I only want our son back.'

'I know,' I reply quietly. 'I know.'

'Let's all have a rest and meet for dinner in an hour or so,' Rob suggests. 'What do you think, Stella?'

'Sounds good,' I reply, getting up.

I empty the safe in the suite and Rob hands me the key card to their old room. I leave them in peace and cross the short landing to my new room. It's a small double with a nice shower room. The decor is similar to the suite, with rich colours and framed paintings of Venice. Instead of a Grand Canal view with a balcony, there are two tall windows that face the side street, high above the hotel entrance. I peer down to see a few people walking past. It feels more peaceful in this room. More cocoon-like, which suits me fine.

I wonder if I should have a nap, but worry that if I fall asleep, I might not wake in time for dinner. I'm also scared that if I close my eyes now, I might not be able to fall asleep later. Because the nights here are even worse than the days. The dark hours are when my mind runs down terrifying alleys.

Instead, I decide to have a long shower and change into something smart for dinner. The act of washing and drying my hair, putting on some make-up and picking an outfit might help stop my brain spiralling.

Once I'm clean and dressed in a black jumpsuit and pale-green blazer, I open one of the windows, fold back the shutters, and let the cool evening air sweep into the room. The chatter of tourists drifts up from below, mingling with the fainter sounds of clattering cutlery, the shouts of the gondoliers and the rushing breeze off the water. I inhale and exhale, trying to clear my mind. To expel any hint of bubbling emotion. Because if I let myself give in to it, I'm going to sink on to the carpet and sob.

Ever since Austin left that first night, I've been barely keeping it together. Trying to remember to eat, to drink, to talk, to do all the things that normal people do. As if I'm balancing on the edge of a precipice, about to plummet to my death. If Austin's parents weren't here, I think I would let myself give in to the fear. But I promised Vicki that I would be strong. That I would help them. So that's what I'm going to do. I'm so glad the Lewises came. I'd be a mess without them.

A knock on the door rouses me from my thoughts. I open it to see that Austin's parents look a little better than earlier. They had the same idea as me – to freshen up and try to put on some semblance of normality.

'Did you have a nice rest?' Vicki asks. 'I hope this room's okay for you. Let us know if you'd rather swap back.'

'No, I love the room. It's perfect, thanks.'

'Good,' Rob replies. 'Let's get some nosh and talk about what we're going to do tomorrow.'

In the restaurant, we're all intent on the menu. I opt for water instead of wine, and the Lewises also order soft drinks. No one wants a repeat of last night. I choose lemon linguine, Rob goes for cuttlefish with polenta, and Vicki orders the wild turbot.

I can tell that everyone's reluctant to bring up the subject of what we should do next. It just feels like such a mammoth task. Too overwhelming. Should we continue searching? Should we focus on social media? Contact the news outlets in Italy? Contact the list of charities Gallini gave us? Chase up the police? Chase up the consulate? Chase up Austin's friends? We need to do all of it, but in what order? And who should do what?

The other thing that's niggling at me is the fact that I haven't told my parents yet. The thought of it makes me feel sick. Having to explain. Having to deal with their worry. But I can't keep it from them any longer. Especially as it's been on the local news. I promise myself I'll call them after dinner.

Just as the waiter is setting down our food, I'm startled to see the familiar dark-haired, uniformed figure of Gallini heading towards us, accompanied by a pretty woman with light-brown shoulder-length hair, wearing jeans and a fitted Barbour-style jacket.

Vicki grips the edge of the table. 'Do you think they have news?' she asks, her face rigid with fear.

'Let's hope they've found our boy safe and sound,' Rob says, his voice quavering.

'Good evening,' Gallini says as they reach our table. 'This is my colleague, Detective Anna Fiore.'

'What's happened?' Rob asks bluntly.

'I'm sorry, we have no news on your son yet,' Gallini says.

Both Vicki and Rob visibly sag.

'What about the cash machine?' Rob asks. 'Did you find out whether it was Austin who withdrew the money, or someone else?'

'We should know tomorrow,' Gallini replies.

'Then why are you here?' Rob asks.

'Mrs Lewis . . . *Stella*,' the detective says to me, her accent thicker than Gallini's. 'We would like you to accompany us to the station to answer some questions.'

'You want to talk to Stella?' Rob asks. 'What about? Can't you at least let her eat something first?'

'We would prefer you come with us now,' Fiore says firmly.

My gaze darts over to Gallini, but his expression doesn't give anything away. He gives a tight smile, but his eyes are hard.

'We'll come with you,' Vicki says to me. She looks up at the detective. 'We can come too, right?'

'No, you stay and have dinner,' I say, wanting their company, but knowing they need to keep their strength up.

'We'd just like Stella for now,' Fiore replies. 'But we may need to talk to you another time. Like Stella says, you stay and finish your meal.'

'Am I under arrest for something?' I ask, my vision starting to blur.

'No,' Gallini replies. 'You're helping with our inquiries, that's all.'

'*Si*,' Fiore replies. 'Can you bring your passport?'

'Um, sure,' I reply.

'Do you have your husband's passport?' she asks.

I shake my head. 'No. He had it with him when he went to the restaurant that night.'

'Should I be calling a lawyer?' Rob asks, standing up. 'You realise our daughter-in-law only knows as much as we do. She's devastated.' His voice is rising and, once again, we find ourselves the subject of surreptitious glances and whispers from the diners around us. I think we'll have to find somewhere else to eat tomorrow – if the police even let me come back here. That notion sets my heart hammering in trepidation, but I tell myself not to think that way. Like Gallini said, I'm just helping with their inquiries.

'It's fine,' I say, getting to my feet. 'I'm happy to answer any questions.' My voice sounds as though it's coming from far away.

Like my ears need to pop. I wonder if it's from the cabin pressure on the flight. But, no, it's only just started. It's fear and stress that's causing it. This whole situation is surreal.

After fetching my passport from the room, as though in a dream I walk with the officers away from my in-laws, away from my lemon linguine and away from the hotel, wondering if the police might actually believe I'm responsible for Austin's disappearance.

Chapter Twenty-Six

THEN

'It's so nice of your mum and dad to have the engagement party at their place,' I say, standing in front of Austin's full-length mirror and slipping in my favourite silver-and-garnet earrings.

'They're more than happy to do it,' he says, buttoning his shirt and staring at me in the mirror. 'Anyway, they've got an army of caterers and cleaners, so it's not like they're actually doing that much.'

'That's not true!' I reply. 'It's still a lot of effort. They have to choose the menu, decorate the house, invite people. It's not like waving a magic wand.'

'I guess so, but you know what I mean. Mum loves doing all that stuff. She can't wait to get stuck into the wedding plans.' His phone chimes from his chest of drawers and he picks it up, frowning.

I've already broached the subject with Austin of having a modest wedding, but he just laughed, saying, *Have you met my parents?* I don't want to tell him that my parents don't have the money for anything too lavish, because Dad would hate for my prospective in-laws to know the ins and outs of their financial situation. But I don't see how I'm going to be able to rein in the Lewises otherwise.

Ever since that night last month when I came across that notification on Dad's phone, I've had a gnawing anxiety that forced me to speak to my parents about it. I admitted seeing the message pop up on Dad's mobile and he looked confused, telling me he would never take out a loan and that if I didn't believe them, he'd be happy to show me the balance of ten thousand pounds in their savings account.

The relief was huge. But even knowing they didn't borrow the money hasn't eased my worries completely. Because my parents' ten thousand pounds is going to be swallowed up too quickly by food, flowers, music, venue, cars, not to mention the photographer, party favours and all the other little extras. It's quite clear that if the Lewises have their way, it's going to cost more than double the amount my parents put aside.

'You don't mind Mum being involved in the wedding plans, do you?' Austin asks, putting his phone down for a few seconds while he slips on his suit jacket. 'It's just, with me being their only child, they're keen to make it a day to remember.'

'No, of course not. I just don't want anything over the top.'

'You've changed your tune,' he replies.

'I know, but the more I've thought about it, the more I'd rather go for something simple and understated.'

'Good luck with that.' His green eyes crinkle with humour.

'I mean it, Austin. I need you to have a word with them. Manage their expectations.' I put on the silver charm necklace that Austin bought me for my birthday last year, trying to decide if it's too much, if I need something plainer.

Austin sits on the bed, his eyes glued to his phone again.

I decide to stick with the charm necklace. Even if it isn't quite right, it was a gift from the man I love. I turn to face him. 'Austin? Did you hear what I said?'

'Yeah, sorry, hang on a sec. I've just got this work stuff to . . .' He tails off, tapping out a text, and then finally puts his phone in his jacket pocket and looks up at me. 'Okay, I'm all yours.'

I slip my watch over my wrist and walk over to him, hold out my arm for him to do up the clasp.

'What were you saying?' he asks, clicking the clasp shut, his fingers brushing my skin.

'I was asking you to talk to your parents and back me up on our wedding plans – nothing crazy, just simple and understated.'

'Sure,' he says. 'They'll want to keep it classy. Don't worry.'

I sigh. What I'm trying to get across is that I don't want it to cost a lot, but I can't say it in those words to Austin in case he mentions it to his parents and it turns into a whole thing where they try to pay for the wedding again. I'll have to think of a sensitive way to handle this. But tonight isn't the best time. 'Any news on the Bart front?' I ask instead.

Austin scowls in response. 'Let's not talk about *him* this evening. Tonight's about us. And only us.' He walks over and tries to kiss me, but I push him away with a laugh.

'Don't you dare ruin my make-up. We have to leave in a minute. I won't have time to fix it if you go smearing my lipstick.'

His phone chimes again. He skims a look and puts it back in his pocket.

'Who keeps messaging?' I ask. 'It's not Bart, is it?' I'm paranoid that he's going to gatecrash our party and try to ruin our night.

'So much for not mentioning his name,' Austin replies, tapping me on the nose with his finger. 'It's nothing – work stuff, and Miles sending stupid memes.'

'He does like his memes.' I nod sagely.

'He's the meme king. Come on, let's go.' Austin takes my hand and we walk out into the hall, where I take my shawl from the coat cupboard. 'You look gorgeous, Stella,' he says, twirling me around so my dress flares out around my legs. It's deep-red silk crepe with knife pleats, a lace bodice and spaghetti straps. My heels are high, and I'm wearing my hair in a chignon with wispy tendrils.

'You're not so bad yourself,' I say, running my gaze over his broad shoulders and up to his handsome tanned features, hardly noticing his designer suit. He could be wearing an old tracksuit and I wouldn't care.

'Are you sure we haven't got time for me to ruin your make-up?' he asks. 'What about if I say "please"?'

Heat runs through me, and I'm tempted, but we can't be late. 'Your mum will kill us if we're not there at seven thirty on the dot, like she insisted.'

'You're right,' he replies. 'But I hope, when we're married, you're not going to be this sensible *all* the time.'

'I promise I'll be part sensible, part reckless.'

'Okay. Deal.'

He glances at his phone yet again and I bite my tongue, not wanting to be a nag about it. But I hope he's not going to be glued to it all evening.

Chapter Twenty-Seven

NOW

The interview room is like something out of a TV crime drama, with me sitting on one side of a table and Gallini and Fiore on the other. They've taken my passport and have given me a plastic bottle of water from which I sip slowly, gripping it so hard it's warping and crackling beneath my fingers. It's a good thing I didn't have time to eat any of my pasta as I feel dizzy and nauseated sitting here in this stuffy airless room under the unforgiving strip lights, like I could easily pass out or throw up at any moment.

Back at the hotel, I'd assumed I was going to walk to the usual station with Gallini and Fiore. That it would be relaxed, and we would talk civilly like on previous occasions. Instead, I was accompanied to the hotel dock and helped on to a police launch bobbing on the canal, its blue lights flashing while waiters and diners on the terrace gawped as though we were a dinner show put on for their evening's entertainment.

I was too stunned to feel embarrassed or humiliated. I sat quietly in the back of the craft while they remained standing, gazing ahead and conversing in Italian with the uniformed launch driver, making no attempt to talk to me. I was glad I'd worn my blazer, pulling it tight around me and jamming my hands beneath my armpits to keep warm. Other boats parted to make way for our blue flashing lights. For me. I felt like a criminal.

Instead of stopping near the station, we passed the turning, taking the next left away from the Grand Canal and along a narrower waterway. The launch slowed and cruised along, beneath bridges, past three- and four-storey buildings. Finally, we pulled over beside a white official-looking building, an Italian flag above its entrance, the wind having wrapped it around the flagpole so many times that only a sliver flapped in the breeze. Fiore stepped up out of the launch with practised ease while Gallini took my hand to help me on to the pavement.

Now, on the second floor of the building, waiting for the interview to begin, I wonder if I really am here simply to answer questions, like they said, or if they actually believe I'm guilty of something. I don't know anything about police procedure, British or Italian, other than what I've gleaned from novels and TV series, so I have no idea of my rights. Although they did say I'm only here to be questioned. That I'm not actually under arrest.

Detective Fiore begins by asking me to go over what happened the night Austin went missing. I've already given Gallini this information, but I guess that was right after it had happened, when there was still the possibility that Austin would show up within a few hours. Now that he's been gone for three days – *how has it been three days?* – this seems more like a formal statement. I shouldn't worry. It's good they're doing this. Taking it seriously, eliminating people from their lines of inquiry.

Once I'm done recounting the traumatic events of Sunday night, both officers are quiet for a moment. I wonder if they'll let me go now. I'm looking forward to crawling into bed. To hoping for a better day tomorrow.

'So, that's it,' I say. 'And since then, I've been scouring the city for him. But it's hard to know where to look. He could be any-where. I . . . I just don't understand what could have happened to him. It's a nightmare. I feel like I'm in a living nightmare.'

'We spoke to Mr Randall just earlier,' Fiore says, taking a band from her wrist and using it to pull her hair into a chic ponytail.

'Good,' I reply. 'So you managed to track Bart down.'

'Actually, he came to us,' Gallini says. 'He had a lot to say.'

I don't like the sound of this, but whatever Bart's up to, I won't let him drag me into it.

'Mr Randall said your husband is his business partner,' Gallini continues, leaning back in his chair. 'He says they have been involved in a dispute. He claims your husband has stolen money and has deliberately "gone missing".' He makes air quotes as he says this.

I shake my head in disbelief at what I'm hearing. This feels different to the times I spoke to Gallini before. Then, he was sym-pathetic. Kind, even. Now he's speaking to me differently, like he suspects me of something. I need to shift things back to how they were.

'He said exactly the same thing to me,' I reply. 'But I told him it's absolute rubbish. My husband is the one suing Bart – I bet he didn't tell you that.' I take a breath and try to calm down. Try not to let Bart's lies get to me. He's obviously been bad-mouthing Austin, filling Gallini's head with nonsense. 'In fact,' I continue, 'Bart also admitted that the man who's been following me is a private inves-tigator that he employed.'

'Mr Randall paid for a PI to follow you?' Fiore says, her head snapping up.

I wonder if I shouldn't have mentioned that. Maybe it makes me sound guilty of something. 'Yes. But I have no idea why,' I add.

'If your husband has deliberately gone missing,' Fiore says, 'he should know that as a UK citizen he cannot legally stay in this country for more than ninety days without a visa.'

'*Deliberately?*' I look away, unable to speak for a moment. 'We've just got married. We're on our honeymoon. We're booked to go skiing in the Dolomites next week. Why would he go missing deliberately? Please don't tell me you're taking Bart's story seriously? Austin is out there somewhere and he needs our help.'

Fiore doesn't reply.

Sweat slicks my upper lip and slides down my back. I'm suddenly very, very scared. I'm in a foreign country, in a police station, my husband is missing and these officers think I possibly have something to do with it. Or that I'm somehow in cahoots with him. How have events slipped so out of control?

I realise I want my parents. I need my dad's no-nonsense help and the comfort of my mum. Austin's parents are lovely, but they don't feel like my real family. As soon as I get out of here, I'm going to call them. Tell them how much I love them. Apologise for not letting them know about Austin sooner. *Why didn't I tell them sooner?*

'How long do you need me here?' I ask. 'I'm exhausted. It's been a harrowing few days and I need to eat. And to get some rest.'

'Please wait here,' Fiore says. 'We'll be back.'

She and Gallini leave the small room and I sink into my seat, glancing around at the scuffed beige walls and the pitted wooden door, at the grilles on the windows and the buzzing ceiling lights, trying not to panic further. They'll come back soon and let me go and I'll return to the hotel and call my parents. And everything will be fine. It will all be absolutely fine.

Chapter Twenty-Eight

THEN

The taxi drops us on the pavement outside Austin's parents' house a couple of minutes before seven thirty. Their road is usually empty but, this evening, parked cars stretch in both directions, and I recognise most of them as belonging to friends and family. My parents' blue Vauxhall Astra is parked directly outside, which means they probably arrived early, as usual.

Austin and I walk across the block-paved driveway up to the front door, which is festooned with an arch of silver and white balloons. He takes my arm and we give one another an excited look before pushing open the door and walking inside.

Cheers and hoorays make me almost jump out of my skin, and I'm overwhelmed to see everyone arranged like a class photo in the spacious hallway to greet us, Austin's and my parents in the centre on the staircase.

'Everyone stay where you are!' Rob calls out, beckoning us over to stand with them. 'The photographer's just going to take a few pics.'

We pose on the stairs, the guests of honour, with everyone else around us, while a photographer – with a proper camera rather than a phone – fires off some shots.

'Thanks for being on time,' Vicki says. 'It would have been hard to keep everyone in position if you'd shown up late.'

Austin and I look at one another, trying not to laugh as we remember the reason we could have been late. 'Bet you're glad I was sensible now,' I whisper in his ear.

'Nope,' he replies, grinning at the camera. 'I wish I could take you back home right this minute.'

I feel my face grow hot, but manage a smile for the photographs.

Finally, we're released from our spot on the stairs and Austin is whisked away by friends and relatives. I hug my parents, and my nana – Mum's mum – who's in a wheelchair at the foot of the staircase. Dad picked her up from the nursing home to join us this evening. My only living grandparent, Nana's in her eighties and very frail, but she's still as sharp as they come. I love her to bits, and bend to kiss her soft, papery cheek, which smells of vanilla and violets.

She grasps my fingers with blue-veined hands. 'Do you love him, Stella?' she asks in her cockney accent – she was born and brought up in the East End of London. 'Is he kind?'

'Yes.' I glance around for Austin to come and say hello to her, but he's disappeared into the crush of friends and family. 'Yes, Nana, don't worry. I love him and he's very kind.'

'Because kindness is the most important thing in a life partner,' she says, still squeezing my hand. 'If he's an arsehole, it don't matter how good he is in bed.'

'Nana!'

'When you reach your eighties, you haven't got time to pussy-foot around. You have to tell it like it is,' she says with a cackle.

'Well, you don't need to worry about me, Nana. I've got a good one. You've met him, so you know how lovely he is.'

'Good. Now, can you sneak me some of that champagne? Your mum said I can't have any because of my medication, but what I wouldn't do for a small glass and a ciggie.'

'I'll see what I can do,' I reply, hoping I can find her something sparkling and non-alcoholic.

'You're a good girl. Now, you should go off and socialise. You don't want to be stuck with an old fogie like me at your party.'

'You're the most gorgeous and interesting one here,' I reply.

She smiles with pleasure and waves off my compliment.

I straighten up. 'Hey, Mum, Dad.' I hug them again, feeling like it's been days since we last saw each other rather than this morning before work.

'We saw Antonia as we were leaving the house earlier,' Mum says. 'I felt so rude not saying where we were going. I'm sure she knew.'

'How would she know?' I reply.

I feel a bit bad not inviting Jake and his mum, Antonia, from next door, but it would have been beyond awkward. Mum and Dad were cross with me for leaving them off the guest list, but I told them I could hardly invite a boy who had recently professed his love for me to my engagement party. That would have just been rubbing his face in it. And it would have been weird to just invite Antonia without Jake. Hopefully, they won't even hear about it as Jake and I don't share the same friendship circles any more.

'Anyway, you look gorgeous in that dress, love,' Mum says. 'Doesn't she, Phil?'

'Yes. I hope Austin appreciates what he's got.'

'He does,' I reply confidently.

'Did someone say my name?' Austin appears by my side. 'Hi, Lindsay. Hi, Phil.'

'Hello, Austin.' Dad shakes his hand and Mum gives him an awkward hug.

Austin clears his throat. 'I just want to say that I'm the happiest man alive, and that's because of your daughter. I want you to know that I love Stella and I know I don't deserve her but I'm grateful that she's agreed to be my wife.'

Tears prick the back of my eyes at his words, and I see they've also managed to penetrate Dad's steely facade.

'Oh, that's lovely, Austin,' Mum replies, patting his arm.

Dad nods. 'Pleased to hear it, lad.' He's never in his life called Austin 'lad'. It's a term he usually reserves for Jake. Could he actually be starting to come around to my fiancé at last?

The rest of the evening is as wonderful as I hoped it would be. The Lewises' home is decorated to perfection with silver and gold balloons, 'Congratulations' banners and fresh flowers, and delicious finger food is being served on platters by uniformed staff. They have a wireless audio system throughout, and Austin gave them an eclectic playlist that starts out as tasteful background music, but will ramp up to dance tunes later on.

All our friends and family are here, including my boss, Millie, and her husband, Darrin; my best friend, Claudia, with her parents and sister, Gina; and Liv and Miles. I also invited my work colleagues, and friends from school. Austin and his family know way more people than my parents and I do, so a lot of the guests I've only met a few times. It doesn't matter, though, as everyone whose eye I catch comes over to congratulate me. The hall table is already piled high with presents, and the bar on the terrace is stacked with booze.

I don't think I could feel any happier right now. I head outside to find Austin as I've barely seen him since he spoke to my parents. But as I cross the patio, scanning the garden for my elusive fiancé, my heart plummets when I spot someone coming around the side of the house who most definitely isn't on the guest list. And I'm one hundred per cent sure they're only here to cause trouble.

Chapter Twenty-Nine

NOW

I slide out of my hotel bed with fragments of yesterday's worst bits replaying in my mind. When the nightmarish interview with Gallini and Fiore finally came to an end, I was handed back my passport and thanked for my time. After Bart's hatchet job – telling the police that Austin had stolen money from him and had gone missing deliberately – I'd been terrified the police were going to arrest me as an accomplice, or keep me in a cell overnight. But once Gallini's mild bad-cop routine was over, he offered to take me back to the hotel – I think he may have felt a little guilty for adding to my stress. I politely declined his offer, having had enough of police company for one day. And anyway, I needed the walk back, craving space and time to myself to decompress, desperate for fresh air after the stuffiness of the interview room.

Now, as I pick out some crumpled clothes from my suitcase to wear, I'm half dreading, half looking forward to my parents arriving later today. I called them last night on the walk back to the hotel. Miraculously, they hadn't caught any whiff of what's happened via the news, and neither of them is big on social media, so it was a total shock for them to hear about Austin's disappearance. But I'm grateful they didn't give me the third degree over the phone.

I told them I'd sort out their flights and accommodation, and that they should get a vaporetto or water taxi from the airport. Vicki offered to book everything for me as I have no credit cards and the replacements haven't yet turned up at my parents' house. I assured her I'd transfer the money from my account, but I don't have anywhere near enough funds to cover it so it will have to be put on my credit card – when it arrives. But I'm not thinking about money right now; I'll worry about finances later.

The Lewises and I divide up the day. Rob volunteers to go out pounding the streets of Venice, and Vicki and I decide to remain at the hotel. She's concentrating on missing persons' charities and databases, while I create more pages and accounts on social media dedicated to finding Austin. We choose to work in our respective hotel rooms, meeting in her suite briefly for a coffee at ten o'clock, and then for a panini at one thirty, where she updates me on her progress and I show her the pages I've created.

'I've invited tons of media outlets to follow and friend me,' I explain, getting up and stretching my legs, walking over to the balcony windows, 'but hardly any of them are interested. I think, after the initial local media buzz, they've moved on. It's so frustrating.'

'We need to think of another angle,' Vicki replies. 'A unique way to get them interested. It's what I do at work sometimes to get outlets to feature our company.'

'Yeah, I guess. It just feels like they *should* be helping. We shouldn't have to look for marketing angles.'

'I know,' Vicki replies, shaking her head. 'This is my son's life.'

My phone rings, and I see that it's Gallini. I mouth his name to Vicki and answer his call, putting it on speaker.

'Stella?'

'Hello. Any news? Have you found him?'

'I'm sorry, no, but I wanted to update you that we've checked the ATM camera, and it was your husband who withdrew the cash after he collected his card from the restaurant.'

'What does that mean?' Vicki asks. 'You said before that he went to a machine in the opposite direction to the hotel . . .'

'We don't know yet,' Gallini replies. 'He could have gone there freely. Perhaps he wanted a walk in the city, or to visit a bar.' He hesitates. 'Or maybe something else.'

There's a pause in the conversation and Vicki's eyes start to glisten.

'You think he might have been coerced to withdraw the money?' I ask.

'We shouldn't jump to any conclusions,' Gallini says.

'But you can't rule it out,' I push.

'No. We can't rule anything out yet.'

Gallini says he'll continue to keep us updated, and he ends the call.

Neither Vicki nor I say anything for a few moments. Digesting the news and trying to figure out what it means.

'I'd better call Rob, let him know,' she says quietly.

I nod and we hug before I leave the suite, giving her some privacy to make the call.

After that unsettling update, we go back to work, where the hours are eaten up online and yet I feel as though I've hardly achieved anything of any use. Although our friends have joined the pages and are sharing the hell out of them, it feels pointless. On the flip side, it has been a relief to stay inside the hotel today. To not feel the fear of being followed. To not drag myself around the city searching for a husband who's not there.

At six thirty, my parents disembark from the water-bus – Mum in black jeans, short grey boots and a checked wool jacket, and Dad in jeans, a lightweight pale-blue sweater and his favourite navy bomber jacket. I shiver as I walk down to the dock to meet them, the wind off the water blowing my hair around my face. I choose the least crowded spot to wait, near the hotel terrace.

Under any other circumstances, my parents would have loved Venice. Dad for the water and the boats, and Mum for the cuisine and the sheer beauty of the city. I'm gutted that they're here for such a stressful and terrible situation.

I can see them glancing everywhere but at me, so I raise my hand and wave. Mum spots me first, her face lighting up and then casting me a look of love mixed with anguish.

I will not cry. I will not cry.

She elbows Dad and points my way. Dad gives a sad smile and I watch as they squeeze a path through the crush and weave their way over to me, wheeling their cases across the flagstones.

Dad gives me a bear hug without words and then Mum kisses my cheek and smooths a strand of hair back from my face. 'Oh, Stella, love,' she says.

I've never been more grateful that my parents aren't the gushy type. That they're relatively quiet and measured when it comes to emotional situations. Their stoicism is what I need right now.

'Shall we check in?' I ask. 'And then we can talk. Our hotel was completely booked up, but luckily a room came free today so you can be with us.'

I take Mum's case from her, and we walk up the street and through the glass doors of the hotel, the suitcase wheels gliding across the marble floor.

'This looks expensive,' Dad remarks. 'We'd have been fine somewhere less posh.'

'I want us all to be together,' I reply, wishing the lobby wasn't quite as grand. Dad isn't a fan of fancy places.

Check-in is quick. My parents' room is on the third floor, just below mine, and they're booked for three nights, until Sunday.

Austin and I were due to check out then, too, to start the second leg of our honeymoon skiing high up in the mountains where there's still some snow this late in the season. But we won't be doing that. Not any more. If we need to stay in Venice any longer, then we'll find somewhere else to base ourselves.

'Are you hungry?' I ask.

'I'd love a cup of tea,' Mum says.

I ask the concierge to take my parents' cases up, and then the three of us head out on to the terrace, where we order a pot of tea for three and some biscuits. I allow myself to exhale properly for the first time in four days. Having my parents here is like being tucked beneath a warm blanket during a snowstorm.

'So what exactly did the police say?' Dad asks, pouring tea for everyone. 'You said they interviewed you yesterday.'

When I called my parents last night, I played down how scared I'd been in the police station. How complicated things have become with Bart's involvement. Because I've never mentioned the court case to my parents, not wanting Austin to appear any worse in their eyes. 'They just said they're trying to find him. Apparently, Austin's been having trouble with his business partner, so they're looking into that,' I say, keeping it vague.

'What kind of trouble?' Dad asks, his eyes sharp.

'I don't know exactly,' I reply.

'Well, you should know,' Dad says. 'Your mother and I are open with each other about finances. You're in a partnership with your spouse; you shouldn't have secrets from each other.'

'It isn't a secret,' I reply, my cheeks warming. 'I just don't know all the nitty-gritty. Anyway, Bart's not a very nice person, but I can't imagine he's done anything bad. He's actually come to Venice to find out what's going on. The police haven't arrested him or anything. He's probably nothing to do with it.'

186

'If he's nothing to do with it, then what's he doing in Italy?' Dad asks.

'He said he was worried after Austin went missing,' I reply, adding a splash of milk to my tea. 'That he only came here to find out what's going on.'

'That doesn't sound likely,' Dad replies.

'Stella,' Mum says, shaking her head. 'How did you get mixed up in all this?'

'I don't know. It's a nightmare. And each day seems to get worse and worse. I can't see an end to any of it.'

'The end will be when the police find Austin,' Dad says. 'I really hope the lad's okay.'

'Thanks, Dad.'

After we've had our tea and biscuits, Mum wants to freshen up, so I show my parents to their room before going up to mine. The Lewises have thoughtfully given us our space for now, but suggested we all go to dinner at a local restaurant later, so I arrange to meet my parents in the lobby in an hour's time.

Back in my room, I open the windows, lie on my bed and close my eyes, letting the cool evening breeze waft in while I try to centre myself and calm my racing mind. It's lovely to have my parents here for support, but I still have no idea what to do for the best. The police say they're still looking for Austin, but what happens if they draw blanks? What happens if they don't?

My phone buzzes with a message from Claudia, checking up on me. She's been messaging and calling several times a day to see how I'm doing. So have Millie and Jake. I'm a little miffed that Liv only messaged once, and that was just a brief, 'We can't believe what's happened. I'm sure he'll be fine. Sending love.'

I reply to Claudia's message with a quick update, and decide to call Liv. It goes straight to her voicemail, so I leave a message:

187

'Hey, Liv, it's Stella. Hope you and Miles are okay. I was just calling for a chat. My parents have arrived in Venice today. We still haven't got any news on where Austin might be. Miss you guys.'

I end the call, hoping she'll ring me back.

After ten minutes of nothing, I video-call Miles on WhatsApp. He's Austin's best friend. Why hasn't he called me to ask about him? After days of silence I don't expect him to reply, so I'm surprised when his face appears on my screen, a blank white wall behind him.

'Stella,' he says tiredly, the skin beneath his eyes shadowed and his shirt rumpled. 'Any news?'

'No,' I reply. 'The whole thing is a shitshow.'

'I'm so sorry. How are you holding up?' he asks, rubbing at his stubbled jaw.

I shrug and shake my head. 'Is Liv okay? I tried calling her, but she didn't answer.'

'She's still in a meeting; it's going to be a late one.'

'Where are you?' I ask. Their place has no white walls. Liv's a fan of colour.

'Work,' he replies. 'Just about to leave actually.'

I nod, getting the sense that he doesn't want to prolong the conversation. That he wants to end the call. 'Everything all right, Miles?' I ask.

'Yeah, of course. Just tired.'

I'm starting to get annoyed now. *He's* tired? What about me? 'Miles, is something wrong?'

'Hang on, someone's calling me. Two secs, okay?' He ends the call abruptly.

I get the feeling that no one was calling him, that it was an excuse. I decide that if he hasn't called me back in one minute, then . . .

A second later, he calls me back and I answer immediately. His face reappears and he looks as though he's about to cry.

'Miles, what's wrong? What's happened?' I'm getting a bad feeling. Is this about him and Liv? Or . . . something else?

'Oh, God, Stella, I've got something to tell you. Something I should have let you know days ago.' He closes his eyes and massages his temple with his free hand before opening his eyes again.

'What is it?' I ask, my mouth going dry.

'Liv wanted me to say something, but I promised Austin I wouldn't.'

'Just tell me whatever it is,' I croak, barely able to speak. '*Please.*'

Chapter Thirty

THEN

'What the hell is *she* doing here?' I mutter to myself, my emotions reeling through shocked, angry and dismayed. How dare she show up at our engagement party.

I glance around for Austin, but I can't see him. He must be inside. I don't know what to do for the best. I turn sharply as some-one grabs my arm, my pulse slowing a little when I see that it's only Claudia. 'Claud, have you seen who's—'

'I know!' Claudia's hands go to her hips, magenta nails bright against her grey silk dress. 'Bloody Keri flipping Wade. You didn't invite her, did you?'

'No I did not.'

'What about Austin? Or his parents? Surely they wouldn't have—'

I shake my head. 'No way they'd want her here. She's nothing but trouble. What shall I do?'

Keri is still at the opposite end of the garden, her head slowly turning left and right like the Terminator scanning for its target. It stops when her gaze lands on me, her eyes narrowing. Keri is dressed for a party, in a black dress with cut-outs at the waist and complicated bondage-style straps, towering gold strappy heels criss-crossing up her calves, and a full face of YouTube-tutorial-style make-up.

'She's coming over,' Claudia hisses, stating the obvious.

'Need some backup?' I turn to see Liv, her hair a mass of seventies waves.

'I don't want any trouble,' I say to my friends. 'I just want her gone.'

'We're on it,' Claudia says, striding over to meet Keri.

Liv stays by my side, holding my hand. 'What's that girl's problem?' she says. 'She just can't stand to see other people happy. Don't worry, Claud will get her to leave.'

'You can't stop me!' Keri cries in response to whatever Claudia said. 'This isn't your house.'

'Keri,' Claudia says, her voice louder now, 'this is a private party. Whatever you have to say will just have to wait for another time.'

'Meh meh m'meh meh.' As Keri mimics Claudia's tone, her hand puppeting the words, I realise she's drunk. 'Oh, piss off, Claudia,' Keri slurs, bashing into her shoulder as she staggers past my friend and continues heading my way.

'If you don't leave, I'm calling the police,' Claudia says, trying to keep up with her and throwing up her hands in frustration when she catches my eye.

But Keri ignores her, striding surprisingly quickly across the patio towards me, her tiny handbag banging against her side with every step.

The music suddenly increases in volume, a heavy bassline thumping through the night air, guests starting to dance on the terrace by the bar area.

'You!' Keri points at me. 'He doesn't love you, you know.'

191

'No,' Liv drawls. 'That's why he asked her to marry him. That's why they're having an engagement party. Because he doesn't love her.'

'Who are you?' Keri snarls, looking Liv up and down. 'This is none of your business. Stay out of it.'

Liv opens her mouth to respond but I interrupt before things get even more heated. 'Why are you here, Keri?' I ask, aiming for a diplomatic tone. The last thing I need is for this to escalate into a screaming match.

'Sorry,' Claudia mouths at me as she catches up.

'*Why are you here, Keri?*' Keri mimics me now, her eyes glazed, a smile on her red lips.

She's obviously trying to get a rise out of me. Trying to cause drama, to ruin my night. But I'm not going to give her the satisfaction.

'Okay, don't tell me,' I reply. 'But I'm telling you that you need to leave.'

She gives a drunken laugh. 'And I'm here to tell *you* . . .' She jabs a finger at me. 'That *you* need to watch out because you don't even know . . .' She blinks and swallows before giving a drunken giggle. 'And you're gonna get your comeuppance. You think your life's soooo perfect, little Miss Stellaaaa—'

'What's going on here?' Vicki shows up in full mama-bear mode, her expression hard.

'Vicki!' Keri cries, her gaze pivoting wildly to Austin's mum. 'It's sooo . . . luvvvly to see you.'

Vicki shakes her head and rolls her eyes. 'Lovely to see you too, Keri. Now let's get you home.' She loops her arm through Keri's, turns and guides her towards the side gate. 'I'm going to call you a cab, and you're going to go home, drink a pint of water and get into bed, all right?'

'Austin loves me,' Keri slurs in response. 'This "engagement" party's a joke. He won't marry that loser.' She waggles her finger at Vicki. 'And if he does, he'd better watch out.'

'Are you okay with her, Vicki?' Liv calls after them.

Austin's mum keeps walking with Keri, but gives us a thumbs up.

I let my shoulders drop a little. Although I won't be able to fully relax until she's gone.

My friends and I exhale.

'Vicki's a boss bitch,' Liv says, taking a slug of her vodka tonic and then offering me the glass.

I have a few grateful sips.

'Totally,' Claudia replies. 'Can I be her when I grow up?'

We manage to laugh about it and head over to the bar, although I'm still shaken, my nerve endings tingling with anxiety. At least Keri didn't manage to get hold of my fiancé and cause a big scene in front of everyone. As dramas go, I think we had a lucky escape. But I worry that she's going to cause trouble right up until the wedding day. What about after that, once we're married? Will she still be trying to inveigle her way into our lives? From the sound of it, she's in serious denial.

Why can't she just leave us alone? Live her own life, not ours. She genuinely still thinks she has some claim over Austin. It's exhausting, not knowing what she'll do next. What with Keri and now Bart trying to make everything difficult, I can only hope no one else comes along to screw up our lives.

Chapter Thirty-One

NOW

My hotel room recedes and all I can focus on is Miles's fearful expression on the screen as he stares at me from his office back in England.

He looks so uncomfortable that I'm dreading whatever it is he has to tell me.

'You might hate me when you hear what I have to say,' Miles says.

I blink and swallow, waiting for him to go on.

'The thing is,' Miles continues, 'I think Austin might have met up with a woman in Venice.'

The sound of church bells filters in from outside the hotel. Loud and discordant, like a death knell. 'A woman?' I echo. 'Like . . . a woman he was seeing?'

'Not "seeing" exactly.'

'I don't believe you,' I say. 'Who the hell meets up with another woman during their honeymoon? And anyway, Austin wouldn't do that. He loves me.'

'He does love you. He adores you, Stella. Whatever else has happened, you have to know that what you and Austin have is the real thing.' Miles stares up at the ceiling, his gaze slowly travelling down again to look at me. 'He loves you and wants to spend the rest of his life with you, but he got chatting to someone online. And she lives in northern Italy.'

'He was chatting to a woman online?' I say stupidly. 'Like on a dating app?'

Miles sighs. 'Yes.'

'That's how *we* met,' I reply quietly. 'Me and Austin.' I think back to our days of flirty online banter. The butterflies. The anticipation of eventually meeting up in real life. And now he's been doing the exact same thing with someone else. 'So you're saying that he's been talking to other women online while he's been with me?'

'I don't know about other women, plural. Apparently this thing started a few months ago, but he only confided in me last week.'

'Did you tell Liv?'

'Yes. But—'

'She knew about this and she didn't tell me?' I cry. 'Some friend!'

'No, you don't understand,' Miles interjects. 'I only told Liv after we found out Austin had gone missing.'

'Oh, well, that's all right then!' I snap. 'She should have told me the minute she knew. The second.'

'She begged me to tell you, but I promised Austin I wouldn't. Liv and I have been fighting about it all week. It's why we haven't been messaging you. It's unforgivable, I know. I'm so, so sorry, Stella.' His eyes redden and he keeps looking down instead of at me.

I want to shake him.

'I'm sorry, I'm *sorry*.' Miles rubs his face. 'I told him not to meet up with her. That it wasn't worth it. I asked him why he was going through with the wedding, but he said that he still loved you. That he would never throw away what you had. But he also said that he had to meet Serafina. Just to—'

'Serafina.'

'Yeah, sorry, that's her name. He wanted to meet her in person. To see . . .' Miles tails off.

'To see if she was any better than me.' I finish his sentence.

'*No!* He wasn't planning on doing anything.'

'How noble of him.' My voice is shaking. 'But he obviously has done something. He's met up with her and now . . . what? They've gone off together into the sunset. Was that the plan? To run off like a pair of lovesick kids?'

'Not at all. He wasn't planning to do anything with her. I promise you. I think it was simply curiosity.'

'Maybe he's fallen madly in love with her.' My head is hot with tears, my hands trembling so violently my wrists hurt.

'I don't know,' Miles replies. 'I'm sorry, I don't know.'

I end the call without saying goodbye and then I go down to my parents' room, my feet bare, my mind feeling as though it's completely divorced from my body. I wouldn't normally tell my mum and dad the ins and outs of my relationship with Austin, knowing how they feel about him, but we've gone way past that point now. I need their support. I need to know that loyalty and trust still exist.

'We have to let the police know about this,' Dad says, after I tell them about Miles's revelation.

To his credit, Dad doesn't comment on Austin's betrayal of me. Doesn't give me any hint of an 'I told you so' look.

My face is blotchy with tears that had already started falling unchecked while I told my parents. My emotions are raw and bloody at the thought of him wanting to be with another woman. 'What about Rob and Vicki?' I say, my voice thick. 'What if they don't believe Miles's story?'

'Why wouldn't they believe it?' Dad asks.

'I hate to say this, Stella,' Mum says, taking my hand, 'but if I were Austin's parents, I'd want to believe it. And I'd take this as good news.'

'*What?* I can't believe you just said that, Mum. I know you're not Austin's greatest fans, but—'

Mum holds her hands up to ward off my tirade. 'I only mean, because if Austin really is off with another woman, then, I suppose, at least he's not lying at the bottom of a canal.'

Dad stands up, his face darkening. 'If he *has* gone off with another woman while you're on your honeymoon, then he'll wish he *was* at the bottom of a canal after I've dealt with him.'

'I know it's no comfort to you, love,' Mum continues, giving Dad a look, 'but as a parent it might give them hope that he's not hurt or worse.'

'That little dickhead,' Dad snarls. 'If he's put you through all this just so he can—'

'Phil, that's enough. You're upsetting Stella.'

I swipe the tears from my face with the back of my hand. 'So should we tell Rob and Vicki, or not?' I ask.

'We have to,' Mum replies.

'Can Miles send us any proof of this affair?' Dad says. 'Like messages or . . .'

'I'll ask him.'

'And then we'll go straight to the cop shop,' Dad adds. 'Hopefully, if it's an online thing, like Miles said, then the police might be able to trace the woman. Get an address.'

My heart is thumping so hard my ears are throbbing and my whole body has started to shake.

'Oh, love.' Mum guides me to the bed and makes me sit. She takes a seat next to me and wraps her arms around me while I cry.

'This was supposed to be the happiest time of my life,' I sob. 'I thought we were in love. I thought I was his everything. Why did he even marry me if he wanted to go off having affairs? What was the point? I don't get it!'

'I know, I know,' Mum says, rocking me gently as I lean into her.

'I'll kill him,' Dad mutters. 'I'll bloody kill him when I get my hands on him.'

'You're not helping, Phil,' Mum says.

But, actually, I feel the same way as my dad. I sit up and take a breath, clenching and unclenching my fists. I hate Austin for what he's done. I feel like death is too good for him. His selfishness has destroyed my happiness and caused misery and pain for his family and mine. What kind of egocentric prick meets up with their online lover when they're on their honeymoon? All the fear and anxiety I've been feeling over the past few days is coalescing into a raging anger that has nowhere to go.

I bang out a quick text to Miles, telling him to send me screenshots of any messages he might have about the affair. And then I get to my feet. 'Let's tell Austin's parents now. Then we can let Gallini know.' Not that I'm particularly looking forward to seeing the police officer again after yesterday's stressful interview.

◆ ◆ ◆

Vicki and Rob are visibly shocked after we break the news. Silent at first. Unsure how to react.

'What does this mean?' Vicki asks finally.

'You think he's gone off with another woman?' Rob asks, confusion spreading across his features. 'No. No, I don't believe it. That's bollocks, excuse my language. Stella, you can't believe that. He loves you. He's just married you, for goodness' sake. Miles must have the wrong end of the stick. Or he's got some other agenda. Maybe it's Miles who's having the affairs and he's blaming Austin to divert attention.'

'I wish that was true,' I reply. 'But Miles has just sent me these screenshots of Austin's chats with him. Talking about how he was going to meet up with this Serafina woman while we were in Venice.' My voice breaks. 'It's horrible!'

Vicki's shaking her head and crying. 'No, no, this all feels wrong. Austin wouldn't do that, he wouldn't.'

'If he did go off to meet her . . .' Mum says to Vicki gently. 'It probably means he's safe.'

'Or he's been catfished,' Rob says darkly.

'What's that?' Mum asks.

Rob looks from her to his wife and shakes his head. 'Nothing. I shouldn't have said it.'

'Rob . . .' The distress on Vicki's face morphs to fear. 'Answer Lindsay. What is that?'

Rob grits his teeth. 'I saw a documentary about it. It's where someone creates a fake online identity. They pretend to be someone else to trick the other person out of money, or . . .' Rob leaves the end of the sentence hanging.

'You think he's been lured somewhere?' Vicki asks, her voice shaking. 'What if he's been taken by someone . . . or worse? We need to go to the police, right now.'

'I thought it might be something like that,' Dad says, 'but I didn't want to worry anyone by speculating.'

Vicki chokes out a sob. 'What if he got in some kind of trouble and made up that story about Serafina as a cry for help? Maybe she's blackmailing him or something and he was forced into meeting up with her.'

We stare at one another, everyone appalled by the possibilities and implications.

Chapter Thirty-Two

THEN

I'm standing at the bus stop making small talk about the glorious weather with Mrs Jefferson, who lives at number 42, when I get a text from Millie. Apparently, there's a burst pipe at the studio, so all classes have been cancelled today.

I'm actually quite disappointed as I have my seniors' class this morning, and we always have a laugh. I know they'll be disappointed too. If it were up to me, I'd have suggested using the nearby park instead, but Millie's already informed everyone of the cancellation.

I say goodbye to my neighbour, who's off to town to do her weekly shop, and head back home, wondering what to do with my unexpectedly free day. I think I'll give my room a bit of a spring clean and then maybe sit in the garden with my book. I never seem to have time to read these days so that will be a treat. Although it's Mum's morning off, so maybe we should do something together. Austin's busy at work this week, meeting new clients in Devon, otherwise I'd have suggested meeting up with him for lunch.

It's been a few weeks since the engagement party and thankfully I haven't laid eyes on Keri Wade since she showed up drunk.

I considered contacting her to try to come to some kind of truce, but after talking it through with Claudia and Liv, we decided it was probably best to leave well alone. I'm hoping that after Keri's embarrassing display at the Lewises', she's keeping a low profile. I'd feel sad for her if she wasn't always so aggressively mean.

I turn into our little road, enjoying the feel of the morning sun on my skin, thinking about how this time next year I'll have left home and be a married woman living on the other side of town with my gorgeous husband. Everything feels so grown-up all of a sudden.

Just as I reach the house, a bank of cloud blots the sun, a northerly breeze making me shiver. I open the front door, rubbing away the goosebumps on my arms, and head straight through to the kitchen, where Mum's cleaning the countertops, still in her dressing gown.

'Hey, Mum.'

'Hi,' she replies, without turning around.

'There's a burst pipe at work, so today's classes are cancelled,' I say, wondering why Mum didn't ask why I'm back. In fact, she's acting quite strangely, kind of hunched over. 'Mum? You okay?'

'What? Yes. That's a shame about the pipe.' Her voice sounds thick. She sniffs a couple of times and reaches for a square of kitchen paper.

'Mum, is something the matter?'

She still hasn't turned around. 'Just a bit of annoying hay fever.'

'You don't get hay fever.' I cross the room and try to look at her face, but she turns away, pretending to clean another area of already pristine countertop.

'Mum! What's wrong?'

'Nothing.' She swallows and sniffs, widening her eyes as she turns to me. 'I'm fine, just having a moment.'

'What moment?' Seeing Mum like this is making me nervous. She never cries. 'Are you and Dad okay? Did you have an argument?'

'What?' She smiles. 'No, nothing like that.'

'Nana?' My heart stops for a second.

'Nana's fine. Still giving the staff at the nursing home hell as far as I know.'

'So what's wrong?'

'Nothing. Like I said, I was just having a moment. Being silly. Shall we have a cup of tea?'

'Mum. Tell me what's up. I'm not going to pretend that you crying alone in the kitchen is nothing. You've always been there for me, so now I'm here for you, okay?'

Mum puts down the kitchen cloth and shakes her head, staring at her slippers. A tear drips off her nose.

'Right . . .' I take her arm and steer her to the kitchen table. 'Sit down. I'm making tea, and you're going to tell me exactly what's upset you.' Although I have a horrible sinking feeling it might be something to do with that notification I saw on Dad's phone a couple of months ago.

My parents have already transferred the ten thousand pounds into our wedding account, and it's almost all been used up as we needed to put down deposits for the venue, the flowers, the band and everything else. We've had to accept that Austin's parents will also be chipping in a sizeable amount. But I'm not going to tell my parents about that.

Mum fiddles with a strand of her ash-brown hair, wrapping it around her finger so tightly it looks like she's cutting off her circulation. 'I don't . . . your dad won't be happy if I talk to you about this.'

'Well then, we won't tell him,' I reply, lifting the kettle to check there's enough water.

'And I don't want you to worry either,' she adds.

'Too late,' I reply, switching on the kettle and reaching for two mugs. 'And I'll worry more if you don't tell me.'

The kettle boils and I make two strong teas, bringing the mugs over to the table and sitting opposite Mum, waiting for her to elaborate.

'Oh, love, I hate having to tell you this.' She blows her nose.

'Whatever it is, we'll sort it out.'

'You sound like me.' She gives a short, strangled laugh.

'I learned from the best,' I reply, giving what I hope is an encouraging smile.

'Well, the long and the short of it, Stella, is that there was no savings account for your wedding. Your dad and I . . . we borrowed the money.'

I'd already guessed that must be the reason for her tears, but it's still a shock to hear her confirm it. To know that my initial suspicion was correct. 'I wish you hadn't done that,' I say. 'I mean, I really am so grateful, but the last thing I wanted was to cause you and Dad any stress.'

'I know, love. It's not your fault. I told him not to do it,' she says through gritted teeth. 'I begged him. Sorry if that sounds harsh. There's nothing I'd like more than to be able to pay for my only daughter's wedding.' She breaks off and takes a breath. 'But we can't afford it. Not in the long term. Not for the next *seven* years. The thought of it is too much. Your dad's already taking on extra shifts, and I'm going to have to do the same.'

'Oh, Mum.' I get up to give her a hug.

'It's bad enough now, but once you move out . . .'

'You won't have my rent.' I finish her sentence.

She throws her hands up in the air. 'So now you know. Your parents aren't so perfect after all.' She gives a bitter laugh and my heart feels as though it's breaking.

'You'll always be perfect to me,' I reply. 'I love you, Mum. And I'm really sorry that you're in this predicament because of me.'

'It's not your fault, Stella. You never asked us for the money.'

'I'd call the whole wedding off if it would make a difference,' I say. 'But we've already paid out the deposits.'

'Don't be daft,' Mum says. 'It's supposed to be your happy day, and we've put a blight on it.'

'No you haven't. You tried to do a nice thing.'

'The road to hell is paved with good intentions,' Mum says. 'And it's so crazy, because you know what your father's views are on getting into debt.'

'Yeah.'

'But this was something he really wanted to do for you. I hope you also know that we absolutely cannot tell him that you found out about this.' Mum wraps her hands around her mug and blows across the surface of her tea.

'Why not?' I reply, frustrated. 'Don't you think it's better to get it all out in the open? He can't jeopardise your financial security. We need to sort this out. Please, let me fix it, Mum. You can soften Dad up while I speak to Austin's parents.'

'If you go cap in hand to the Lewises behind your father's back, he'll never forgive you,' Mum says. 'Or me.'

I shake my head, but I know she's right. I don't know why I even bothered suggesting it. If only Austin hadn't told my dad that he could provide me with a better life. That comment really got under Dad's skin. I know Austin was only trying to let Dad know that he was going to treat me well, but his choice of words was so unfortunate. 'Okay, fine. We'll come up with another way. In the meantime, I'll give you more of my wages, and you can tell Dad you've picked up an extra shift, or had a pay rise or something.'

'I can't ask you to do that, Stella. This is our mess, not yours.'

'Of course you can, Mum. It's my wedding that's caused all this grief.' *That and Dad's pride*, I add silently, sipping my tea.

If only I could ask the Lewises to pay for the whole thing, like they wanted. They could easily afford it. But Dad would be horrified. It would be bad enough if he discovered I knew about the loan. He'd feel diminished. Not to mention furious at the fact that Mum told me about it. I could put up with Dad's displeasure. But it's not fair on Mum, so I'll keep quiet. For now at least.

Chapter Thirty-Three

NOW

After another night of terrible nightmares where I'm being chased down dark alleyways, my limbs leaden, my voice missing, I wake to the sound of frantic knocking and my mum's voice calling through the door. For one blissful moment, I think I'm back home in my childhood bedroom and Mum's waking me for work. But then reality washes over me like an icy wave closing over my head. I'm in Venice on my honeymoon. Without my husband.

I drag myself from the mess of tangled sheets and run a hand through my sweaty hair as I open the door.

Mum comes in, wide-eyed and jittery. 'Thank goodness you're here,' she says, taking in the dark, shuttered room.

'Where else would I be?' I croak. 'Ugh, my mouth tastes horrible, I need to brush my teeth.'

'I've been ringing and texting, knocking on the door,' she replies. 'I thought something had happened to you.'

'Why? What's going on?'

'You need to get dressed. The police are downstairs, wanting to talk to you.'

I'm pulled into alertness. 'They're here now? What's the time?' I blink and check my phone to see streams of missed messages.

'Quarter past nine,' Mum replies, her whole body radiating anxiety.

'I overslept,' I say, giving myself a shake. 'Okay, where are they? In the lobby?'

'Yes.'

'Give me a few minutes to get ready.'

Five minutes later, I'm riding down in the lift with Mum by my side. In the lobby, the Lewises are sitting with my dad. Seated opposite them are Gallini in his uniform and Fiore, smart as usual in grey jeans, a pale-pink shirt and a fitted navy jacket. Ordinarily, keeping people waiting would have me apologising and feeling terribly guilty, but right now I can't worry about that. My adrenaline spikes, same as it does every time I see the officers, wondering – and dreading – what news they have.

Last night, with both sets of parents sitting anxiously nearby, I called Gallini to tell him about Miles's revelation – that Austin had been talking to an Italian woman online. Even thinking about it makes me sick to my stomach. Gallini said they would look into it, and that they would call Miles directly to get the information straight from his mouth. I guess they thought he may have been holding some of the details back from me, in case they were too upsetting.

After brief hellos, Fiore starts talking. 'We wanted to let you know that after speaking to your friend Miles Grey, our tech guy has had some luck with the dating app company. We've managed to find Austin's online relationship with this person calling herself Serafina.'

Hearing the name makes me flinch. 'Did Austin use his real name?' I ask.

'No,' Fiore replies.

'What name did he use?' I ask.

'I can't disclose that information at the moment.'

'We're his family,' Vicki says. 'We have a right to know. What if this woman was catfishing? What if she's hurt him?'

'Let's not jump to any conclusions,' Gallini says. 'I know this is hard, and you want answers, but right now the best thing you can do is let us do our job.'

'So what are you going to do?' Rob asks, sitting forward on the sofa and fixing Gallini with an intense stare.

'We'll discover the identity of the woman,' Fiore replies. 'And then we'll track her down and try to get to the bottom of where your son is.'

Rob gives a single nod and gets to his feet. 'Good. How long do you think that will take?'

'Not long, if she's a real person. If not . . .' Fiore shrugs.

'What do you mean, "if she's a real person"?' I ask.

'She could be a fake profile.'

My breathing goes shallow and my palms are suddenly damp with sweat. 'Why would someone do that? What would they want with my husband?'

'Like my colleague said,' Fiore replies, standing up, 'let's not worry about *what if this* and *what if that*. Let's wait and see what our investigation turns up.'

The officers say goodbye, and the five of us are left in the lobby, reeling from their information.

'I can't stand this,' Vicki says, letting her head drop forward and gripping the underside of the sofa. 'It doesn't feel real. This is Austin, our son. We know him. All this meeting up with women from the internet – that's not him. It's not. Something's happened to him, someone's done this, made it look like he's a bad person when he's not. I really think that Bart could be behind this.'

Rob nods grimly. 'I agree. It's too much of a coincidence that Austin's suing Bart, and now Bart has shown up in Venice.'

'Exactly!' Vicki cries. 'Why aren't the police pursuing that line of inquiry?' She turns to me. 'What do you think, Stella? You know that Austin worships the ground you walk on. He'd never jeopardise your relationship for some fling with a woman he'd never even met!'

'What about Miles?' I say. 'He's Austin's best friend. Why would he lie about that?'

Vicki frowns for a moment. 'Maybe . . . maybe Miles and Bart are in on it together.' She pushes her fingertips against her forehead. 'Bart could have . . . I don't know, he could have paid Miles to lie for him.'

I listen to Vicki making excuses for her son, searching for ways to prove that he's innocent, and I don't bother trying to correct her any more. I can't cope with the pain and humiliation of any of it.

None of us says anything further, the weight of Austin's betrayal hanging between us. First is the pain of not knowing what's happened to him. Second is the realisation that whatever did happen to him, or whatever he did, there's no good outcome for *me*. Because in either scenario, he left to meet up with another woman.

I stand abruptly and leave the lobby on shaky legs, weaving across the grey marble floor, past the reception, avoiding the gaze of Paola and the rest of the staff, and heading straight to the lifts.

My parents catch me up and we stand in silence, waiting for one of the lift doors to open. A memory flashes through me of when I was a child and we'd sometimes go to Beales department store in Bournemouth for a coffee on the top floor next to the toy department. We'd wait on the ground floor in the perfume department next to a bank of about four or five posh lifts, and we'd have to guess which one would arrive first. Dad always seemed to get it right and we'd accuse him of having inside information. The store isn't there any more. It's been turned into flats.

Here, the second lift arrives with a ping and the doors open. But no one cares about guessing games today. Not when there's a real-life mystery to be uncovered that involves my new husband, and an affair with either a beautiful Italian woman or an unknown shadow.

Chapter Thirty-Four

THEN

It's today. I'm getting married *today*. I know most of my friends stay over in fancy hotels the night before their wedding but, conscious of money, I insisted on getting ready at home. I said it would feel nicer, more meaningful. I could tell Mum was touched. But she's also been quite stressed, rushing around, beautifying our little house before my friends arrive.

I've told her not to worry, that Liv and Claudia aren't bothered about how our house looks, but Mum wouldn't listen, and has almost had a nervous breakdown with all the extra work she's given herself. Every time I've tried to help, she's told me to relax, that I need to be rested before my big day. It's been exhausting, and I half wish I'd chosen the hotel option just to save Mum's nerves. Dad's been working all the hours God sends, so he's been knackered when he gets in.

But here we are, all in one piece – just – on the morning of my wedding, on what should be the happiest day of my life. And yet I can't stop thinking about the amount of money my parents have spent on this and how they're going to pay it all back. I actually feel physically sick at the thought. Or maybe it's just pre-wedding jitters kicking in and I'm focusing on my parents to take my mind off my anxiety. At least, I hope it's just that, and not the other thing I'm trying to ignore.

The past few months have been stressful. I made Millie's day by accepting her offer to increase my number of weekly classes, which has meant I've been able to slip Mum extra cash each month to help with the loan, easing her worries. But, even with that, there's still nothing left over in my bank account. So, what should have been a fun time of meeting up with friends and getting excited about the wedding has instead seen me working longer hours and turning down invitations to go out because I don't have the funds, the time or the energy.

The knock-on effect of accepting Millie's offer has also seen the quality of my teaching suffer because I don't have as much time to hone my choreography. Thankfully, my students still seem to be enjoying themselves, and the popularity of my classes hasn't diminished – *yet*. But my own enjoyment has plummeted. I'm hoping things will get better after the wedding. But I'm also terrified that they won't.

'Come on, sleepyhead.' Mum knocks on the door. 'Time to get up. It's your big day!' She pushes open the door and comes in with a tray of breakfast for me – toast, fresh berries, orange juice and a mug of tea. Dad follows her into my room and eases open the curtains a little, making me screw up my face against the light.

'It's sunny,' I say, sitting up and hoping it's a good omen. 'What's the time?'

'Eight o'clock,' Dad replies.

Mum places the tray on my lap and hovers at my side, while Dad sits on the end of the bed. They're both in their dressing gowns, their familiar faces a balm for my nerves. I feel the years concertina out behind me. Aside from my time at university, this is the only home I've known. And today is the end of that chapter.

I'm praying and hoping for a wonderful new life with Austin, but I'll miss the unshakeable comfort of being with my mum and dad. The knowledge that these two people love me more than they love themselves. Leaving home will be like unbuckling a safety belt and leaping into the unknown. I think if I'd moved out when I was younger, I wouldn't have thought too deeply about it. But leaving now, combined with my wedding day, seems momentous.

My parents are lost in thought too, and I feel like I should say something.

Dad beats me to it. 'Well,' he says. 'Your mum and I are very proud of you, Stella.' He clears his throat. 'You're the best daughter a parent could have, and we want you to have the happiest life. But we also want you to know that we'll always be here for you, if you need us.'

My skin tingles at his words. My heart expanding.

'Oh, Phil, you big softie,' Mum says, giving him a watery-eyed smile before turning back to me. 'But he's right, Stella.'

'I love you guys,' I manage to squeak.

'We love you too,' Mum replies. 'Okay.' She claps her hands. 'Enough of this. We've got a wonderful day ahead of us so, Stella, you eat up your breakfast while your dad and I get dressed.'

The morning rushes past too fast for me to savour. Liv and Claudia arrive to help me get ready, while Dad pops to the nursing home to collect Nana. Mum spoils us all with snacks and praise, and then, before I've had a chance to catch my breath, the cars arrive and we're ready to head to the priory for the ceremony.

I walk down the stairs in my ivory lace wedding dress with its boned corset and full skirt. It was made by one of Mum's friends, who copied a dress I'd seen in a bridal magazine. It turned out better than I could have ever imagined for a fraction of the cost and I feel like an actual princess.

My friends sigh, Mum takes photos and Dad actually cries, too choked up to speak.

But minutes later, as we cruise through the pretty streets of Christchurch towards the priory, I feel like I'm driving blind towards a cliff in a car with no brakes. And I don't know if that's normal. I don't think you're supposed to feel like this on your wedding day.

Chapter Thirty-Five

NOW

Up in my room, my parents look on helplessly as I sit on the bed and pull my knees up to my chest. I can't help thinking back to my wedding day last week. In fact, I realise it was exactly a week ago today that I was walking down the aisle towards my handsome husband, whose eyes lit up with joy when he saw me. Who made vows that sounded so sincere. Who told me he would love and cherish and protect me forever. But the reality is that those vows were worthless scraps of paper to be tossed by the wind into a muddy puddle and stomped upon.

'Stella, love,' Dad says, sitting beside me.

I don't reply. I just stare at the tops of my knees.

'I think we should go home,' he says.

'Home?' I echo. The word sounds alien to my ears. *Home.* I consider what it will be like there now. Back in my childhood house, living next door to my childhood friend, in the same town where I grew up with all the same people. Who will soon discover what's happened. Everything will be different when I go back. Me included. And not in a good way.

'I should have taken that job,' I blurt out.

'What job?' Dad asks gently. I feel him looking at Mum, wondering if I'm losing my marbles.

'You know – that *job*. The one you told me I'd regret turning down.' I huff out a breath. 'Touring as a dancer. If I'd taken it, I probably would never have stayed with Austin. I'd have been travelling the world, meeting new people, making a name for myself. You were right, Dad, about the job, about Austin, about all of it . . . and I was very, very wrong.'

'You can't start going through all the what-ifs,' Mum says. 'I know it's tempting to play that game, but we're here in the now so we have to deal with what's in front of us, not look back at a life we never lived.'

'Your mother's right.' Dad stands up. 'There's nothing you can do here, Stella. There's no point going out searching for him any more. Not after what he's done.'

'And what if it was someone catfishing?' I ask. 'What if they've done something bad to him? Something terrible.'

'Look,' Dad says. 'If he'd planned to meet up with some other woman on his own honeymoon, for Christ's sake, then whatever's happened . . . well, that's on him.'

'*Phil*,' Mum says, a warning tone in her voice.

'*What?*' Dad replies. 'He's broken our Stella's heart. Humiliated her. Made a mockery of their marriage.'

'All right, Dad, we get the message,' I snap.

'Sorry, love. But he doesn't deserve our tears or our energy. We need to get you back home. Think about what you're going to do next.'

'I can't think about any of that! I can't even think about the next second, let alone the rest of my life.'

'Fine, no, of course not. I just mean, well, we need to get you home, away from all this . . . nastiness.'

Like I just told Dad, right now I feel numb, incapable of making any decisions. All I want to do is sink into my bed and sleep for a thousand years. That decides me. I uncurl my body and straighten my legs. 'Yes. Okay, let's go home.'

Both my parents sag with relief.

Dad manages to book us on an evening flight to Heathrow. He goes down to speak to Paola to let her know we'll be checking out today, while Mum helps me pack. It's not straightforward because I'm not sure what to do with Austin's stuff.

'Keep it all in his case,' Mum says briskly, 'and I'll take it down to the Lewises to look after.'

'What about you, Mum?' I ask. 'Don't you and Dad need to pack?'

'We didn't bring much, and we didn't unpack anything other than our pyjamas and a few toiletries.' She starts making up the bed.

'You don't need to do that, Mum. They're going to wash all the bedding once I've gone.'

'Force of habit,' she says, reluctantly letting go of the sheets.

'And Rob and Vicki?' I say, feeling queasy at the thought of abandoning them. 'We need to let them know what we're doing.'

'They'll understand,' Mum says grimly. 'And if they don't, well, that's too bad.'

I know Mum and Dad are just being protective of me, but I can't help feeling bad for Austin's parents. He hasn't only hurt me; he's shattered them too.

Finally, an hour later, we're packed and ready to leave, standing on the dock in the lemony sunshine, a cool breeze whispering off the water, ruffling our clothes and whipping my hair in front of my face as we wait for our water taxi to arrive. As we wait to flee the most beautiful city in the world.

Our flight isn't for hours, but now that we've made the decision to go, we just want to leave as quickly as possible.

I gaze down at the rippling turquoise surface of the Grand Canal, at the tourists queuing for their half-hour gondola rides that will stay imprinted in their memories for a lifetime, at the medieval palaces and churches that we never got to visit. I view it all through the lens of my devastated heart.

Vicki and Rob were surprisingly understanding about us needing to go home. They promised to keep us in the loop, although part of me doesn't want updates. Why should I have to hear about his infidelity? I just need to put the whole sorry business behind me. I'm not even considering the legal implications of still being Mrs Stella Lewis. Dad has already broached the subject of a possible annulment, but I'm not getting into all that now. All I'm thinking about is crawling into my single bed at home and staying there.

A boat skims towards the dock and I take a breath, mentally preparing myself for the journey ahead. But as it draws closer, I can see that it's not our water taxi. It's a police boat. On it stand the familiar figures of Fiore and Gallini, their faces unsmiling as they look our way, exuding an atmosphere of seriousness.

My whole body starts to quiver, and I suddenly feel icy cold.

Something has happened.

Something bad.

Chapter Thirty-Six

NOW

The launch draws alongside us, and Gallini loops a rope over one of the posts before stepping on to the dock and holding out a hand to help Fiore up.

Her gaze travels down to our cases. 'You are leaving,' she says, like an accusation rather than an observation.

Dad squares his shoulders. 'After what we heard about our daughter's husband meeting up with another woman, we decided it was best to go home. Obviously, Rob and Vicki Lewis are staying on.'

A 'blink and you'd miss it' glance passes between Gallini and Fiore.

'Is there somewhere we can talk?' Gallini asks me. He looks somehow different this afternoon. More unsure of himself.

'What's happened?' Mum asks. 'Have you found Austin?'

'Are his parents at the hotel now?' Fiore asks, without answering Mum's question. 'It's better if we speak to all of you at once.'

'We can go up to their room,' I say, sounding more normal than I feel, my heart pounding like a battering ram against my ribcage.

A taxi pulls up to the dock, its young driver looking up at us, his gaze landing on Dad. 'Mr Goldsmith? Airport?'

Dad peels some euros from his wallet, reaches down and hands them to the man. 'Sorry, we have to cancel for now. I hope this covers it.'

The driver does a quick count of the notes and looks up again, his eyes drawn to Gallini's uniform. He gives Dad a dissatisfied nod and takes his mobile from his pocket, no doubt trying to arrange another fare.

We walk with the police officers into the hotel, wheeling our cases back through the lobby. Mum calls ahead to Vicki, explaining that we're on our way up with the police. I wonder if their news will be minor enough that my parents and I will still be able to leave. That we'll be able to make this evening's flight. I'm craving the safety of home right now. But from Fiore and Gallini's manner, I'm already anticipating the worst.

Up on the fourth floor, Rob and Vicki are waiting, white-faced, in the doorway of their suite. They move back to let us in, and there's a moment of awkwardness as the suitcases become wedged together in the door. Gallini lifts them easily, and places them out of the way by one of the huge armoires. If we'd been thinking straight, we'd have left them down in reception.

'Please, sit.' Fiore gestures to the seating area as though this is her suite.

We do as she asks. I sit next to the Lewises on the chaise longue while my parents sit in the club chairs, angling them towards the officers, who both remain standing. The balcony doors are open, bringing in a fresh breeze and the blurred sound of chatter and laughter from below.

Vicki and Rob's hands are threaded together so tightly their knuckles are white.

'Have you found him?' Rob asks, his voice barely above a whisper.

Fiore speaks. 'Earlier today, we pulled a man's body from the canal.'

'Oh my God, no!' Vicki cries, shaking her head.

Fiore continues, 'It was found floating in the Grand Canal close to Santa Lucia railway station in the early hours of this morning.'

'Is it him?' Rob asks. 'Is it Austin?'

'The body will need to be identified,' Fiore says.

Her words float over me without sinking in.

Austin's parents are clinging on to one another, dry-eyed. Shocked.

'It won't be him,' Rob mutters. 'It won't be him.'

'Stella,' Gallini says, 'I'm sorry, but will you come with us now to the mortuary to identify the body?'

My throat constricts. I can't seem to speak.

'We're coming,' Vicki says, letting go of her husband and standing up, wiping imaginary dust from her jeans. 'Like my husband says, it's probably not even him.'

'We can take three of you,' Gallini says.

'Me, Rob and Stella,' Vicki says. She looks at me beseechingly. 'You'll come, won't you?'

'Do you need us to be there too, Stella?' Dad says. 'We can take a taxi, if you give us the address.'

I swallow, finding my voice. 'No, Dad, it's okay. I'll go with Rob and Vicki. But you won't . . . you're not going home yet, are you?'

'Of course not!' Mum replies. 'We'll speak to Paola on the desk, see if we can get our rooms back.'

The journey to the mortuary only takes an hour or so – a short way by boat and the rest by car – but it feels as though it lasts forever. I stare out of the window the whole way without seeing anything. Fiore drives and Gallini sits in the passenger seat. They talk to one another in Italian, occasionally switching to English to ask if we're comfortable – too hot, too cold, thirsty etcetera – until finally we arrive.

I get out of the car, my eyes scratchy, my face dry, aching from stress. Rob helps Vicki out of the vehicle. We're all mute with shock as we walk into the building with the officers. I can't feel the ground beneath my shoes. I don't even feel like I'm here. Are we really doing this?

We enter the building through a set of glass doors and walk along several empty corridors, the soles of our shoes squeaking, until we reach a metal bench outside a closed door, where we come to a stop.

Fiore tells us to wait here for a moment. She knocks and enters the room, and I shiver, wondering if that's *the room*.

Rob walks over to a vending machine a little way along the hall and gets a bottle of water. He glugs half of it and offers the rest to Vicki, and then to me, but we both shake our heads, even though I'm as thirsty as hell.

The three of us stand by the door with Gallini. Waiting. Everything and nothing spins through my head.

Moments later, the door opens and Fiore exits the room, accompanied by a tall man with greying hair, in dark-red scrubs.

My hands have started trembling.

'Please,' the man says softly, 'come in whenever you're ready.'

Chapter Thirty-Seven
NOW

Vicki and Rob hold hands as I follow them into the room, where a body lies on a steel gurney covered by a sheet. Vicki slows and reaches for my hand too. I thought my fingers were cold, but hers are icy. The coroner ushers us to the side of the body.

'Are you ready?' he asks gently.

Rob nods and Vicki's hand squeezes mine. I want to scream, *No, I'm not ready, I don't want to see!* But, instead, I nod too. Vicki gasps back a sob and gives her nod.

The coroner peels back the sheet to uncover the face.

'NO!' Vicki's legs give way and Rob has to hold her up.

My hand flies to my throat and I let out a whimper. It's him. It's Austin. But it's Austin from a nightmare. Not the charismatic, handsome Austin who was my boyfriend for four years. This version is bloated and waxy. His skin a blue-grey colour, like a life-size model created for a horror movie. I don't want to look any more, but I can't seem to drag my gaze away. My whole body is stiff, like his.

Vicki is moaning in Rob's arms. Wailing, sobbing, noises that don't sound human. It's painful to listen to.

I can't stay in here. I walk out of the room and sit back on the bench, my hands gripping my knees, Austin's inanimate face burned into my brain. I already know that image is going to stay with me for the rest of my life. It's going to rob me of my appetite and stop me sleeping at night. It's going to torment my waking hours and haunt my dreams.

'I'm so sorry for your loss.'

I look up to see Gallini offering his condolences, his eyes soft with compassion, but I'm too shocked to reply.

Fiore stands further down the corridor, speaking to someone on the phone. I think about the fact that this is simply a working day for them. They must have to deal with this kind of thing on a regular basis. Witnessing death. Watching lives shatter. Breaking bad news. But then . . . they also get to catch the bad guys.

I'm vaguely aware of Austin's parents finally coming out of that awful room, Rob supporting Vicki as she staggers through the door.

'No, no, no, no, no,' she cries over and over, louder and louder, until the words disintegrate into sobs.

Rob looks broken. He guides Vicki to the bench, where we sit either side of her, leaning into her, frozen, like an art installation on grief.

'I'm sorry for your loss,' Fiore says to us. 'Thank you for coming here. It's not an easy thing.'

'Who did this?' I ask, looking up at her. 'Was it deliberate or an accident? Can you tell? Do you think it was the woman he was talking to online? Why would she have done this?'

'There is some further information that we need to tell you,' Fiore replies.

Rob and I look up at her, and even Vicki quietens her sobs to hear what the detective has to say.

'The coroner has identified a puncture wound in Austin's side that indicates he may have been stabbed.'

'He was murdered?' Rob cries. 'My God!'

'*Who?* Who could have killed our son?' Vicki wails. 'This Serafina, or whoever she really is? You have to find her!'

'You'll catch whoever did this to our boy, won't you?' Rob croaks. 'You have to make them pay. What about Bart? What about . . .' He breaks off, and chokes out a sob.

'Please don't worry about that,' Fiore replies. 'We've already alerted the public prosecutor. They'll head up a team and work with the UK police to complete a thorough investigation, interviewing everyone involved. In the meantime, we'll take you back to your hotel whenever you're ready to leave.'

The journey back is bleak. Rob and Vicki seem to have diminished in size since we saw Austin's body. The life is draining from them as surely as it's drained from their son.

And I . . . I don't know how to feel. Austin was the love of my life. My husband. The person I trusted most in the world, aside from my parents. But he betrayed me in the worst way possible. He made a mockery of our love. Of our marriage.

I message my parents to tell them that it's Austin, and that the police think he was murdered. I also let them know that I'm not sure what time I'll see them tonight. That I want to be alone for a while.

Back at the hotel, I leave the police boat and the Lewises to their private grief. I walk alongside the Grand Canal, threading my way through the tourists, allowing my mind to stay numb. I have months to process this. Years. The rest of my life, even. So a short time of nothingness will be a reprieve from what's to come.

I walk and I walk and I walk.

As darkness falls, gold and silver lights from the buildings reflect on the water, shimmering on the surface, gilding the darkness beneath.

This is my honeymoon. And I'm a widow.

Chapter Thirty-Eight

THEN

I watch my new husband slip on his suit jacket and leave the hotel room, the door closing with a definitive clunk.

My phone shows that it's only 11.15 p.m., but it feels much later.

I touch my lips, thinking back to Austin's kisses. To his body against mine. To the promise of our night together. To the thought of our lives together. When he proposed to me last year, I didn't imagine it was possible to be so happy. How did a regular girl like me end up with a handsome, successful man like Austin Lewis? I sink back down against the pillow, my eyes wanting to close, my brain wanting to shut down.

But then I blink and stretch out my arms. I can't fall back to sleep. Not yet.

Not when I don't trust my new husband.

I get out of bed and quickly pull on jeans, a hoodie, a pair of trainers and a backpack. Lastly, I take the expensive blonde wig that's hidden in a bag in my suitcase, and carefully arrange it over my auburn locks. I place my regular phone on my bedside table, take my burner phone and leave the hotel.

With my head down, I walk quickly along the quiet streets towards the restaurant until, with a jolt of relief, I catch sight of Austin up ahead, striding purposefully across St Mark's Square, ignoring the lone flower seller and avoiding the late-night stragglers. I keep to the shadowed cloisters, hope vying with fear. Please let him be heading to the restaurant like he said he would.

I follow him to La Terrazza di Stella and I exhale, my jitters receding. So he wasn't lying about leaving his credit card at the restaurant. I slip into a narrow alley and wait for him to exit. I don't have to wait long. Hopefully, he'll head straight back to the hotel now. To me. And I can pretend that none of this ever happened.

He doesn't. Instead, he heads in the opposite direction to our hotel. I tell myself it's okay because he also said he was going to buy a phone charger from the supermarket. But would they even be open at this time? Surely he could wait until tomorrow morning.

I realise deep in my bones that it's hopeless. That my husband is not a trustworthy person. He's not the man I fell in love with. Even knowing what I know, I'm still giving him the benefit of the doubt. But it looks increasingly like he's going to fail me.

As he crosses a bridge, I hang back, watching him move easily, confidently, *eagerly*. Once he's on the other side, I follow, head down, my deep hood pulled forward, a sick feeling in my gut that's contracting into something harder.

Ten minutes later, I see Austin's silhouette at the end of an alleyway leading to a quiet stretch of canal. There's a lantern strung halfway along the passage casting a wash of gold down one wall, throwing light and shadows on to the ground.

I take a breath and enter the alley. My footsteps are muffled, my breaths loud and uneven. My palms are clammy and I want nothing more than to turn around and head back to the hotel. To crawl into bed and pretend to sleep. But I don't do any of that. I keep on walking.

As I draw closer, Austin turns to look at me, his face barely visible under the waning crescent moon and pinprick stars. For a brief moment, I think that it's not him. That I've been worrying for nothing. That my husband is back at the hotel and this is some other random stranger I've been following by mistake. The relief is so huge that I'm not even scared about being alone in an alley with a strange man. But then I realise that it's just the darkness playing tricks on me. Of course it's Austin.

The expression on his face is different to the one he normally uses on me these days. I remember this Austin from when we first met. His look of anticipation exudes hunger and desire. But as he gazes at me, his expression suddenly falters. Confusion clouds his features and, even as I stand here in the unfolding ruins of my life, I find myself taking a perverse pleasure in wrong-footing him like this.

'Stella, is that you? Are you wearing . . . a *wig*?'

I resist the urge to put a hand to my hair. 'What are you doing here, Austin?' My voice is surprisingly level.

'Were you following me?' He squints, his brow wrinkling, and then he looks beyond my shoulder to the alleyway.

We're standing on a narrow ledge alongside a canal that looks as black and thick as treacle on this dark night. The brick wall behind us is blank, the other side is studded with boarded-up windows. A yellow lantern hangs from the wall a couple of hundred yards away, throwing out a weak light.

'Looking for somebody?' I ask.

He gives himself a shake. 'What? No. I thought I saw someone in the alley, that's all. You still haven't told me why you're wearing that wig.' He reaches out to touch a lock, but I flinch away. 'I'm not complaining,' he says. 'It suits you. It's sexy.' He gives me a smile designed to make me want him.

'Why are you out here, Austin? I thought you were getting your credit card from the restaurant.'

'I was. I have. I came to get it and then got lost trying to find a supermarket. This city's like a maze.' He gives a short laugh.

'So why are you lurking at the end of an alleyway?'

'I'm not. I mean, I am, but that's because I realised it was a dead end, so I turned around and was about to walk back. But then I saw you walking towards me, and thought I'd better wait because it's not wide enough for two.'

'Liar,' I say, with just the barest whisper of lightness in my tone so that he's not sure if I'm angry or I'm joking.

He gives me a nervous look.

'I know what you're doing here, Austin,' I continue. 'You're waiting for your online lover.'

He snorts and folds his arms across his chest. 'You've got an overactive imagination, Stella. We're on our honeymoon. I think a lover is probably surplus to requirements. Come on, let's go back to the hotel, get some sleep, and you can apologise to me in the morning with make-up sex.'

I've suspected for a while now that Austin has been sleeping around. It hurts almost as much to hear him lie to my face like this. 'I know you're lying, Austin, so you can cut the crap.'

His face hardens. 'Stella, I don't know who you've been talking to, but—'

'I'll tell you who I've been talking to – Keri Wade, your charming ex-girlfriend.'

Austin rolls his eyes. 'Oh, well, that makes sense. It's not like Keri has an agenda or anything. Oh, wait a minute . . .' He places his forefinger on his chin. 'Yes she does. She's trying to split us up.'

I ignore his sarcasm and keep talking. 'I met her a few months ago to ask, no, to *plead* with her to stop trying to sabotage our relationship. Instead, she showed me proof that you two were still sleeping together.'

'That's ridiculous!' Austin snaps.

'Funny, that's what *I* said. I didn't want to believe it. But she showed me proof. Dates, texts, voicemails. You can deny it all you like, Austin, but I know it's true.'

His face grows redder, his fists clenching and unclenching by his side.

My throat aches as I let out all the stress and pain that I've been holding on to for the past few weeks. As I confront Austin with everything I've discovered about our sham of a relationship. 'Keri also told me that you're addicted to dating apps, that you're always meeting new women online. She said she didn't think you'd ever give it up, marriage or no marriage. I didn't believe her but it turns out she was right.'

'I can't believe you've fallen for her lies,' Austin says. But he doesn't sound so sure of himself any more. He rubs the back of his neck and shifts uneasily.

I think back to that horrible meeting with Keri at her apartment in December. She was so smug. So happy to break apart my world. I told her I didn't believe her, but she showed me his dating profile. He's been using a fake name, like he had with me when we met. Back then he was Firestarter888, now he's using Speedboatboy456. The photo was taken at an angle so it's not obvious that it's him. But I could tell that it was.

Keri told me she could give Austin what I couldn't – the freedom to be himself. To flirt and sleep around if that's what he wanted. As long as he always came back to her. She asked me if I would be prepared to give him that freedom. Because she said that's what it would take to keep a man like Austin happy. Either that, or turning a blind eye. Pretending that everything was just fine.

Even as my world was collapsing, I made up my mind then and there that I would never be that kind of woman. If Keri wanted him under those terms then she was welcome to him. But that wasn't the life I wanted.

Austin is still casting surreptitious glances down the passageway, and it's making me furious.

'Why do you keep looking down there?' I ask.

'Down where?'

'Down the alley, where else?'

'I'm not.'

'How many lies have you told me tonight, Austin?'

'I've had enough of this,' he mutters, his jaw clenching. 'Are we going back to the hotel, or not?'

'Are you looking for Serafina?' I ask.

He freezes and stares at me like a rat in a trap.

Chapter Thirty-Nine

THEN

'What did you say?' Austin asks.

'You heard me. I asked if you were looking for Serafina.'

He swallows, his face a shade paler than it was a moment ago. 'Who?'

I give a bitter laugh. 'I hoped you wouldn't come here tonight. I really hoped that after we were married, that after we'd made love tonight, you would have left all your cheating behind you.'

'I don't know what you think you know, Stella, but you're mistaken. This is just Keri putting ideas in your head.'

'Just. Stop.' I stare at my husband. This stranger who's been my everything for so many years.

He shakes his head, trying to look outraged, like he's the one being wronged by his overly jealous wife, but I can tell he knows the game is up. 'Stella, you've got this all wrong. If you'll just—'

'I'm Serafina,' I say.

Austin falls silent, his lips clamping together.

For a moment, the only sounds are our breathing, the soft slap of water against the stone sides of the canal, and my breaking heart.

'Who?' he replies eventually, frowning.

'You know who.'

'Stella, I have no idea what you're talking about.' He sounds genuine, but his eyes are panicked and his jaw tics where he's grinding his teeth.

I ignore his denials and continue talking. 'I wanted to be sure of your fidelity, so I created a fake online lover. Someone you'd be instantly attracted to. I made her sexy and funny, charming and mysterious. I know your likes and dislikes, so I tailored your perfect match.'

It's like I can see the cogs whirring in Austin's brain. The sheer horror of realising that I read every cheating word he typed to 'Serafina'. His flirty banter that gradually morphed from light-hearted to sexy and dirty, to passionate and loving. I watched his online affair play out in real time. I shaped it.

'There's no point denying it any more, Austin. I know. I have proof. And I can see in your eyes that you know I'm right.'

He closes his eyes for a moment. Takes a deep breath in and then out before opening them again. 'You're Serafina?' he asks, his voice barely audible.

'I thought the hard part would be getting you to agree to meet up in Italy,' I say. 'I thought, *surely he won't be so crass and unfeeling, so cold-hearted and selfish as to text Serafina to try to meet his online crush during our honeymoon.* But – surprise! – you were.'

'You catfished me. You ruined our marriage before it's even begun! What kind of person creates a fake girlfriend for their fiancé? How could you do that?'

'*How could I do that?*' I spit. 'What about an apology for cheating on me with your ex? How about being sorry for sexting virtual strangers? For living this secret life? For betraying me?'

'Coming here tonight was a stupid, spur-of-the-moment thing,' he replies.

'No it wasn't,' I say.

'You have to believe me. I never planned to come here, but then, when I left my credit card at the restaurant—'

'Stop. Lying.' My fingers curl into a fist. I have to stop myself from punching him in his lying mouth. 'Yes, you really did leave your credit card at the restaurant. But I'd lay bets that you did that on purpose and planned the whole thing so you'd have an excuse to go out.'

'That's ridiculous. You sound paranoid.'

'Can you blame me?'

He pauses and lets out a sigh. 'Look, Stella, I admit, I've been less than perfect. I've been tempted in the past, but now that we're married—'

I choke out a bitter laugh. '*In the past? Now that we're married?*' I can hardly believe the garbage that's spilling out of his mouth. 'In case you hadn't realised, this is the first night of our honeymoon and here you are meeting up with some random woman you've met online.'

He swallows and tries to take my arm, but I shake him off. 'But she's not some random woman, is she?' Austin says softly. 'She's *you*.'

'Are you really trying to justify—'

'Just hear me out, Stella.'

I grit my teeth.

'I felt an affinity with Serafina. The knowledge that she could be my person. And now I understand that the only reason I felt that was because she was you.'

'No she wasn't,' I hiss. 'I made her up. I gave her all the pathetic, weak, sycophantic traits that I knew you'd love. I gave her all the characteristics that I don't have.'

'That's not true.' Austin's face darkens.

'And if she reminded you of me, then why did you need her too? Why aren't I enough?'

'You are enough. Now that we're married—'

'There you go again with the "now we're married" crap. We *are* married, so what are you doing here?'

He bows his head. 'You're right, Stella. Of course you're right. I honestly don't know what came over me. I got in too deep with her. I couldn't just break it off online. That's why I wanted to see her tonight. I thought it would be better to do it in person.'

My heart shrinks further at yet another lie. At his attempts to wriggle out of his infidelities. 'After we slept together tonight, you crept out of our bed, showered, wore your nicest suit, drenched yourself in aftershave and snuck out to see her. So don't try to tell me you were trying to do the right thing. I'm not one of your parents, blindly believing everything you tell me.'

Austin's shoulders slump. 'I know. I have no excuses. I . . . I don't know what's wrong with me. You have to believe that I do love you, I do want to be married to you, and I want this to work. If I could rewind everything and start again . . .'

I've lost count of the number of times I wished he would confess everything to me. Beg me for forgiveness. Ask to start over. But not like this. Not after I've already confronted him with the truth. This apology sounds like a last resort. A way out after I've backed him into a corner.

'I really am sorry, Stella.' His body wilts and he seems so genuine, but Austin's always been good at winning people around.

'Then why all this?' I ask, spreading my hands wide. 'Why the affair and the online flirting?' I ask. 'What's the point of it? If you want the freedom to do all that, then why have you been stringing me along for the past four years? It's not fair. I don't deserve it. Go and live the single life if that's what you want!'

'I can't explain it,' he replies, shaking his head. 'It's like . . . I want marriage and kids. I want a family with you, the woman I love. But I'm also . . .' He swallows and looks down at his feet. 'I'm

237

addicted to the thrill of being with other women. Maybe it's the buzz, the fear of getting caught . . . I don't know.'

'And now you have been caught,' I reply. 'So how does that feel?'

'Like shit.' He gives a bitter laugh and looks up to catch my eye. To see if any part of me finds what he says amusing.

I don't. I realise that Austin is never going to change. I know he loves me and that he wants to be my husband. But he also wants to enjoy himself. The trouble is, his whole life he's always been given whatever he wants. He likes women and fun and the good life. But now he also wants a family and stability. He thought he could have both, without any consequences. He thought I was a mug.

'You're shivering,' he says softly.

Some part of me registers that it's cold. That *I'm* cold. But I'm not consciously aware of it.

He reaches for me and I let myself be held. Let my head rest against his fast-beating heart. Desperately wanting to stay like this. Not wanting him to ever let me go. But I know what I have to do, and I'd better do it quick before the opportunity slips away.

I breathe in his familiar clean, warm scent one last heartbreaking time before I pull the folded hunting knife from the pocket of my hoodie, flick it open and plunge it into his side.

Chapter Forty

THEN

As I withdraw the knife, Austin grunts and jerks away from me, doubling over and clutching his side.

'Something just . . .' He tails off and looks at me. 'Did you . . . ? *What . . . ?* His blurred gaze goes to the knife in my hand, dripping blood.

Before he can react further, or stagger off, I slip off my backpack and try to loop it over his head. But it's too heavy and he's ducking out of the way, elbowing me, his hands still clamped over his wound. His eyes are wide and wild as he realises what I've done. That I've stabbed him.

I manage to prise one of his hands away and hook the backpack over his shoulder, yanking the strap tight and looping the other one partway over his other arm before shoving him backwards into the glassy canal, hoping the rubble-filled bag will pull him under quickly. I curse myself for not getting the strap over his head, but everything happened so quickly and, despite his wound, Austin still has a surprising amount of strength.

My breaths are ragged, my body drenched in sweat and adrenaline as I watch him fall, his mouth open in a silent scream, his eyes disbelieving and terrified. He breaks the surface with a deep splash, submerged quickly into the dark water that's like a greedy mouth swallowing a tasty morsel. Bile rises in my gorge as I suddenly understand what I've done.

This isn't a theoretical plan any more. It's a reality. It's happened. I've done it. There's no turning back. In my head, I'm telling myself that it's fine. That this is all on him. I try to get back into the frame of mind where doing this all made perfect sense.

Back home, I was hurt, betrayed, *devastated* by Austin's infidelities. I never wanted to marry a cheater, and I didn't dare tell my mum and dad that they'd been right about him all along. I would have called the wedding off, but my parents had already gone into debt to pay for it. Why should they have to suffer for Austin's sleaze?

And, anyway, I knew what Austin and his parents were like. If I'd accused him of cheating, they would have denied it. The whole thing would have been somehow twisted to make him look good and me look bad. Leaving me and my parents with a bucket-load of debt and a bad reputation. A scandal in a small town that would have had me painted as the bad guy.

This way, he can just disappear and no one will know what happened. As long as that rucksack with the rubble stays on him. Keeps him down there at the bottom of the canal. I googled that the canals are around five metres deep, so it's a long way down. My head swims at the thought.

Why couldn't Austin have been satisfied with his charmed life? Why did he have to go chasing after more? Why wasn't I enough for him?

I realise I've been standing here too long. I peer into the canal, but there isn't so much as a ripple there now. With shaking hands, I crouch and rinse the knife in the dark oily water before folding it closed and tucking it into my jacket pocket.

Noticing a few spatters of blood on the narrow walkway, I lean forward to scoop up some water in my hands, sloshing it over the stone ledge, trying to rinse away the blood. After a few attempts, it appears clear enough, but it's impossible to know what it will look like in daylight. I reach forward for one last handful of water, shivering at the thought of Austin being down there. I see a pale face floating up to the surface, a white arm reaching out to pull me in. I shudder and step back, cursing my overactive imagination for playing a sick joke on me.

I stand and turn, hurry back along the alley, reliving each second with every frantic footstep that beats out across the smooth flagstones. My legs propel me forward, but my mind is locked in place back there by the canal.

I realise I'm making too much noise, panting, thudding, jumping at shadows and cats.

Calm down. Breathe.

I keep walking, but slower now. The clear fresh night smells to me of blood and steel and water. Of betrayal and darkness. Of death and sorrow. Even of regret.

I stop. Heave out a breath. Dry retch, before getting hold of myself again, staring at a puddle of lamplight on the pavement. I gaze up at the black sky, at the fingernail of cold moon and the winking stars, before glancing wildly around the unfamiliar street and up at the blank windows. People are sleeping all around me while I'm in turmoil. While my heart judders and sweat still oozes from every pore.

I tell myself to stay calm. To be relieved that my plan worked out without a hitch. This whole night, I've felt like Alice tumbling down the rabbit hole. One minute the implications of everything are too huge to contain. But now my emotions are contracting so fast I can barely get a hold of them. I think I'm going into shock.

Before catching up with Austin tonight, I ducked into an alleyway and took off my hoodie, beneath which I was wearing a slim backpack with a change of clothes – leggings, a T-shirt and a thin blazer. I replaced my blonde wig with a dark brunette one, and changed my trainers for a pair of sliders, then I stashed my discarded clothes in a plastic bag on a window sill behind a planter. I then headed to the end of the alley where I'd scoped out a building site earlier today on an afternoon walk while Austin was having a brief siesta. I filled the backpack with loose rubble from the site, and zipped it up.

I'd already done a lot of research on Google Maps before the wedding, using my burner phone on public Wi-Fi to scout locations – the same phone I used to set up my fake profile on a free dating app to conduct the affair. The upsides of Venice are the dark alleyways and deep canal, but the main downside is all the cameras. I think – I *hope* – I've managed to conceal my identity well enough using the two sets of disguises. One disguise to leave the hotel, and the other for meeting up with Austin, on the slim chance we were seen together. Also, my fake profile picture of Serafina showed a stunning brunette and my dark wig fooled him right up until he looked at my face.

Now it's over, all I have to do is change back into the blonde wig and jeans, get back to the hotel, and then I'll sink both sets of clothes and wigs, along with the knife and burner phone, into different parts of the canal before I need to call the police and report my husband missing. I only hope I can be convincing enough. My fear and panic are real though, so I won't have to fake that. I risked bringing the knife with me from the UK, packing it in my checked luggage along with my toiletries.

Back when I discovered what Austin had been up to with Keri, shoving him into a canal seemed far too good for him. I was raging, furious, devastated. My plan seemed so reasonable. Fair, even. As

Serafina, I would encourage him to meet me, but as Stella, I would show him how much I loved him. I would give him every reason not to meet up with her.

After our blissful wedding and exciting first day in Venice, I was convinced Austin was going to stay loyal. Especially after we made love and then curled up in bed together, happy. But then I woke up and saw him dressed and ready to go out. Even then, I wanted to believe his story about the credit card, until I checked my burner phone and saw his text wanting to meet 'Serafina'. I think I must be naive. Stupid. Or perhaps I was simply too much in love to be clear-headed.

I still can't believe he did that to me. If he had stayed true, he would still be alive. Even up to the final minutes, I didn't think he would actually go through with the rendezvous.

Killing Austin was a last resort that I never truly believed would happen. It started as a revenge fantasy in my head that has somehow become a reality. When I plunged the knife into his side, I truly believed he deserved it. But now it's over, I'm overcome with a heavy sense of dread. Maybe it's just a hangover from all the adrenaline, but reality is punching home. I've carried out this string of actions that now seem almost preposterous.

What have I done?

Chapter Forty-One

NOW

It's a sunny Saturday morning as I sit in the kitchen of my parents' house scrolling through Rightmove properties on my phone, light streaming in through the windows, lazy dust motes floating in the rays. It's been almost a year since my honeymoon, and life has only just begun to resemble anything near normal again.

After that traumatic day when Austin's parents and I identified his body at the mortuary, the police requested that I remain in Venice while the murder investigation proceeded. My parents wanted to stay with me too, but I sent them back home as there was nothing they could have done but worry and stress along with me. I promised to call them every day to keep them updated. The Lewises insisted on staying, though, renting us a two-bedroom apartment as none of us wanted to remain at the hotel, and the cost would have been too much anyway.

It was a stressful, horrible time. I had to process what I'd done, while living with Austin's bereaved parents in another form of hellish limbo. I spent most of my time out of the apartment, walking the city, sitting in coffee shops and staring out over the water. But the city felt as oppressive as the apartment as the days grew busier and hotter.

In between long days of waiting, the police would periodically contact me to ask questions – some as formal interviews, others more casual. The UK police searched Austin's flat and his parents' house. They even searched my parents' place. But there was nothing to lead them to Serafina. They were unable to trace her, or her true identity, as I'd covered my tracks well with the burner phone and prepaid Italian SIM card – paid for in cash – that are now at the bottom of a canal. Austin was using one of the anonymous free dating apps that don't require you to register your real details, which suited my purposes perfectly.

The police case stumbled along until it finally limped to a dead end and I was informed, several weeks later, that I was free to leave the country.

Rob and Vicki were naturally unhappy with the police's lack of progress. They still believed that Bart had something to do with it and they hired a private investigator of their own. He's still in their employment, but nothing has come to light.

'How's the flat-hunt going?' Mum asks, coming into the kitchen, her hair newly highlighted, her skin glowing after the spa treatment we had at the Harbour Club hotel yesterday.

'I've got two viewings lined up for this afternoon,' I reply. 'One in the centre of town, and the other one up near the rowing club at the back of the Quomps.'

'How exciting. If you want me or your dad to come with you for a second opinion . . .'

'That's okay, Claudia said she'll come.'

'Anyone making tea?' Dad asks, popping his head around the back door, his face tanned, his eyes bright. He's been getting into grow-your-own recently, and the back garden is now filled with raised beds of veggies. He's even planted a couple of small apple trees near the back fence.

'I'll make you a cup, love,' Mum says to him. 'Stella, you having one?'

'Yes, please.'

After returning from Italy, I moved straight back into Mum and Dad's. As I'm officially Austin's widow, I inherited his apartment and his business. But I didn't want to live there. To be honest, I didn't want to set foot in the place ever again. Although the flat was legally mine after probate, I offered to give it to the Lewises as it didn't feel right to keep it for myself after what I'd done. But they turned me down. Told me they would be even more unhappy if I didn't take Austin's inheritance. They said I deserved it after what I'd been through, which made me feel even worse.

I put it on the market and it sold within a week. Went to a bidding war. I used part of the money to buy my parents the house they'd been renting for the past thirty years. Some of the rest I used to pay off the wedding debt, telling Dad that I knew all about the loan and that after what Austin had put me through I didn't want to hear another word about me paying it off. He took one look at my face and capitulated.

'There you go, love.' Mum puts a mug of tea down in front of me and takes Dad's out to him in the garden. I hear them chattering together through the open door, happy that they're finally free of money worries. Working less and enjoying life more now that they have no rent or mortgage to pay.

I'm using the remainder of the money from Austin's property as a healthy deposit for a flat of my own. I'll need to continue working at the dance studio to cover the mortgage, but Claudia's going to be my lodger, so she'll help with the bills. I'm hoping it will be fun, the two of us living together.

The other person who's been a rock throughout all this is my neighbour, Jake. There's nothing romantic going on as I absolutely am not ready for another relationship, but it's lovely that he treats me like a normal person, not treading on eggshells or asking how I'm doing all the time. Instead, he makes me laugh and takes the piss. Makes me almost forget about what happened.

It turns out Austin wasn't only lying to *me*; he'd been lying to Bart too. Poor Bart had been telling the truth about Austin all along. I looked into Austin's business affairs with a forensic accountant, and it became clear that Austin had been the one using their business account for personal pleasure – trips with Keri, and with friends, a boat purchase, flying lessons, various hotel stays and restaurants that were very possibly with other women, the list went on – passing them off as client business expenses.

When Bart called him out on it, Austin turned the tables to scare him into backing down. It would have worked too. Despite being innocent, Bart was prepared to turn a blind eye to Austin's crimes as he said he just wanted an end to the stress of a court case hanging over his head. I'm not even sure if Austin would have gone through with the case as it would have highlighted his own crimes. But he realised that victim blaming would muddy the water just enough to take the heat off him.

As soon as I could, I made sure the case against Bart was dropped and I signed over Austin's shares in the company to him. He and Patsy both cried with relief that their nightmare had finally come to an end. It's nice to know there's no bad feeling between us.

Every one of my friends now knows the official version of what happened on our honeymoon. That Austin was catfished and murdered, his killer never apprehended. That he'd been having multiple affairs. That his parents and I have suffered through a nightmare.

There was another bout of local media interest when I returned from Italy, but I spurned all offers of an interview and the stories eventually died down, thank goodness.

Back in Italy, after Austin 'went missing', I had hoped the Serafina part of it would stay hidden from public knowledge. I hadn't banked on Austin confiding in anyone about his online affair, let alone Miles. So when it was clear the police would have to be told about her, I was sure that it was only a matter of time before my involvement came out. I pictured myself locked up in an Italian prison for decades. Especially when Austin's body surfaced. I'd never been so terrified in my life.

If I had only managed to get the rucksack strap over his head, Austin would have stayed at the bottom of the canal instead of being washed up. But maybe it was a blessing that they found his body. At least I don't have to live with the fear of him bobbing to the surface one day and opening up the whole case all over again. Also, this way, I'm officially a widow rather than Austin being a missing person. Plus, Rob and Vicki got some kind of closure. Even if it was closure of the worst kind.

I have to live with my secret every day. It feels like a dead weight lodged in my chest, being the only person in the world who really knows the full story of what happened to my husband. Knowing I can never tell anyone about it.

I'd always thought of myself as a simple, regular girl. Turns out I'm a deceiver, a schemer, a murderer. If I'd never met Austin, would I ever have discovered that about myself? I swing between being appalled at what I did and feeling like he deserved everything he got. But mainly, I feel utterly amazed that I actually got away with it.

Epilogue

I tug my baseball cap down low on my head and hang back in the shadows, watching Austin Lewis turn down an alleyway. I draw closer, preparing to follow, but he halts at the end by the canal. I can't get a decent view of him from back here, but I can't very well stand at the entrance to the alley or he'll see me.

After a few moments, it's clear he's not going any further. Maybe he's waiting for someone. I need to get a clearer view. I walk a little way along the deserted street, light on my feet in soft-soled trainers, until I come to a parallel alley that looks like it leads to the same stretch of canal. Hurrying along the passage, I'm relieved when I reach the end and discover that I now have a nice unobstructed view of him, while remaining perfectly concealed at the end of the alley. I think I might be getting the hang of this job now.

What is he even doing down here on his own in the middle of the night? A business meeting? Unlikely at this hour. This is my very first stint as a private investigator. My boss, Pat, will be pleased if I manage to get some photographic evidence of Austin doing some kind of dodgy deal. Apparently, Pat's client, Bart Randall, is Austin's business partner, but they've had a falling-out. Bart's convinced Austin has been ripping him off so he wants photographic and video evidence of everything he does and everyone he meets. Bart's trying to build a case against him because Austin's denying any wrongdoing. The whole situation sounds messy.

While I've been thinking about Bart and Austin, I see that someone else has joined him. A dark-haired woman. Annoyingly, she has her back to me, but I'll make sure to get a shot of her face somehow. Hopefully, she'll turn around at some point.

What's he doing meeting another woman while he's on his honeymoon? I know he's been having affairs back home, as Pat got me up to speed on all Austin's activities, but this is shady behaviour even for him.

Maybe he's buying drugs. Hang on, looks like they're arguing. I hold up my digital camera, zoom in, take a few photos and then start filming.

I'm too far away to hear what they're saying, they're speaking in low tones so I'm only getting snatches of words. But it's obvious she's unhappy with him and he's trying to appease her. More like trying to wriggle out of something he's done. Maybe she's a lover who's discovered he's in Venice with his wife.

But . . . no, it looks like he's got away with it as they're embracing now. I wonder if they'll kiss . . .

I startle as Austin suddenly staggers back, his hands clutching his side. Zooming in, I see the glint of silver steel and the shocking drip of scarlet blood. The woman is holding a knife! I almost cry out. Almost drop my camera, or, I should say, Pat's camera. He lent me his spare with strict instructions to take care of it. But a camera is the least of my worries. What should I do?

Don't panic. Stay calm, like Pat taught me when he gave me a crash course in surveillance. Whatever you see, *Pat said,* if it relates to the case, always keep filming. You're an observer, a collector of information. You're not paid to have an opinion. You're not a good Samaritan or a hero. *I'd nodded along at the time, but surely this is different. This is* murder. *As much as Austin is a sleazeball, I should help him, right? Call the cops, or an ambulance or something.*

They tussle as the woman shoves some kind of bag at him and then pushes him into the canal. She leans over the edge, watching him disappear beneath the surface.

I realise I'm panting. The whole thing was so shocking and brutal. So quick. Unreal. I double-check to see if my camera's still recording. It is.

The woman starts scooping up canal water and sloshing it over the footpath, washing away the blood. She looks up and I freeze, worried that she's spotted me – it feels as though she's staring right at me. But now she's glancing back the other way and soon resumes her clean-up.

Something strange plucks at my brain, like a memory, and when she looks up again I realise why. That woman is wearing a wig. And, what's more, I know her. It's Austin's wife. It's Stella! I almost call out her name, but manage to stop myself just in time.

My heart thunders in my chest. I now have video evidence of Stella murdering her husband – not that the slimy creep didn't deserve it. But murder? I could make some serious money out of this from Pat, or I could even go straight to Bart. Sell him the footage. But do I really want to do that? Would I want to send Stella to jail?

I heard about Pat Foyle's job for Bart through the security grape-vine – Christchurch is a small town where everyone knows everyone. It was a long shot, but I approached Pat to ask if I could work for him. He told me he worked solo, but I persisted, threw in a bit of flattery. Told him I'd already practised a bit of surveillance on my neighbours – I'd even followed Stella a few times, but I wasn't very good back then. I think I might have freaked her out once or twice, which wasn't my intention. Anyway, I told Pat I wanted to learn properly from the best. That I'd be prepared to work for free for a while. Pat turned me down again. But then, a few weeks later, he got back in touch, said he had a gig abroad that he couldn't handle on his own as it entailed twenty-four-hour surveillance.

Knowing what it was, I jumped at it. And so, now, here I am in Venice, tailing Austin Lewis. Or at least I was, until Stella killed him.

I blink and try to refocus my brain. I think I'd better get out of here and be really careful she doesn't spot me. Because it wouldn't do for Stella to recognise me. Which wouldn't be hard as I've lived next door to her since she was born.

Before I arrived in Italy, I shaved off my dark curls, and I've been wearing a baseball cap and sunglasses to further disguise myself. I think I've done a good job so far at blending into the background, but I don't want to push my luck. Especially not now, after what I just witnessed.

I've already decided I'm not going to tell Pat or Bart about what I saw here tonight, and I'm not going to turn Stella in to the police. How can I possibly do that while I'm in love with her? While there's a real chance now that Stella and I could finally be together – Jake Pirelli and the girl next door, our happy ever after, just as it was meant to be.

But I'm not stupid, I'm not a mug. It won't hurt to save the footage and send it to myself. Just in case.

ACKNOWLEDGEMENTS

Thank you to my wonderful editor, Sammia Hamer. I've loved working with you on *The Honeymoon* – I hope it didn't spoil your Venice trip too much! Huge thanks to my developmental editor, Hannah Bond, for all your brilliant suggestions and guidance. Thanks a million to Eoin Purcell, Rebecca Hills, Nicole Wagner and the rest of the fabulous team at Amazon Publishing who helped bring this book into the world. I'm forever grateful.

Thank you to Jenni Davis for doing a fantastic job on the copy-edits, and to Sadie Mayne for an excellent proofread.

Endless gratitude to author and police officer Sammy H. K. Smith for advising on the police procedure. As always, any mistakes and embellishments are my own.

Thank you to The Brewster Project for my beautiful cover – I'm head over heels in love with it. Huge thanks also to Jonathan Pennock and the team at Brilliance Publishing for another incredible audiobook.

I'm so thankful to my beta readers, Julie Carey and Terry Harden, for always having the time and enthusiasm to comb through my books with such care. Thanks also to my readers, bloggers, reviewers, sharers, recommenders and tweeters – none of this would have been possible without you!

As always, huge gratitude to my friends and family for your constant love and support. Thank you to my rock, Pete Boland. To my children, who are starting to forge their paths in the world. And to the Empress Jess, my fluffy and demanding writing companion.

A LETTER FROM THE AUTHOR

I just want to say a huge thank you for reading *The Honeymoon*. I hope you enjoyed it.

If you'd like to keep up to date with my latest releases, just sign up to my newsletter via my website and I'll let you know when I have a new novel coming out. Your email address will never be shared and you can unsubscribe at any time.

If you enjoyed my book, I'd be really grateful if you'd be kind enough to post a review online or tell your friends about it. A good review absolutely makes my day!

Shalini xx

ABOUT THE AUTHOR

Author photo © Shalini Boland 2018

Shalini Boland is the Amazon and *USA Today* bestselling author of nineteen psychological thrillers. To date, she's sold over two million copies of her books.

Shalini lives by the sea in Dorset, England, with her husband, two children and their increasingly demanding dog, Queen Jess. Before kids, she was signed to Universal Music Publishing as a singer/songwriter, but now she spends her days writing (in between restocking the fridge and dealing with endless baskets of laundry).

She is also the author of two bestselling sci-fi and fantasy series as well as a WWII evacuee adventure with a time-travel twist.

When she's not reading, writing or stomping along the beach, you can reach her via Facebook at www.facebook.com/ShaliniBolandAuthor, on Twitter @ShaliniBoland, on Instagram @shaboland, or via her website: www.shaliniboland.co.uk.

Visit Shalini's website to sign up to her newsletter.

Follow the Author on Amazon

If you enjoyed this book, follow Shalini Boland on Amazon to be notified when the author releases a new book!

To do this, please follow these instructions:

Desktop:

1) Search for the author's name on Amazon or in the Amazon App.

2) Click on the author's name to arrive on their Amazon page.

3) Click the 'Follow' button.

Mobile and Tablet:

1) Search for the author's name on Amazon or in the Amazon App.

2) Click on one of the author's books.

3) Click on the author's name to arrive on their Amazon page.

4) Click the 'Follow' button.

Kindle eReader and Kindle App:

If you enjoyed this book on a Kindle eReader or in the Kindle App, you will find the author 'Follow' button after the last page.